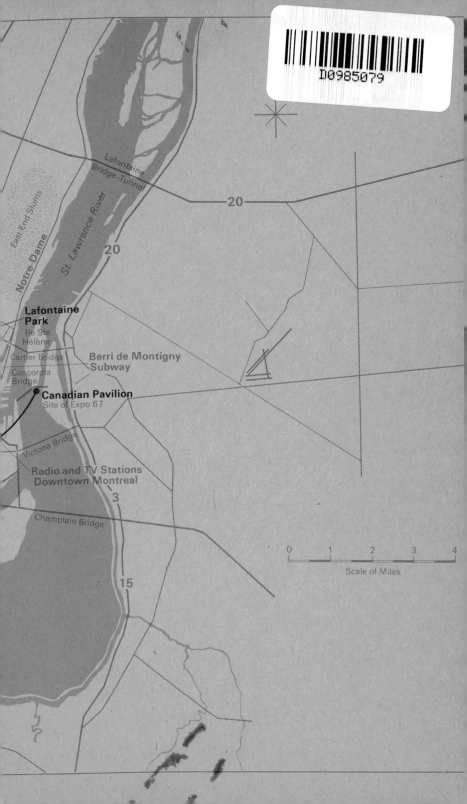

F
1053
.M6   Moore, B.
(1)   Revolution Script

THE
REV
SCR

Brian Moore

THE REVOLUTION SCRIPT

Holt, Rinehart and Winston
New York/Chicago/San Francisco

F
1053
.M6
(1)

Printed in Canada

For Cynthia and Sean

Books by Brian Moore

The Lonely Passion of Judith Hearne

The Feast of Lupercal

The Luck of Ginger Coffey

An Answer from Limbo

Canada (with the editors of *Life*)

The Emperor of Ice-Cream

I Am Mary Dunne

Fergus

The Revolution Script

Note

When these extraordinary events occurred, hostages, ministers of state, police chiefs, lawyers, and news commentators, crowded the screens and pages of the communications media. But the leading actors – four young men and a girl who set these events in motion by kidnapping James Cross – remained faceless. Even in the last act of this drama, the most publicized event of its kind in history, they still seemed shadows, figments of our imagination, fleeing into exile and silence.

This book uses the techniques of fiction to bring these young revolutionaries on stage. Many of the scenes and incidents are, necessarily, of my invention, and are not the result of special information gained from revolutionaries, politicians, or police.

I was in Montreal during the period at which most of these events took place. I conducted interviews and studied newspaper files, court transcripts, television film footage, and radio broadcast material. Later, I interviewed persons who knew the kidnappers of James Cross, and, also, others of their generation who share their frustrations and political beliefs. Some of the experiences and sentiments attributed to the kidnappers of James Cross in these pages were revealed in a ninety-minute taped discussion which was sent by the kidnappers to the weekly newspaper *Choc*.

I am particularly indebted to friends on Montreal newspapers and in the news and public affairs departments of the Canadian Broadcasting Corporation for granting me access to their files and to their sources of information. I will not attempt the long roll call of their names. However, I do wish to thank, in particular, William Weintraub, who accompanied me on many trips over the various routes and to the locations where the communiqués were placed. And, finally, I would like to thank Aaron Asher and Tom Maschler, who encouraged me to undertake this project and who helped from first to last.

B.M.

1

Shortly after seven on the morning of Monday, October 5, 1970, Marc Carbonneau drove a cab out of a garage belonging to the LaSalle Taxi Company of Montreal. The regular driver did not know the cab was missing. He would not come on duty until ten. A few blocks away from the garage, Marc parked at a street corner and removed the driver's police identification card and photograph from its position on the left-hand side of the ceiling. Then he got out and dialed a number in a public telephone booth. Jacques Lanctôt answered the call. "It's me," Marc said.

Marc then drove the cab to the top of University Street, opposite the Montreal Neurological Institute, a hospital area. Taxis were constantly coming and going there. Marc parked. Ten minutes later, an old, wine-colored, 1962 Chrysler sedan pulled in across the street. Marc, seeing a free space behind the Chrysler, put the taxi in gear and drove over, reparking directly behind the old car.

Jacques Cosette-Trudel, at the wheel of the Chrysler, sighted the taxi in his rear-view mirror. He nudged Louise, his wife, who sat snuggled up to him in the front seat like a high-school date. Louise said something and suddenly all four, including the two boys in the back seat, turned and looked at Marc.

When he saw the four faces, framed as in a photograph, staring out at him from the rear window of the old Chrysler, Marc Carbonneau was afraid: they were so young. When he was a kid at school, the priests used to talk about bad companions who led you into mortal sin. The bad companions were always older boys. He was thirty-seven, twelve years older than these boys, with a lot of his hair gone and a wife and four kids he had left behind. Yet, until this summer, what he had done was sound. Like the street demonstrations a year ago this month, when he and Jacques Lanctôt organized all the taxi drivers in town to get up on their hind legs and smash the Murray Hill Limousine Company's monopoly at the airport. Violence, sure. Burned buses, wrecked cabs, Molotov cocktails, looting, police baton charges. A real struggle. The Mouvement de Libération du Taxi. And they'd won.

"But this plan is different," he had told Jacques Lanctôt.

"How is it different?" Jacques said. "You saw *The Battle of Algiers.*"

"Saw it! That damn movie, I saw it three times," Marc said.

"All right," Jacques said. "At the start, there in the Casbah, there was no big demo. It was just a few guys who would go the limit. Like us."

"It was a movie," Marc said.

"But it was real. They freed Algeria! It started with a few guys, Marc. Think of it!"

Yes. He'd thought of it. Now, he watched Jacques Lanctôt and Yves Langlois as they got out of the old Chrysler.

2

Jacques, slender and handsome, his eyes hidden behind large, dark, hexagonal sunglasses, carried the false birthday present, a box, four feet long, wrapped in fancy silver gift paper. Yves followed behind, big and boyish, a jolly young monk out on a morning jaunt. But inside the rolled-up rugs under Yves' arm was a .30 caliber M-1 semiautomatic rifle with sawed-off barrel and cut-down stock. Also in the rugs was a gas mask, its eyepieces blacked out with masking tape. Cosette-Trudel, whom they called C.T., cool as a cat despite his schoolboy stammer, was the last one to leave the Chrysler. He kissed Louise on the cheek, then sauntered empty-handed, over to the taxi. Jacques Lanctôt got in front beside Marc, placing the wrapped box on the floor. Yves and C.T. got in back. Leaving Louise in the front seat of the Chrysler, they turned the cab and drove down University Street, cruising, waiting for Jacques Lanctôt's signal.

"Well, we're back in the taxi business," Marc said, and everybody laughed, glad to break the tension. But Jacques Lanctôt, staring ahead, thought: *without that I wouldn't be here.* In the last two years his life had changed. He could date it from the time he started driving a taxi to make some bread. Suddenly, he wasn't a French kid in the East End any more, but up here in the rich parts of town, places he'd never known, like Westmount, Hampstead, Town of Mount Royal. Driving the big shots around, seeing how they live, an education he'd never had in school – an education, as Pierre Vallières said, that taught him more than all the theoreticians. And Pierre should know. Pierre's book was the theory behind this new revolutionary spirit here in Quebec. Pierre wrote down what it was like to be French Canadian, a second class citizen in your own country. And what must be done. Revolt. But to know what he meant you had to live it yourself. Like Marc Carbonneau, a cab driver, who had been a Communist when Jacques was still a kid in school. All cab drivers are slaves,

Marc said. All of them suffer the same things. The big shot fare who throws your money into the front seat so that you'll have to bend down to pick it up: the English Canadians sitting in the back seat, talking to each other about their crooked deals and asking where they can find a girl to fuck. And five times out of six, the whore getting into your cab with some sixty-year-old Anglo is an eighteen-year-old French Canadian girl just out of convent school – kids the age of your kid sister who've been taught to do any shameful, dirty thing to these old bastards for a twenty dollar bill. Yes, you sat there driving the cab while some Westmount Anglo bastard was groping a kid in the back seat, and if he saw you look at him through the rear view mirror, he'd just wink, because what does he care, to that Anglo you're just some smelly young peasouper, a servant. You drive, that's all. And the girls – those thin little French girls in see-through blouses with miniskirts up to their navels. Or sometimes it's a woman in her thirties, somebody's wife making a few extra dollars on the side, and when you speak French to her she looks afraid, at first, in case you might be someone who knows her husband. But then, four times out of five, she winds up giving you a fifty-cent tip and asking you to steer her to another client. Yes, it made him sick, it made him want to kill those Anglo bastards, for wasn't it just as Pierre said, we're their white niggers. French Canadians are just shit to them. Yes, real education began, not in school, but in those months I drove a taxi. And as Marc pointed out, it's not only taxi drivers who learn who the real bosses are – it's the bus drivers too and the boys from Chambly Transport and the clerks who work for the Quebec Government Liquor Commission and the Lord Company guys who were on strike for such a long time. Solidarity with all of *nous autres*, that's what Marc taught me we had to go after. Solidarity with the working people of Quebec, with the people who don't know about unity yet, but who will. Because what will happen this morning is going to make a big difference, it's going to make Trudeau run to the Anglo-Saxon and American capitalists and tell them things are getting out of hand in La Belle Province de Québec. And they're going to listen, you bet. Because this time it's one of them.

Jacques Lanctôt checked his watch, although his sense of time was so sharp he had no need of a watch this morning. It was five to eight. This operation wasn't like putting bombs in mailboxes to scare the Anglo-Saxon capitalists out of Quebec and make them move to some other province of Canada. All those bombs did was get prison sentences for the guys now in cells at Saint Vincent de Paul Penitentiary. For what? No, this was something else.

Time to go. Jacques Lanctôt signaled Marc.

The taxi began to climb the steep incline of Upper Peel Street. It passed huge Victorian mansions, now converted into university student residences. Today, the very rich of Montreal live even higher up on the mountain. The taxi was going there. At the top of Peel Street it made a left turn for one block, moved along Pine Avenue, then climbed up again into Redpath Crescent, a quiet, curving street, an enclave of diplomats, industrialists, and people of inherited wealth. The houses on Redpath Crescent are of gray fieldstone, with black paint trim on doors and windows; houses which, in contrast to the older mansions below them, manage to minimize their considerable size. When Marc Carbonneau first drove the taxi past Number 1297, he had no idea of what he would find inside. Later, he read in the newspaper that the house has twenty-two rooms. "Twenty-two rooms, that's a hotel," Marc said.

The black taxi with its orange dome light and LaSalle Company markings passed 1297, drove around the loop of the Crescent, and came back again. Jacques Lanctôt had noticed an elderly gardener raking leaves in the front path of the house opposite. Jacques hated heroics. "Unnecessary violence defeats the Movement," he used to say, quoting from an article he had read on the Tupamaros, the urban guerrillas of Uruguay. During the taxi wars he had warned the cabbies, "Never hit a cop unless his back is turned." The other cabbies thought that Jacques was a bit crazy on the subject of cops. It was so bad he couldn't even look at one without going tense. Now, he stared at the gardener across the street. The gardener was a balding man in his sixties, doing his job, minding his own business. But he would see too much. Plan! Plan! Jacques warned himself. Don't make a mistake. Remember, two attempts at this operation have failed because there was a flaw. That's why François, Claude, and André are coming up in court this morning. It's taken months to get to this point: security, transport, financing, hideout. Now, right now, we pass from plan to deed. Is anything wrong? Have I forgotten anything?

The taxi, moving very slowly as though searching for a house number, again drifted past the gardener. Jacques gave the go signal. Marc stopped the taxi beneath the stone steps and iron stair railing which led to the ivied front entrance of the three-storey house. No one spoke. Jacques nodded to Yves. He and Yves got out of the taxi. Jacques carried the long, gift-wrapped box. C.T. and Marc remained in the cab, as the other two boys climbed the front steps. They watched, as Yves rang the doorbell. The time was eight-fifteen.

While he waited for the front door to open, Marc Carbonneau leaned over from the front seat to the back and unwrapped the heavy rugs, picking up the M-1 concealed inside them. Greatly shortened as it was, it was still a conspicuous thing to carry. He got out of the taxi, but did not go up the steps. His stomach hurt, indigestion knifing him, causing him to bend over in pain as he waited for Yves' signal.

C.T. got out of the cab, but only to shift from the back seat to the front, replacing Marc at the wheel. Whistling through his teeth. Shut up! Marc thought. He looked up at the front door. Jacques Lanctôt was ringing the bell a second time.

When the front door opened, Jacques Lanctôt expected that the maid who answered would be French Canadian, like themselves. He planned to speak English to her. But the girl who opened the door was, he sensed, not one of *nous autres*. Not English either. Some foreign woman. "We have a gift for Mr. Cross," Jacques told her. "You'll have to sign for it."

As he spoke, he and Yves stood outside the half-opened door, nervous, excited. So nervous that, at first, Jacques forgot to hand her the receipt pad. When he did remember to pull it out and give it, he did not offer the maid a pencil. That was part of the plan. The maid said she had no pencil. "I have one," Jacques said. Then, with the maid and Yves watching him, he put his hand into his coat pocket and took out the small, black .22 Beretta pistol, raising it, pushing it against the maid's stomach. He felt uncomfortable. After all, she was a woman.

The maid, a Portuguese immigrant called Analia Santos, stared at the gun pressing into her flesh. Yves, slipping on his gloves, knelt and ripped the gift paper from the box. He opened the box and lifted out the longer M-1 automatic rifle, then, rising with the rifle in his hands, turned and nodded to the street. Marc Carbonneau, waiting for this signal, ran quickly up the steps, hugging his sawed-off M-1 to his chest, hoping to hide the sight of it from the gardener across the street. Jacques Lanctôt had already begun to back the maid into the house.

"Mamma?"

The maid's little girl, five or six years old, was standing in the front hall behind her mother. Somewhere, upstairs, a dog barked once.

"Pick her up," Jacques said and the maid, grateful, scooped her child into her arms. "Where's Mr. Cross?" Jacques asked. She turned, pointed up the staircase. "Watch them," Jacques told Yves and, turning, ran upstairs, the pistol in his hand. He saw a bedroom, an adjoining bathroom, a dressing room, and a man, in pajamas, moving out of the bathroom into the bedroom. Jacques followed him in.

There was a woman in the bedroom, a small, stout woman. The man turned as Jacques entered. Both saw the gun. The man was the one whose photograph Jacques had studied, the one they had come for. Jacques pointed his black pistol at James Richard (Jasper) Cross, Senior British Trade Commissioner in Montreal. "We're the FLQ," Jacques said. "Lie down on the floor."

Cross looked at him, his heavily lidded eyes studying the gun; the dark-haired, handsome, very nervous youth; the frightened face of his wife as she watched. Heard his dog. The dog, a big spotted Dalmatian, jumped up on the bed, teeth bared, growling.

Cross lay down.

"Turn over. Lie on your face."

Jacques went to the door and called: "Bring them up."

Yves came upstairs, boyish and bespectacled, his M-1 at the ready, nudging the maid ahead of him, the maid carrying her child in her arms. As Yves brought them into the bedroom, the Dalmatian began to bark.

"Get hold of that dog or I'll shoot it," Yves said, staring at the dog, which had its feet firmly planted on the quilt, its head down, snarling.

Mrs. Cross went to the dog and put her arms around it, holding it, gentling it.

"Get up," Jacques Lanctôt told Cross. The commissioner rose and Jacques asked, "Where are your clothes?" Cross pointed to the dressing room. Jacques nodded and Cross, followed by Jacques, went towards that room.

Yves waited. A woman with a dog and a woman with a child. Holding the dog, holding the child: four living things who were afraid of him. As I am afraid of them, Yves thought.

A minute or two later, Jacques came out of the dressing room with Cross. The commissioner wore dark slacks, a shirt, and a dark-green checked sports jacket. "You can say goodbye," Jacques told him. As Cross went to kiss his wife, Jacques stared at him: a big man, six feet tall and overweight, with graying hair. He was a few days past his forty-ninth birthday. That was why they had brought the present that was not a present. He was nearly as old as Jacques' father.

Jacques took out the handcuffs and went to Cross. Cuffed him, hands locked behind his back. Cross looked over at his wife, like a man pondering a decision. Jacques tugged the sleeves of the jacket down to hide the steel bands.

"All right," he said. "Let's go."

Marc, waiting below in the front hall, had drawn on his gloves so as not to leave fingerprints. As always when his stomach hurt, he walked bent over, dragging his left foot slightly as though he had a limp. What a place this was! Holding his M-1 in front of him, he moved into the main hallway. The boys were upstairs. It was his job to find the back door and make sure there was no one on this floor. He went into one room, another, another. No, there was nobody. He found the kitchen and the back door. Man, what a house! The carpet must be two inches thick. And the pictures, big oil paintings. *Grande luxe.* He had never been in a place like this in his whole life.

He went back towards the front door. It was going just the way they'd planned it. Jacques was already coming downstairs with the big shot. Marc heard Yves telling the women: "You are not to telephone or notify anyone for an hour. Otherwise Mr. Cross will be shot. Do you understand?"

Jacques took a raincoat off a peg in the hall and threw it over the commissioner's shoulders. He nodded to Marc. Time to go.

Marc went outside. The street was empty except for the old

gardener across the way. C.T. had the taxi engine running. Marc nodded to Jacques, who at once put his gun in the prisoner's back. They took Cross out and down the steps and put him into the rear of the taxi. They pushed him down between the seats and put the rugs over him.

Yves came out of the front door, big, boyish, M-1 at the ready. Myopically he squinted around, ran down the steps, looked back. At an upstairs window he saw Mrs. Cross waving frantically, trying to attract attention. He jumped into the front seat beside C.T. The taxi started off, went around the circle of the Crescent, then came back down the street towards Pine Avenue to meet the morning traffic.

As Yves looked back through the taxi window he saw the gardener staring up at the window where Mrs. Cross was. But, amazingly, the old man went back to raking leaves. Still, in five minutes, either Mrs. Cross or the gardener would do something. Someone would phone the police.

It was eight-thirty. A taxi was normal, even invisible, coming out of this rich man's street. In silence they drove in an easterly direction, doubling back on a two-way street, passing student residences and university buildings, seeing files of Mc-Gill students, many of them long-haired Easy Riders ambling to morning classes, books under their arms, English Canadian students who, despite their Berkeleyian cool, were bent, as always, on acquiring those skills – engineering, management, and scientific – which in a hundred years of so-called parity, few French Canadians have mastered. The taxi moved past the gray Victorian turrets of the Royal Victoria Hospital, then turned up University towards the dead-end street where, outside the Montreal Neurological Institute, the old wine-colored Chrysler was parked.

The commissioner lay quiet. He'd better, Jacques decided. As long as he behaves, we'll treat him like a prisoner of war. Geneva Convention. We will be correct at all times. *"Est que vous parlez français, monsieur?*" Jacques asked the figure under the rug.

"*Oui.*"

"Well, then," Jacques said, in French. "We're going to change cars here. Do as I tell you and you'll be all right."

The taxi stopped. C.T. waved to Louise, who sat staring at them from the front seat of the Chrysler. C.T. went to take the wheel of the old car, while Marc limped over to replace C.T. as driver of the taxi. Jacques Lanctôt bent down and said: "When you get up, keep your eyes closed, do you hear?" He then took the rug off his prisoner and raised him up. Cross kept his eyes shut. There are a great many sick people going in and out of the Neurological Institute. No one paid attention as two youths led an older man from a waiting taxi. They put him down as before, but this time they covered his face with the gas mask, its eyepieces blacked out. They pulled the rugs over him. Jacques signaled to Marc and the taxi moved out, leading the Chrysler down University Street. The taxi kept going downtown, but the Chrysler turned left on Pine, passing McGill Stadium, entering an underpass to emerge on the far, unfashionable slope of Mount Royal. They drove up through Parc Jeanne Mance, going towards another Montreal, the Montreal these boys were born in, a Montreal that Commissioner Cross did not know, would never know. In silence they passed a last Victorian relic of English Canada, a circular bandshell, circa 1900, where, long ago, English Canadian regiments entertained the populace with Elgar airs. Then, on Park Avenue, the Chrysler entered that everyman's land which divides French from English in Canada's largest city, a belt of streets, boundary between east and west, running from the center of the Island of Montreal down to the docks, streets in which Poles, Greeks, Portuguese, Jews, Italians, Yugoslavs coexist in something of the polyglot confusion of lower East Side New York six decades ago. The ethnic divider: a few

11

blocks more and the Chrysler was in French Montreal, the largest French-speaking city in the Americas; indeed, one of the largest in the world. The car turned right on Boulevard St. Joseph, one of the arteries that run along the spine of the metropolis. Only ten minutes from Redpath Crescent but already Senior Commissioner Cross had been snatched from perhaps the best that Canada can offer visiting proconsuls: from mountainside with a view of the city and the St. Lawrence River, from mansion, from the enclave of English privilege, into an anonymous jigsaw of lower-middle-class living, of cheap duplexes and triplexes, signs in French, Caisse Populaire Banks, green-domed Catholic churches bearing the names of improbable French saints, church halls for Tuesday bingo and rinks for Saturday hockey, first communion dresses, wedding tuxedos for hire, taxis for funerals, and masses for the repose of the souls of the dead.

In this dormitory of cheap labor were congregated the human statistics of these young men's rage. Forty per cent of Canada's unemployed live in Quebec, despite the fact that the province, twice as big as Texas, is as rich as it is vast. It is also, lamentably, a haven for foreign capital and a source of non-union labor. American corporations own 60 per cent of the province's industry. English Canadian companies own or control most of the remainder. English Canadians, who make up only 17 per cent of the population, provide the vast majority of managers and executives. The language of command in this French speaking province is, astonishingly, English. Unemployment hovers chronically around ten per cent among the French workers. Half of these unemployed are under twenty-five years old. Many have never held down a real job.

"Turn on the radio," Jacques Lanctôt said. Louise moved to obey him. Sometimes, her husband complained, you'd think you were married to him, not to me. How could she explain?

Jacques was her older brother: he had been her hero as long as she could remember.

"Try CKLM," Jacques said.

But the radio crackled with such static they could not hear even the blaring French commercials. Perhaps it was because of electrical interference from the building coming up on their right, the Angus Locomotive Repair Shops of the Canadian Pacific Railway; vast, sprawling over blocks, a bedlam of rivets and heat, of soot and steel, in which thousands of French Canadian workmen toil out their lives. C.T. looked to his right as he drove past; saw the huge ANGUS SHOPS sign, like a title in the sky.

He thought of Pierre. What would Pierre say when he heard about this? Pierre Vallières' face swam onto the retina of C.T.'s mind's eye, remembered with the devotion a monk affords a vision of sainthood: a heavy, sullen face with an inward-seeing glance, eyes weak behind heavy spectacles: Vallières as a thirty-two-year-old lumpen-intellectual, violent in the courts, shouting like a madman against his judges. Vallières as a revolutionary who in New York with his friend Charles Gagnon picketed the U.N. in an effort to gain support for the Quebec Separatist cause. Vallières who in four months in prison in Manhattan's Tombs wrote an autobiographical polemic, *Nègres blancs d'Amérique,* which bears witness against these same Angus Shops where his father labored out a lifetime, working a night shift from four p.m. until five a.m., rarely seeing his angry, disaffected son.

"I just th-thought of P-Pierre," C.T. said aloud over the inane crackle of the radio. Louise nodded and turned the radio down. She smiled and looked at her brother in the back seat. In her family they had often spoken of Pierre's book. It was their testament, their sword.

"The police will pick him up again," Yves Langlois said.

13

"You watch. When they hear about this, they'll blame Pierre. They'll revoke his bail."

"He doesn't c-care," C.T. said. "When he hears that s-s-someone has done this, it will be blood in his veins."

"*Tais toi*," Jacques said and pointed warningly at the prone figure under the rugs. The less the prisoner knew, the better. They must remain anonymous, faceless, lay figures. In Brazil, the National Liberation Alliance men wear hoods. Their victims never see their faces. Never.

Suddenly, like a man reaching for a gun, Jacques jammed his hand into his side pocket. The homemade mask which he hadn't even taken out. The first, most obvious precaution and he had forgotten it – all of them had forgotten! "*Les cagoules*," Jacques said softly and looked at Yves, who turned and looked at C.T., who lowered his head, startled, so that Louise, watching her husband, suddenly realized what it was. "Oh my God," Louise said. "You didn't forget?"

"Shut up!" Jacques Lanctôt said. "But from now on, do you hear, everybody! At all times!"

Sick, they sat, each in his private pool of fear, as the Chrysler turned north off Boulevard Saint Joseph onto an even larger boulevard, named long ago in honor of Christ's vicar on earth Pope Pius IX. Traffic moves fast on Pie IX Boulevard. One might be in any big city in North America, on any expressway moving out of town. The Chrysler passed a slurb of small houses, built ten years ago and already showing signs of age, then went through a place called Ville St. Michel where Colonel Sanders' face loomed up on a roadside sign, string tie, Vandyke beard, finger-lickin' smile. But the sign over his head read LE VILLA DE POULET. The sign seemed to say it all, as did the adjoining California-style, four-times-larger-than-life-size mannequin of a gas-station attendant named Monsieur Muffler: America, yet not America. Canada, but not Canada. Quebec.

14

At 8:45 a.m., some miles away from the Chrysler as it moved north, Marc Carbonneau, driving the borrowed LaSalle taxi, stopped outside the garage and replaced the driver's photograph and police identification card. Five minutes later an alarm would go out across Montreal for five men in a LaSalle taxi. Marc, a meticulous planner who mapped out logistics for the cell, expected this, and now, on schedule, he drove into the garage, waved to the dispatcher in such a way as to screen his face, and drove down the ramp to his friend the parking jockey, who had loaned him the key to this cab. "Thanks," Marc said. "I sure appreciated it." The parking jock nodded. He was an old friend, a veteran of last year's taxi wars. Marc had driven a cab for five years before he left to make this revolution. He had told his friend he needed this cab to take his mother to Hotel Dieu Hospital. The parking jock was one of *les gars:* he knew how to keep his mouth shut. Even if he read something in the papers, he would not gossip. The dispatcher did not see Marc leave the garage. At eight-fifty, he walked out clear.

An alarm was on the wire. At eight-thirty-five, Desk Sergeant Seville Brabant at Police Station Number 10 on de Maisonneuve Boulevard received a phone call from a hysterical woman who spoke in a foreign accent. "She was all mixed up," Sergeant Brabant said. "She told us they had been told not to interfere for an hour. She told us to send somebody, then not to send somebody." The woman mentioned something about "Greek" so, while she was still talking, the police began calling the Greek Consulate. Then she said "Redpath Crescent." Plainclothesmen went at once to that street and at first checked on the home of John L. Topping, the new U.S. Consul General. Then, they moved to the Cross house. By nine a.m., members of the 100-man police Mobile Squad, and the Combined Anti-Terrorist squad of Montreal and the Royal Canadian Mounted Police had spread out across the city, taking up posts at bridges and roads leading off the Island of Montreal, hoping to box in the kidnappers.

But the kidnappers did not plan to leave the island. At nine a.m. as the alarm went out, C.T. drove the old wine-colored Chrysler into the suburban area of Montreal North, a working-class community which is almost exclusively French. Only three blocks away from the red-brick Hôtel de Ville and the adjoining Montreal North Police Station, C.T. drove down Avenue Gariepy, passing two new schools, built in that bright, international, modern style which seems equally indigenous to Denver, Colorado, or Reading, England, but somehow odd and out of character in this trailing entrail of the hybrid city of Montreal. The schools were large: they were the Ecole Scolaire Pie IX and the nearby high school, the Ecole Benjamin de Montigny. One block away from the morning cries of children in the large outdoor playgrounds of these schools, the Chrysler entered a quieter street, Des Récollets, a residential street of modest, three- and two-unit apartments. It was not a slum: it was small, anonymous, a no-place place, two minutes from the big boulevard, a street where, in contrast to Redpath Crescent, one sensed that the rooms inside these dwellings would be even smaller than they seemed from outside.

Halfway down the block, the Chrysler stopped outside a red-brick, three-unit apartment building, with green paint trim on windows and a green-painted entrance-hall door with chrome trim and side panels of opaque ripple glass. On the wall were numbers of the three apartments within: 10947, 10945, 10949.

Louise Cosette-Trudel got out of the car, and using her key, entered 10945, the lower and the largest of the three apartments. She went down to the garage which belonged to this apartment and opened the door. The old wine-colored Chrysler drove in. The door shut. At ten minutes past nine, wearing their masks, Yves and Jacques took James Richard Cross upstairs. The apartment contained three small bedrooms, a kitchen at the rear, and a double living room in front. They led Cross into the rear bedroom. It was a room eight feet long by twelve feet wide, with a closet and a small rear window which had been completely boarded over so that the prisoner would never know if it was day or night. There was a mattress on the floor with a sheet folded beside it. The door of the room had been removed and leaned against the wall so that one could look in at any time to see if the prisoner was where he should be. This room was next to the one bathroom in the apartment, and was the farthest room from the front door. In one corner was a small table on which sat a pack of cards. A chair for the guard had been placed by the door.

Jacques and Yves removed the commissioner's gas mask. They placed a hood over his head, much like a monk's cowl, which limited his angle of vision as blinkers limit a carthorse. They unlocked the handcuffs and re-cuffed him, this time with his hands in front of him. They placed him lying down on the mattress in the middle of the room.

"You are not to look at us. If you turn your head around to try to see us, you will regret it. Do you understand?"

"Why are you doing this?" the prisoner said.

"Wait. You'll see."

The prisoner, handcuffed, with the peculiar vulnerability of the bound man who at any time can be struck and cannot raise a hand to protect himself, lay on the mattress on the bare floor, his head held obediently in the required position. He saw the shoes, cheap, with turned-up toes, of one of his captors, as the man moved in front of him and switched on the television set, tuning it to a French-language station. He heard the other man leave the room; then his guard moved behind him. He heard the man sit, heard the hard steel sound of the gun being placed on the bare floor. Involuntarily, with an instinct stronger than his will, his head twitched as he sensed the enemy settle in at his back.

"Don't turn," the guard said. "You heard what we told you."

"I'm sorry."

"All right."

Jacques Lanctôt had left Yves on guard. He went into the double sitting room which was almost bare; two kitchen chairs and a table with a typewriter on it. There were also some paperback books. In the other part of the room was a television and three small radio sets, which Louise had tuned in to

CKLM and CKAC, both French-language stations, and to CJAD, a local English-language station which was good on spot news. The television showed a children's cartoon show. Jacques sat down facing the typewriter and pushed back on his brow the large, almost black-lensed hexagonal sunglasses which he habitually wore as though to screen from others his extraordinary, handsome, boyish face. Now, his large dark eyes dreaming as he picked up the four large brown envelopes and placed the communiqués in them, he had the air of a young correspondent who had just finished his dispatch and was preparing to file it. Indeed, this room, from this day on, was to serve as their pressroom, their communications center. He folded the last copy of the communiqué. Like those that would come later, it was typed on stationery at the top of which was printed the slogan FRONT DE LIBÉRATION DU QUÉBEC: COMMUNIQUÉ. Jacques had asked the printer, a Separatist and an FLQ sympathizer, to add, along the left side of each page, the words OPÉRATION LIBÉRATION, and, occupying almost the entire remainder of the page, a shaded line-drawing in a style reminiscent of *Little Orphan Annie,* a *habitant* Quebec farmer of the 1837 rebellion, dressed in tuque and sabots, but carrying a modern rifle and, disarmingly, smoking a pipe. This was Jacques' special stationery, with these added touches, supplementing the simple FRONT DE LIBÉRATION DU QUÉBEC, which his FLQ predecessors had used in their bomb warning communiqués in the sixties. He was proud of his additions.

He sealed the envelopes and folded them in three, the better to fit them into a letterbox. At last they had done the thing which gave them strength. Now, the world must be told. As C.T. had said in his excited stammer, they "had the greatest ch-ch-chance of any kidnappers, anywhere, ever." Nothing like this had ever happened in a country where television was in every home, even the poorest, and where, unlike South America, almost everyone in the country could and did read. C.T. was a college type; he liked discussing the media and rating

19

Trudeau as a television performer. Jacques frowned: the difference between me and C.T., he thought, is that when I went to that place where they had the guitars, that coffee-espresso club, I put on my best clothes, my Sunday suit. He put on blue jeans and a shitty, dirty shirt; he plays at being poor: jeans and a dirty shirt, those are working clothes for me.

"Any news on the radio?" Yves asked, coming in the living-room door.

"Jesus Christ!" Jacques Lanctôt jumped to his feet. "I told you to stay in the room with him!"

"All right, all right," Yves said. He slouched back into the dark bedroom. With Cross tied up and the television blaring away, what was so dangerous? Yves thought. Our greatest danger will be from ourselves, if the government stalls or doesn't give in. Why does Lanctôt have to be so nervous all the time? I'm nervous, but I don't scream at people. Besides, he's not so great, he makes mistakes like anybody else. He forgot the masks.

But I was the one who was seen. I stood there with Madame Cross and the maid looking at me. And in the street I was the one who covered with the M-1, while that old gardener stared right at me. The gardener in the witness stand, pointing, adjusting his glasses to peer. "Yes, your Lordship, that's the guy. Yes, he had a machine gun in his hands."

In the dark, bare, back bedroom, the only light came from the blue flutter of daytime television. The Canadian Broadcasting Corporation, the government-owned network, was showing a Disney cartoon dubbed into French. Bugs Bunny winked at Yves and at the bound prisoner. Relax, Yves warned himself. Nothing has happened yet.

He was right. In a sense, nothing had. But in the theater of confrontation, the curtain was going up.

At nine a.m. Marc Carbonneau got into a cab, this time as a passenger, in downtown Montreal. Thirty-five minutes later he paid the driver off in Rue Martial in Montreal North, outside a little dry-cleaning store: DE RAY'S VALET SERVICE — RÉPARATIONS DE TOUS GENRES. He surveyed Rue Martial and liked it. He had only been here once before, three days ago, when he and Jacques Lanctôt held a general meeting in the apartment on Des Récollets Street. Jacques had picked out the area, and C.T., Louise, and Yves had been living there, off and on, for a month, ever since Louise and Yves had rented the place, posing as man and wife.

It was funny, though, the way their plans had changed. At first they had held on to Jacques Lanctôt's original idea, which was to kidnap Harrison Burgess, at that time the American Consul General in Montreal. But the police had got wind of that plot. Marc had worried that perhaps there might be Americans, CIA or FBI, guarding the U.S. Consul now. Still, they went on with their plans. Hideout, transport, guns, money: all was planned for the American.

Only a few days ago, they had switched to this man. "Let's take the British Consul General," Jacques said. "That way we'll be serving notice on English Canada that we're after *them*." It was funny to think they knew so little about the British setup that they didn't realize there was no such thing as a British Consul General in Commonwealth countries like Canada. It was C.T. who found out that the nearest equivalent to a British Consul General was a man called James Richard (Jasper) Cross, who was Senior British Trade Commissioner in Montreal, who lived at 1297 Redpath Crescent, and who had celebrated his forty-ninth birthday a few days ago.

Yves still wanted to take the American. "If you kidnap an American big shot, the whole world will hear about it on television."

"But every-b-body's anti-American; even the English C-C-Canadians are anti-American," C.T. said. "On the other hand, they look up to England. If we take a real live B-B-British official, papers like the *Star* and the *Gazette* will f-finally come out in the open against French Canadians. And the people of Quebec will learn who's really in ch-ch-charge here."

A lot of people wouldn't agree with that, Marc knew. The trouble with these kids, they didn't understand how ordinary people felt. Last summer when he'd been up at La Maison du Pêcheur, Paul Rose's camp in the Gaspé, there were kids sitting around discussing the kidnappings in South America and praising the Panthers in the States and saying how we needed something like the Tupamaros here. All of those kids believed the best thing would be to capture a Cabinet Minister of the Canadian government. Like Trudeau!

But Marc did not agree. A Minister was a Canadian; some were French Canadians, and kidnapping our own people might just scare the shit out of the ordinary French Canadians we

22

need on our side, the same people who were scared for the last seven years while the Front de Libération du Québec bombed mailboxes and blew up armories and stole guns and dynamite. Let's face it, he told the others, the bombings of the sixties achieved only one thing. They put a lot of young guys in jail for life. Which is one reason for this operation. We want to get those boys out.

So they had switched to Cross. And now, Marc thought, we have him. Jesus!

He walked past the Meo Pet Shop, seeing a tank of tropical fish in the window and, inside, cages of budgies and canaries. Next door to the pet shop was Le Chaton, a small snack bar. They could get newspapers there. Across the street, on the corner, was a place called Carlo's, a nice clean grocery with a big freezer, lots of Lowneys Ice Cream which Marc liked, and a neon sign which said: BIERE ET PORTER. He turned the corner, feeling his stomach ache like a wound, and with his odd dragging limp walked along Des Récollets. He rang the bell of Number 10945, giving the signal. Louise opened up.

"That was quick."

"Yes," Marc said. He went in and saw Jacques sitting with the communiqués on his knee. "Any news?"

"Not yet," Jacques said. "You?"

Marc shook his head.

"Any trouble?"

"None," Marc said. "It was perfect. But, the taxi I took to get back up here cost nine-fifty with tip. We should use the bus and subway from now on, unless it's an emergency."

Jacques laughed. "I always knew you were a counter-revolutionary against us taxi drivers."

"I'm serious," Marc said. "How's our friend?"

"Fine."

"Who's with him?"

"Yves."

"*Just* Yves?" Marc's voice rose in anger. "We agreed there should be two. Always two!"

"We're not an army," Jacques said, crossly.

"You're goddamn right we're not. If we were, we'd carry out a simple order. Suppose Yves dozes off. Man, we *discussed* all this!"

"Okay, you're right," Jacques said. He remembered how Yves had slouched in, a minute ago. "C.T., will you go in?"

"Right," C.T. said and got up, carrying his air mattress. He went out of the room. Jacques looked at Marc.

"Nobody's perfect," Jacques said.

"I know. Sorry, I got mad."

"I don't mean that. Did *you* wear your mask up at Redpath Crescent?"

"*Tabernacle!*" Marc said. Like many French Canadians he was fond of liturgical curses.

"Hey, come here," Louise called from the other room. "Something — "

In French, an announcer, speaking indistinctly over the noise of the competing radios. Louise ran around lowering the other sounds — ". . . three armed men who kidnapped the Senior British Trade Commissioner in Montreal have announced themselves as belonging to the FLQ, the Quebec Liberation Front. The British High Commissioner's office in Ottawa has informed police that the men who broke into Mr. Cross's house and kidnapped him in the presence of his wife and a servant said they were members of the FLQ. However, until now, neither the British nor the Canadian government has received any notification from the illegal organization as to responsibility for the kidnapping or, indeed, a reason for it. . . . Medical specialists on strike this morning, announced . . . ." Louise lowered the sound and ran to turn up another radio. But there was nothing further.

"You heard that," Jacques said. He handed Marc the communiqués. "Better give them our calling cards."

Marc put the communiqués into an old plastic sales envelope.

"*Three* men?" Louise said.

"Journalists are always wrong."

"I'm off," Marc said.

"Take a taxi," Jacques said, grinning. "If you want I'll get Marcel to authorize it."

Marcel was the friend who had raised this money. Marcel knew people who were Separatists and maybe more than Separatists: anyway, they were emotionally in favor of the FLQ. A doctor, Marcel said, and a few young businessmen and a professor and a television announcer – they'd all given him two or three hundred dollars apiece. And others had given smaller sums. In all, Marcel had raised over $2,000 for this operation. It couldn't have been easy for him to get that cash. The FLQ wasn't a movement that attracted the rich. "We have a responsibility for this money," Marc told Jacques.

"Responsibility, shit!" Jacques said. "The sooner we let the authorities know who we are, the sooner this operation will be over. Take a cab! You're like an old woman, worrying about pennies."

Louise went to the door with Marc. "You know," she said. "Jacques thinks the world of you."

"*Nous vaincrons,*" Marc said. He smiled at her and showed her the clenched fist.

"*Nous vaincrons,*" she said.

This morning, we've made a start, Marc thought. Maybe we *will* conquer.

But he worried. No wonder my guts ache, he thought. Security's one thing but, sometimes – there are, maybe, thirty guys in prison, thirty who've gone to jail because of things they did for the FLQ. Supposing those thirty guys, and us, and maybe ten or fifteen other people sitting around wanting to do something, supposing we're all there is. We – maybe only twenty of us out of jail – *we are the* FLQ. This isn't *The Battle of Algiers,* no matter what Jacques says. It's Quebec. America is next door. The people here don't know they're slaves. They don't *think* about a revolution.

And again: Would the federal government under Trudeau, a French Canadian, ever take a French Canadian revolution seriously? What if Trudeau tries to laugh this off?

C.T. had told Marc: "Trudeau will take this hard. He's the *Roi Nègre*, the Nigger King, the one the English Canadians put on the throne because he knows how to handle us niggers. He'll kill us, if he can, will Pierre Elliott Trudeau. He's one tough nigger himself."

We will see, Marc said to himself. At least we should know soon. Say in forty-eight hours. Well, three days at the most.

On Avenue Gariepy an empty cab rolled past Marc. He signaled it. It was hard to find a cab out here in the sticks. Marc Carbonneau was a small man. The wanted posters would describe him as being only five feet five inches tall and weighing one hundred and forty-five pounds. He habitually wore cheap, short-sleeved, open-necked sports shirts, Ban-Lon sweaters, department store basement slacks, and Hush Puppy loafers with cushion insoles for his tired feet. For many years he had cultivated a pencil-thin mustache on his long upper lip. The mustache was fuller now, in an effort to emulate the revolutionary élan of the more hirsute Cuban guerrilleros, and his hair, curled long about his neck, was combed over a bald patch. But Marc was still the last man an Anti-Terrorist Squad policeman might eye in a crowd. He could be a short-order cook, perhaps. Or a waiter. This morning he wore a green nylon windbreaker against the October breeze. Eyeing him through the rear-view mirror as he sat, tense, with the plastic sales presentation envelope on his knees, the cab driver concluded this little guy was a messenger.

It was nine-forty-seven. Marc had told the boy he thought of as Ti-Chrisse to wait for him between ten and eleven. The name, Little Christ, had come to mind the first time he saw this kid with his Jesus beard and his long fair hair down to his shoulders. He reminded Marc of the holy picture of Our Saviour which used to hang at the head of Marc's parents' bed at home, that big double bed around which he and his brothers had to kneel and recite the family rosary. Of course, Marc did not call the boy Ti-Chrisse to his face. He knew only that the kid was a student at the University of Montreal and that his first name was André and that he had been recommended by Alain. The boy knew Marc by the name Jean. That way, they followed the FLN's rule, as they had seen it done in *The Battle of Algiers: No one knows more than he needs to know.* That way, in the movie, it was hard to destroy more than one cell, if somebody were tortured or talked. Of course, that presupposed that there was more than one cell. Who knew? It was easy for guys to sit around in taverns and talk revolution.

They always met in taverns; taverns are the Quebec workingman's club. The Boucheron, on St. Denis Street; it had begun for him there. He was on his way there now. He first began to be a Boucheron regular at the beginning of the taxi strike; at that time he'd just about given up on the Parti Québecois. Separatist Party. *They* thought things would be solved if Quebec became an independent country, separate from the rest of Canada. Marc had been a Marxist for years. He knew that an independent Quebec in the capitalist system would remain an American satellite. The same American companies would run things, just as they did now. No, Quebec must become a Cuba. And the only group pointed in that direction was the FLQ. They weren't orthodox Marxists; there was too much old-fashioned nationalism and dislike of outsiders in their makeup. But still. They were anti-capitalist. He worked with this kid, Jacques Lanctôt, during the taxi strike. Jacques was FLQ *and* radical *and* a Marxist. Then, one night, sitting in the Boucheron tavern, Marc read in the paper that Jacques Lanctôt and a man called Pierre Marcil had been arrested while driving a

27

rented panel truck in the East End of Montreal. The police had stopped the truck and searched it. Inside they found a wicker hamper, big enough to put a man in, a sawed-off shotgun, and a document in Jacques Lanctôt's pocket. The document was an FLQ communiqué for something which had not yet happened. It read:

```
OPERATION TELEPHONE

FLQ News Service: Kidnapping of the Consul and
Trade Commissioner of Israel, Moïse Golan, 6858
Hudson Road. Details will be found in an envelope
under the shelf in the telephone booth located at—
```

A few days later he read that the *flics* had charged Jacques Lanctôt and Pierre Marcil, not with an attempt to kidnap, but with possession of an illegal weapon. They were released on bail. Marc ran into Jacques at that time and Jacques laughed and said the only reason he'd gotten bail was because this was Canada and the Quebec Sûreté just wasn't prepared to believe that some dumb French Canadians would dare to kidnap a foreign big shot. This wasn't a banana republic, after all, this was the peaceable kingdom, with the most obedient population in the whole wide world. "Just let them wait and see," Jacques said. And Marc said, "You're serious?" Jacques laughed. "Of course," he said. "I always was. But last time there was an informer. Somebody turned us in." Marc didn't believe him. He thought it was just bad luck, the cops stopping the truck. Or maybe Jacques' bad driving.

But a few weeks later, in the tavern, someone said Jacques Lanctôt had gone underground. That the police were hunting for him because they'd found out something that changed their minds about the kidnap charge. Pierre Marcil was re-arrested in March, then released on July 15, when a new group called Movement for the Defense of Quebec Political Prisoners got up $2,000 for Marcil's bail.

Towards the end of June, three weeks before Marcil's release, a new kidnap attempt was made public. Police broke into a rented summer cottage in the Laurentian Mountains north of Montreal. They broke in with Fire Commissioner warrants, which meant, Marc knew, that they were looking for bombs or stolen dynamite. The newspapers reported that there were two young girls in the place, a thirty-year-old man called Pierre Carrier, and three boys: François Lanctôt, twenty-one, a laborer; André Roy, twenty-three, a taxi driver; and Claude Morency, nineteen, a laborer. François was Jacques Lanctôt's young brother.

The police found dynamite sticks. They also found 150 copies of an FLQ manifesto in the cottage. The manifesto said the FLQ had just kidnapped "the disgusting representative of the U.S. in Montreal, Harrison Burgess." The manifesto was headed Operation Marcil-Lanctôt and indicated that the plan was to kidnap Burgess during the July 4 weekend. Carrier was sentenced for contempt of court. The police let the two young girls go. They kept François, André, and Claude.

When the arraignment came up, Marc limped down to court to have a look. He saw the three boys in the dock, showing the clenched fist, shouting what sounded to Marc like Maoist slogans. He saw them being dragged back to cells. God help them now, those kids. He left court feeling sick, but excited. There were other kids like these. Maybe a revolution *was* possible. A real revolution.

A few nights later, through a friend, he asked if Jacques Lanctôt was around. The following afternoon he met Jacques in the Boucheron Tavern. "This time there was no question about the informer," Jacques told him, his mouth grim under his dark hexagonal shades. "Choquette, the Justice Minister, offered money for information three weeks ago. Somebody led them right to the cottage."

"What are you going to do? Cool it for a while?"

"No," Jacques said. "I'm going to form a new cell. Are you interested?"

"You still want to get the American?"

"American companies *own* this province. American capitalism owns *Canada*, for God's sake. Get the top American and you have something."

"Right," Marc said. He did not even think it over.

"You in?"

Marc nodded. "Good," Jacques said. "It will be you and me and C.T. and my sister. And Pierre Seguin will be the backup man."

"Who's he?"

"Do you really want to know?"

"Yes."

"Well, he goes under that name. His real name is Yves Langlois. He's been to Europe. He was in Algeria."

"*Battle of Algiers*," Marc said and laughed.

"You saw the movie?"

"Three times."

"I saw it four times," Jacques said.

Marc's taxi turned off the boulevard now, going down towards the waterfront, moving through the residential slum streets of French Montreal, old streets of uneven little red-brick houses with small windows, double-paned to keep out the terrible winter winds, streets of uneven façades amateurish as a drawing by a six-year-old, streets in which many and multifarious families are crammed into airless, pokey Dickensian warrens which remain unchanged amid the fine false fronts of the Expo 67 years; which are still as they were in Marc's childhood; streets like Ontario. Premier Duplessis, that Boss Tweed of Quebec, could rise from the dead and walk along Ontario in his gray grave pallor and know his city had not changed. Look into these stores. Elsewhere the window dresser's homosexual chic may have transformed store windows into fantasy rooms where price and sale are rarely mentioned. But to stare into the windows of Ontario Street is to see into the lives of the French poor who shop there: all is cheap, all is gaudy, all is old-fashioned. There are plastic flowers and imitation mahogany sideboards and shiny bedroom suites and strangely lapelled men's suits of cheap fabric: *Mode Géométrique.* It is a street where the barbershops have last year's Christmas cards still in the display window beside the poster – WRESTLING-CATCH – of two years' vintage. It is a street of People's Credit Jewellers, and Bagues de Mariage, et Fiançailles; it is Caisse Populaire banks on the corner, and the one building which has size, stature, and some sense of graystone grandeur is, you can be certain, called The Church of the Sacre Coeur, or Visitation, or St. Jean Baptiste. The food stores are crammed with cheap comestibles, with specials on beer and ground chuck. There are restaurants: they sell pizza and *Chiens Chauds Stimés* (Steamed Hot Dogs) and *Mets Chinois* (Chinese Food) and *Les Hamburgers,* everything ticketed in that special dogsbody language which results when French Canadians literally translate from the English or the American. And above all there are the special playthings of this harsh land: cheap wooden hockey sticks, skates, and ski boots, selling now at third and fourth hand. Toystores abound: many children are the rule. Toystores with windows filled with cardboard games and plastic dolls, all of these things so strangely old-fashioned that it is a shock to notice that the toy airplane hanging on a thread is a model of the supersonic Concorde. The toys are made in Japan, the United States, and England, but what Japanese or American or English child can one see playing with these ghost playthings? To whose child could one give one of these boxed games, the very

31

colors of which seem to age and fade as soon as they are set out in the windows of Ontario or St. Hubert Streets?

Above all, these streets cry family: weddings, funerals, confirmation dresses, layettes, anniversaries, birthdays, remembrance cards. There is no sign of the ratfilth of other big cities: no skid-row midday cowboys lie in doorways or lurch in mindless anger down these snow-slush pavements. Dirt, yes, but mostly it is something other than dirt: it is cheapness, always cheapness: it is the obverse of beauty, of style, the paradigm of those pinched lives for the blessing of which generations of French Canadians were told by their clergy to give thanks to God, told by their rulers, Duplessis, Taschereau, Godbout – a line of grafters and public-trough swillers that goes back over a hundred years – yes, told by these, their own politicians, to be grateful for the bounty brought them by the party in power. The fathers of these kidnappers – yes, and their uncles and aunts and cousins, including the one who is a Sulpician Brother and the niece who left and went to live in Tenafly, New Jersey – all of them accepted these streets, accepted this mean little life down here in the shadow of the mountain, below the big English mansions, accepted this white niggerslum, this *nous autres* existence.

The kidnappers will not.

On St. Denis Street, Marc paid off the taxi and limped into the Boucheron Tavern, a gloomy men-only barn where one drink is sold: strong beer. It was five after ten and the tavern had just opened, but Ti-Chrisse was already sitting slumped in a captain's chair at a corner table, an untouched glass of draught beer in front of him, reading, as always, a paperbound book. Winter and summer his appearance did not change. Moccasins, dirty blue jeans, and a Kit Carson, fringed buckskin tunic with long tassels hanging from chest and back: these were his clothes for all seasons. This morning he was carrying his handbag, a woollen knitted pouch made in Greece, which he wore on a long shoulder strap.

"*Salut!*" he said and kicked a captain's chair free of the table, indicating that Marc should sit there.

"You heard the radio?"

"*Oui. Félicitations!*" Ti-Chrisse said. He seemed both amused and excited and it occurred to Marc, as it had before, that Ti-Chrisse enjoyed acting out his conspirator's role. Sometimes, on their infrequent meetings he behaved like a child, despite his nineteen years, as though the FLQ was merely a prolongation of long-ago afternoons when he and other kids played cops and robbers at the back of some used-car lot.

"You want my beer?" Ti-Chrisse said.

"No. Let's deliver this mail."

Ti-Chrisse stood, hitching his Greek satchel, shaking long Jesus locks from his forehead. Marc had met him, two years before, up in the Gaspé at La Maison du Pêcheur, a sort of hippie haven for kids who talked up the FLQ. Marc and Jacques and C.T. had decided, some time ago, that long hair and a hippie style were a convenience for the *flics*. "If you want to make a revolution don't advertise it," Jacques had said. "Dress square, act square. Beards are a uniform, a badge. Let's make it tough for them."

But in Ti-Chrisse's world it was Marc who stood out as odd. When they reached the Lafontaine Pavilion of the Université du Québec on Sherbrooke Street, Marc hung back. Ti-Chrisse took the envelopes and went on, moving in a thick stream of

33

his familiars through the front doors of the technical school building, going into the yellow-painted reception hall where a receptionist sat behind a glass window, answering the switchboard and giving directions. Beneath her window was a long wooden box with four white name tabs for mail:

CENTRE VILLE   ARTS   LAFONTAINE   EXTERIEUR

Ti-Chrisse, casual, waited until the receptionist was busy on the phone, then walked over and slipped the four folded brown envelopes into the mailbox marked LAFONTAINE. He turned and walked out, a student among hundreds. He met Marc on Sherbrooke Street, walked to the nearest phone booth with him, took from Marc a stack of dimes and went in to make his calls. Watched from outside by Marc, he phoned, first Pierre Pascau, the program director and news commentator of CKLM, a French-language radio station which Marc considered friendly to the FLQ, or, at least, to the Separatist movement. Then Ti-Chrisse phoned *Québec-Presse*, a left-wing French-language weekly. Then CKAC, another French-language radio station. On each call Ti-Chrisse said the same thing. "Look in the Lafontaine Pavilion mailbox in the University of Quebec for a message from the FLQ." Then came out of the booth, with a hop, skip, and a jump.

"Curtain going up. Let's go see the fun."

"You go," Marc said. "I don't look like the student body."

"Right," Ti-Chrisse said. And loped off, Kit Carson scouting the pavilion's front entrance.

There were four envelopes in the box. The fourth was for the authorities who had not been called. The authorities would find out soon enough. The important thing was to make sure the media got the communiqué. That way it would be publicized, not suppressed. But as Marc waited, the first car to show up was, he was sure, an unmarked police car. It skidded to a stop and two men got out and ran inside. They were *flics,* members of the Anti-Terrorist Squad. The fucking radio journalists had called the *flics!*

The police stayed in for a good five minutes. Ti-Chrisse did not come out. Then a second car raced up. This time it was lettered: CKAC RADIO. A reporter went into the building. Marc waited. The cops came out first, with envelopes. Then the CKAC reporter came out. He had an envelope. Then Ti-Chrisse, loping along, grinning as he came up to Marc.

"They thought it was a bomb," he said. "They were scared shitless."

"But the cops got the stuff?"

"So did Peyrac," Ti-Chrisse said. "He's the CKAC reporter. Relax. You're in business."

"*Merci*," Marc said.

"Okay. Call me anytime," Ti-Chrisse said. "And good luck."

Marc watched him go. I won't call him, though. Why involve more people than I have to? I should have done this myself. We must find some easier place to leave communiqués. Let's keep it simple.

But the worry was back: his stomach knifed him. He was sure he had an ulcer. Worry, the old, the same worry: they had got their hostage, they had started this thing moving. But would it work? This is a country that never had a revolution, a country that stayed passive even through the American Revolution. And on top of that, this is Quebec and Quebec has no heroes: all our heroes were losers. We always lose. We lost in our little uprising in 1837, so small it was a joke. We're colonized, all right, we're exploited and cheated and robbed by our own leaders and we're cheap labor for everybody else and I know it and it makes me sick, but do the Quebec people know it, will they ever know it? You can't have a coup d'état in Quebec, that's what they say. This isn't Africa.

It wasn't even noon and he had already spent twenty dollars on cabs. He went back to the hideout by subway and bus.

The Minister was worried. There was something oddly ridiculous about this situation. No wonder, when it had been announced this morning, many of the news media people thought it a hoax. There had been these scares before: that business of the American Consul General in the summer and, before that, the Israeli Consul. It was not something one should panic over. This was not Uruguay. Or even America. Such deaths as there had been in the past ten years, these local bombings and so forth, had been, make no mistake about it, largely accidental. One hardly envisaged that this morning's affair would be different.

Still, he was calling a press conference this afternoon. It would be carried on radio, but it scarcely merited live television coverage. The Minister was a skilled negotiator. He had studied at the best lycée in Montreal, had been admitted to the Quebec bar when he was only twenty years old, had obtained a degree in economics from the Sorbonne in Paris, and completed his postgraduate studies at the Columbia School of Business Administration in New York. He was fluently bilingual. His position as Minister of Justice in the Quebec Cabinet was roughly equivalent to that of a State's Attorney-General in the United States. However, he had more power.

Nevertheless the Minister, Jérôme Choquette, was not an impressive public performer. If people can be compared with objects, the Minister was a shovel, a heavy-jawed man of forty-two, with a plodding, deliberate manner. He preferred to minimize the political aspects of this kidnapping. After all, he was not a federal minister but Minister of Justice for the Province of Quebec. And this was a criminal offense committed in his province. He announced, briefly, the fact of the kidnapping. He said an FLQ manifesto and a communiqué listing several ransom demands had been found in the Lafontaine Pavilion of the Université du Québec in Montreal. He refused to release these documents to the press. He summarized what he said were the kidnappers' ransom demands:

1. Publication in all Quebec newspapers of the political manifesto which the kidnappers had enclosed, spelling out the aims of the Front de Libération du Québec.

2. That certain "political prisoners" be released from jail.

3. That a chartered aircraft be provided to take these prisoners to Cuba or to Algeria.

4. That $500,000 in gold bullion be placed in the departing aircraft as a "voluntary tax" on behalf of the departing prisoners.

5. That 450 truck drivers belonging to the Lapalme Service, a private postal firm, who lost their jobs in a recent dispute with the Federal Post Office, be given federal jobs at once.

6. That the name and photograph of an informer whom the FLQ believe led police to discovery of a recently smashed FLQ cell, be published at once.

37

7. That the police manhunt for the kidnappers of Mr. Cross be called off at once.

The Minister told the press that the kidnappers had given "the authorities" forty-eight hours to accede to these demands. There was no indication, he said, as to whether the kidnappers meant the provincial authorities (the state government of Quebec) or the federal authorities (the government of Canada). The Minister asked the kidnappers to "at least show some elements of human decency" by providing Mr. Cross with Serprasil tablets, a drug necessary to control his high blood pressure.

The Minister refused to answer any questions put to him by the press.

He said that earlier in the day he had held meetings with senior officials of the three police forces concerned: The Royal Canadian Mounted Police, the provincial Sûreté du Québec, and the Montreal Police force. He said he would leave immediately for the provincial capital, Quebec City, where he would report that evening to the Quebec Cabinet.

In the double living room of 10945 Rue des Récollets makeshift blinds had been pulled across the front window to prevent passersby from seeing in. Jacques Lanctôt sat in a high state of excitement, cross-legged in front of the radio which carried the Choquette press conference, his hexagonal sunglasses pushed high on his forehead. Whenever Marc Carbonneau or Louise or C.T. interrupted to comment, Jacques tried to block out their voices. Choquette, the Justice Minister, was speaking to him! He had waited a long time to make these fascists jump, a long, long time. His first arrest had been when he was sixteen: he and another boy were picked up by the *flics* on the corner of Mountain and Sherbrooke Streets, right in the downtown Anglo stronghold, shouting stuff like "Down with democracy! Long live Socialist Quebec! Down with the police Gestapo!" It had been his first declaration of war. He was taken to Station Number 10, beaten and thrown in a cell. On the following day he was fined $25 and bound over to keep the peace.

And I have not kept the peace, he thought, as he listened to Choquette trying to cover up, trying to minimize their communiqué. I wrote that! You'll have to read all of it, you sonofabitch! Do you hear me, Choquette?

When the press conference was over, he asked C.T. and Marc to come with him into the kitchen. They left Louise to monitor the radio and television. "What do you think?" he asked Marc. He trusted Marc. The guy had a good head: he was more Old Left than New Left: a dialectician. "Well," said Marc. "Choquette is the stooge. Now he must speak to his boss, Premier Bourassa, in Quebec City. Then Bourassa will talk to *his* boss, the Prime Minister, Trudeau, in Ottawa. Kidnapping a diplomat is a federal matter. Finally, it's up to Trudeau and to nobody else. They can't just pass this off as a criminal case."

"That makes sense," Jacques Lanctôt said, nodding. He did not want the others to know the rage he was in. "Our communiqué was eight pages long," he said, trying to sound composed. "Yet Choquette tried to make it sound like a criminal's ransom note. Think of the trouble we took with that communiqué, knowing it must be read to the people."

"And the manifesto," C.T. said. "The s-statement of the issues, you n-notice the way he handled that?"

"He ignored it."

"Exactly."

"But we didn't ask that he read the manifesto right away," Marc said. "We asked that it be read on television at a proper time. Prime time."

"Marc is missing the p-point," C.T. said, grinning at Marc, then turning to reach in the refrigerator for a Coke. C.T. was different from them: snotty, educated, with a Jesuit's self-conceit. "Our f-first demand was the search be called off. So he mentioned that. It didn't worry him at all. But our s-second demand did. It said, and I quote:

" 'That the p-political manifesto which will be delivered to the authorities by the FLQ appear in its entirety on the f-front p-pages of the leading Quebec newspapers.' Now he did mention that. But, casually. Then we went on to d-demand, and, again, I quote:

" 'We ask that our manifesto be read in its entirety and commented on by the p-political p-p-prisoners before their departure from the airport in a radio and television p-program of at least thirty minutes' duration, live or on v-v-videotape, between eight p.m. and eleven p.m. on the CBC national French network and on its member stations in Quebec.' "

"That's just what I meant!" Jacques said. "Choquette ignored that. The most important part!"

"Precisely," C.T. said in his irritatingly assured way. "It's our o-p-p-pinions they're afraid of. He didn't even mention television, because he knows its p-p-power. And you notice *he* didn't appear on television. Just radio."

"If we can't get our message across to the people, we're finished!" Jacques said.

"Exactly. We're du-dead!"

"Well," Jacques said, "we won't be the only ones." He jerked his thumb at the prisoner's room. C.T. looked noncommittally at the room, then put down his Coke bottle and went to the window, staring at the backyard outside. Marc coughed. It had not been said before: none of them wanted to think about it. But we will *have* to think about it, Marc decided. All of us.

Jacques put the M-1 rifle under his chair, stood, moved past the prisoner's mattress, and turned off the television set. It was after midnight. The prisoner, handcuffed, lay on the mattress, his face towards the wall. Earlier, Jacques had read him their manifesto and the communiqué. In full. Afterwards, they had talked politely, addressing each other as "monsieur." But it was difficult to talk to someone who was bound, who was hooded, who could not turn his head to look at you. And whose first language was not French. He had told the prisoner that they were Marxists; had differentiated between Marxist practice in Russia and in China. The prisoner had said he had a degree in political science. It had been an abstract conversation, without rancor. He wondered if Cross would be able to sleep, or would he lie awake, afraid that if he closed his eyes it might be his last sleep ever?

He himself would not sleep at all that night. How could he, with this happening? Or not happening? How could he sleep until he knew what the authorities were going to do? He looked again at Cross and thought of the one pistol they owned, the little Beretta. That would be what we would use, he thought. He shivered. Cross always had his back turned. Would it be easier to shoot a man in the back? Or would one, when the moment came, feel obliged to call out, to ask one's victim to turn and face the barrel, the bullet?

After supper, he, C.T., and Louise had sat together in the rear living room, switching from television to radio, from newscast to newscast, like kids playing one-arm bandits in search of a payoff. There had been some small gains. The news commentators said the story of the kidnapping was on the front pages of the newspapers in England and in France. Marc went out then and phoned Ti-Chrisse, who went to the Metropolitan News Stand at Peel and Ste. Catherine Street and bought three dollars' worth of newspapers. Ti-Chrisse reported that the story was on the front pages of newspapers all over Canada. *And* in *The New York Times.*

At eleven on the national television news, the kidnappers learned that the provincial Cabinet of Quebec had held a three-hour meeting to discuss the situation. "You hear that?" Yves said. "Deliberations for three hours. Imagine their faces if they knew they'd spent three hours discussing the demands of a bunch of kids."

Justice Minister Jérôme Choquette was interviewed after the meeting. He said he could say nothing at the moment. "We are in close touch with the federal government. And any action taken on the kidnapping will be a joint effort."

C.T. cheered ironically. "That means we're in the r-r-ring with Cassius Clay Trudeau."

Ministers came and went. Outside the ramparts of the Quebec Legislature the media representatives stood in half-darkness, holding out their microphones like Merlin wands. A man came into the circle, a big burly man, a man whose face the kidnappers knew, whom all Canada would know a week hence. Ironically, like Macbeth on the lonely moors, Pierre

Laporte, Minister of Labor and Immigration in the Bourassa government, was asked his opinion of these events. He stared, pondered, and in a sentence which would stand as his epitaph, said: "This is a wind of madness blowing across the province. I hope it won't last long."

The prisoner, shifting on his mattress in the semi-darkness of the room, uttered a small cough which Jacques had come to recognize as Cross's way of indicating that he wished to speak.

"Monsieur?" Jacques said.

The prisoner wished to go to the toilet. Jacques untied him, after first making sure that his own mask was on straight. It was humiliating for both of them, this business of the toilet. But someone had to be in there with him. Jacques prodded the prisoner ahead of him and switched on the bright light of the bathroom. The newspapers had said that Cross was Irish. Now he asked Cross if this were true. Yes, the prisoner said. "But we are *for* the Irish," Jacques said. He quoted from memory from the communiqué, the one which Choquette had refused to make public. "The Quebec Liberation Front unconditionally supports the American blacks and those of Africa, the liberation movements of Latin America, of Palestine and of Asia, the revolutionary Catholics of Northern Ireland, and all those who fight for their freedom, their independence, and their dignity."

"You see?" he said, when he had finished. But the prisoner, hooded and patient, merely nodded and stared at the bathroom wall. "I'm sorry," Jacques said. The poor bastard only wanted to go to the toilet, not to hear a speech. "Go ahead," Jacques said, and turned away. Of course the Irish must have their Trudeaus too, their sellouts, their *maudits vendus.* The newspaper said Cross fought for the British during the war. And was in Malaysia. I must give him Fanon's *The Wretched of the Earth.*

43

Cross washed his hands. He asked permission to wash his face. Jacques, making sure that his own mask was on straight, went to the prisoner and removed the cowl hood which Cross always wore. He stared at Cross as the prisoner bent over the sink. Cross looked pale and shaky. They had already tried to find the pills he was supposed to take. How like Choquette to appeal for us to have common decency and give this man pills. I'd like to know how his *flics* are treating our boys down there on Parthenais Street. Bastards!

❊ ❊ ❊ ❊ ❊

That night Minister Choquette flew back late from Quebec City. He went to his suite of offices in the Justice building in Montreal. He slept on a couch, waiting for a telephone call which did not come.

❊ ❊ ❊ ❊ ❊

On Redpath Crescent, Lord Dunrossil, of the British High Commissioner's Office in Ottawa, also waited near a telephone. It was possible the kidnappers might try to contact Cross's wife. So Dunrossil spent the night in Cross's house. Waiting.

❄❄❄❄❄❄

Deputy Undersecretary A. E. Ritchie, a senior official of the Department of External Affairs, had also made up a make-shift bed. His was in the East Block of Parliament, in a second-floor suite normally used as the communications office of the department. Now it had been designated Operations Center. Deputy Undersecretary Ritchie waited out the night.

None of these logical points of communication would ever be used. Kidnappers and the authorities, like table-tappers in some spiritualist séance, would, henceforth, speak only through media: the many, garbled, and hyperactive tongues of television, radio, and the press.

4

In his dream Yves saw himself back at work as a court stenographer, taking down dictation in Superior Court of Montreal. But the details he was taking down were of the kidnapping and, when he looked up at the bench, his uncle was the judge, staring at him from beneath a huge crucifix. The Crown Prosecutor was the manager of a small Montreal hotel where Yves had worked last winter. The witness was James Richard Cross, handcuffed, his face masked by a cowled hood, made out of the leg of a pair of trousers which had belonged to Yves. Cross wept behind the cowl as he told the judge of Yves' cruelty. "I asked him to let me write a letter to my wife but he did not permit it. He said he had been ready to kill my dog and now he was ready to kill me. It was his revolutionary duty, he said. The Canadian government had refused to ransom me. Therefore they had no alternative. They had drawn lots and he had been chosen. It was his revolutionary duty."

Yves woke with a start and groped blindly for his thick-lensed spectacles. His brow and neck were wet with sweat. His hair, cut in a thick bob, was now damp and sticky. There was sunlight in the room. He lay on an air mattress in the front room of the apartment on Des Récollets Street. In the room across the hall he heard the constant muffled music and voices of the radio and television sets. He looked at the cheap skindiver watch he had purchased for this operation. It was almost four, which meant he had slept three hours since coming off guard duty at noon. Noon today, not noon tomorrow, he thought, with sudden gratitude. It's only the second day. Noon tomorrow is the time we set for doing away with Cross.

He got up, trembling, and went to the window, looking down the street for a parked car or some walker who might seem to loiter. But if the police were about, they were well hidden. On the sidewalk below him, two children tried to balance on one skateboard. They fell and laughed as they rolled over. He turned from this normal scene and went into the living room. There was an M-1 automatic rifle leaning against the wall inside the door. The television screen showed a white-haired astrologer examining the palm of an improbably big-breasted high-school girl who was dressed in the uniform of a drum majorette. He thought of the scenes he had watched last night on television: the Redpath Crescent house, police, photographs of James Richard Cross. It had seemed real then. Now, remembered, it was like a television show. The three radios, muted, scrambled rock music and commercial announcements. Jacques Lanctôt and Marc Carbonneau were sitting on the floor, drinking lime drinks and discussing the young Premier of Quebec, Robert Bourassa, whom they had just heard in a broadcast press conference.

"That millionaire's asslicker," Jacques said. "You see his priorities. It's not Cross, it's not even catching us. It's that this is bad for business. It might scare off American investors."

"And all that bullshit about his own life being in danger," Marc said. "Christ, I wish it were!"

Yves asked what had happened. He was told Bourassa had said that despite the kidnapping he was not going to cancel his scheduled trip to New York the next day. The purpose of the trip was to raise further American investment funds for Quebec. What interested Jacques and Marc in the press conference was not what the Premier had said but a chance remark by a French Canadian reporter who said the Canadian Broadcasting Corporation had got hold of all or part of the FLQ's unpublicized communiqué and manifesto. "That reporter said that to warn *us*," Jacques told Yves. "He was trying to tell us that the authorities are trying to screw us – the media have our manifesto but the authorities won't let them put it on television or in the newspapers. And, believe me, if we let them get away with it, then we might as well call this whole thing off."

"I don't agree," Marc Carbonneau said. "The first aim of this operation is to get our comrades out of jail and out of the country. Including your kid brother, for God's sakes! Our first responsibility is to those guys!"

"Our first responsibility is to the Movement," Jacques said, his head swinging around angrily, his eyes hidden by the hexagonal sunglasses. "Our first responsibility is to let the people of Quebec know how they're being screwed by these fascist bastards! To let them know they're no different from the poor blacks of Africa – they're a colonized people, exploited, with no dignity, no pride, and until they rise up in a real revolution nothing is going to change for them!" He paused, out of breath, trembling slightly as though he were giving a public speech. Marc and Yves both nodded agreement. Of course, of course, Yves thought. We all know that.

"And that's *why* the manifesto is first! That's *why* we must get it on television and in the newspapers. In full. The way we ask for it to be done. And if we don't get that, we must be prepared to follow through!"

He stared at them, consumed in his anger.

"You'd kill Cross for the manifesto?" Yves asked. Someone has to say it, he thought.

"Well, we'll cross that bridge when we come to it."

"Pierre Pascau said on his show that the federal Cabinet is meeting in Ottawa right now. About this," Marc said. "So, we'll know soon. Maybe even tonight."

"I see." Yves turned and went into the kitchen. He supposed he should eat something. He opened the refrigerator. Food. Sausages, minced meat, tomatoes, carrots, eggs, relish, peanut butter, soft drinks, cheese spread, bread, margarine. Just like a normal apartment. He could see Louise and C.T. going around some supermarket, picking this stuff out. He shut the refrigerator door, nauseated. My God, am I the only one of us who wonders if I'm dreaming?

He turned and went across the hall to the room where the prisoner was kept. C.T. and his wife were at the rear of the room, both reading, sitting side by side, like children, on an air mattress. The prisoner had been allowed to sit up. He sat, cowled, on a chair, facing a corner. They had given him Pierre Vallières' book: *Nègres blancs d'Amérique*. But he was not reading. He sat like a pupil being punished, his head down. In the other corner, where he could not see it, the second television set flickered. An afternoon soap opera moved in the stately slow motion of a world where there are no kidnappings, no politics: where death is cancer, or an off-screen accident, the doctor removing his stethoscope, folding it, shaking his head, *I am sorry, Lois. There was nothing we could do.*

Yves looked at the jailers, reading their newspapers. "How goes it?" he said. The prisoner, hearing a voice, involuntarily moved his head a fraction to the left.

"Don't turn around," Louise snapped. "He's always trying to sneak a look at us."

She was nervous – more than any of them. She had a double reason: she was a woman and not only her husband but her brother was mixed up in this. Still, Yves thought, I wish she wouldn't be so damn nasty with Cross. He's all right: he's sensible. He won't try to cheat.

"*Bonjour, monsieur,*" he said to the prisoner. "I told the others that you wish to write a letter to your wife. They are going to discuss it and we will let you know."

Cross, his head obediently turned towards the corner, nodded to show he had understood. Yves went out: the prison room depressed him. He went back into the kitchen and stood, looking out of the window. There was a child's swing in the backyard, below the blacked-out window where Cross was being held captive. A dog, its nose tracking some scent, came into the yard, sniffed towards the child's swing, stopped, turned, smelled all over a decaying milk carton which lay on the concrete path, delicately balanced on one hind leg, lifted the other hind leg, urinated on the carton as though disinfecting it, then trotted on, suddenly businesslike, crossing the yard to disappear in the alleyway between the houses. Yves considered the banality of this scene. He thought: I have done nothing until now. It seems only yesterday I was a boy in school. But already I am an ex-student, an ex-wanderer through Europe, an ex-court stenographer, an ex-night clerk in a hotel. I am the Underground Man if ever there was one. And at this moment the Cabinet of my country is debating what to do about me. What happened yesterday is in newspapers and on television all over the world. Yet I'm still just me, a young guy staring out of a kitchen window and if a girl appeared now at one of those windows across the way, and started to take her clothes off, I mean like that red-head I saw last summer out at Chambly – she came into a room across the way and took her dress off and was naked underneath and then went into her kitchen and started to make her supper, naked, taking her time. Goddamn! I mean if something like that happened now, wouldn't I just stand here getting a hard-on, hoping she wouldn't pull down the blind, *praying* that she turn around and give me a look from all angles? I mean, is that the way it is with real revolutionaries, the ones in the history books, the men of the Paris Commune, the Russian Bolsheviki, would they have stood here at a kitchen window, hoping some girl would come into view and take her pants off?

Probably, the answer is yes. Somehow, anything out of the ordinary is unreal to me. The reality is hoping I'll see a girl undress. The unreality is not knowing if, in the next forty-eight hours, I will be chosen to kill that man next door, a man old enough to be my father. Or be on a plane flying off to exile in Cuba or Algeria. Or be imprisoned. Or killed on some shoot-out with the police. Mowed down like the gangsters in that film: bullets, blood. *Bonnie and Clyde*.

Yes, this is real life; yet it's a movie I'm watching on television. And I *am* watching: we all are. Listening to the radio, watching television, reading the newspapers. Waiting for our next instalment.

51

The six o'clock news came and went, with no news. They drifted away from the television room and congregated in the kitchen. Louise heated tomato soup with rice and C.T. made some sandwiches. Suddenly, they heard Yves call: "Hey, Robert Lemieux is on radio!"

They ran into the communications room. Robert Lemieux was their man; their generation, French Canadian, graduate of McGill University Law School, a middle-class rebel who had abandoned an Establishment job with a leading English Canadian law firm to defend the impoverished activists of the Quebec New Left. He was tall; his tab-collared, blue-blazered conservative dress contradicted by shoulder-length D'Artagnan curls and the manner of a sinister Laughing Cavalier. He was angry but level-headed, fast on his feet, completely bilingual, a dialectical swordsman who, in the days ahead, would prove himself a wounding blade in the side of authority.

Now, as they tuned in on his opening conference, Lemieux could be heard telling reporters that "confidential sources inside the Montreal police department have told me that the FLQ ransom demands are for *twenty-one* political prisoners who are FLQ members and, mostly, clients of mine."

"What do you think will happen, Mr. Lemieux, if these demands are not met"

"There is no doubt in my mind that James Cross will be executed if the demands are not met. That is my personal opinion, based on my experience."

"B-b-bravo, Robert!" C.T. shouted.

Would Mr. Lemieux define the term "political prisoners"?

"They are young men who have run into legal difficulties because of their political militancy for the independence of Quebec."

"The kidnappers' forty-eight-hour deadline is due to expire tomorrow morning unless some last-minute delay is granted. Will you comment on that, sir?"

"Well," said Lemieux. "It's a rather scary situation, isn't it?"

On Des Récollets Street, his young audience laughed.

Had he known about the kidnappings beforehand?

"No. I had no foreknowledge. I have no contact whatever with the members of the FLQ who kidnapped Mr. Cross. And I feel that my twenty-one clients, who are in prison, had no prior knowledge that the kidnappings would take place. For the record I would like to say, however, that the kidnapping has agreeably surprised all of them."

"Agreeably!" Jacques Lanctôt chortled. He was enjoying this.

Lemieux then complained that the authorities had misrepresented the FLQ's demands. He said Minister Choquette had mentioned only twelve prisoners as the number to be ransomed, not twenty-one, as was the case. He ended by saying that he had contacted twelve prisoners in jail that day, eight of whom had signed a note saying they would accept any offer to set them free. Four others had given verbal approval. He listed the names of the twelve men willing to go into exile. Among them was Louise's and Jacques' younger brother, François.

"Did you hear?" Louise said, excitedly. "François signed. Oh, God, will we really get him away to Algeria?"

"*Nous vaincrons!*" Jacques said and, around the television set, they all raised clenched fists. They had begun to hope.

But, an hour later, the radio announced that a short statement had been read to the federal House of Commons by Mitchell Sharp, External Affairs Minister of Canada. The statement had been cleared with the provincial government of Quebec and approved by the Prime Minister of Canada, Pierre Elliott Trudeau. A still photograph flashed on the television screen. It was the face of the man who holds a position equivalent to Foreign Secretary in Britain or Secretary of State in the United States. Mitchell Sharp, the first

53

federal spokesman to confront the kidnappers, had a face the young men on Des Récollets could easily hate: tight-featured, English, the face one sees on old ex-servicemen who spend their postwar lives in uniform as doormen and guards of the Canadian Corps of Commissionaires; those officious nobodies who used to wave off Jacques and Marc when they tried to pick up an illegal fare at the airport. Briefly, Sharp summarized their demands; briefly, contemptuously, he dismissed them. "Clearly, these are wholly unreasonable demands and the authors could not have expected them to be accepted. I need hardly say that this set of demands will not be met. I continue, however, to hope that some basis can be found for Mr. Cross's safe return. Indeed, I hope the abductors will find a way to establish communication to achieve this."

"What does he *mean*, c-c-communication?"

"But, it is most important," Sharp continued, "that we should find out whether Mr. Cross is safe and well and whether there is a basis on which he might be delivered on a healthy basis to his family."

"Right," Jacques Lanctôt said, jumping up. "He'll hear from Cross. And from us. Let's get to work!"

❈ ❈ ❈ ❈ ❈

Marc the mailman. He thought of it, grimly amused, as he stood at the mailbox at the intersection of Sherbrooke and Victor Bourgereau Streets and slipped a letter into it. This letter will never be collected by a mailman, he thought.

He turned and, limping, went into a snack bar. From a booth in the rear, he phoned the house of a reporter called Louis Fournier. He knew Fournier slightly, had seen him at the time of the taxi demonstrations – a hip, bearded young guy, an ex-student at the Université de Montréal, and an ex-reporter for *Québec-Presse*, the left-wing weekly. Now he was a reporter at CKAC radio station. A good guy, Fournier. If anybody would help and not fink by phoning the *flics*, Fournier would be the type. Still, Marc did not identify himself when he phoned. He merely told the person who answered that a message from the FLQ would be delivered to Mr. Fournier's home. He hung up.

Shortly afterwards, Louis Fournier opened his door to a taxi driver who handed him a package and left without speaking. Fournier went inside and opened the envelope. When he saw what he had, he at once phoned his news director at the station. The director, Pierre Robert, a twenty-nine-year-old French Canadian, was chatting with Daniel McGinnis, twenty-four, the station's news commentator. They listened to what Fournier read, then recorded it over the telephone on magnetic tape. Fournier then telephoned the police and handed over the package.

As Fournier was doing his civic duty, McGinnis performed his journalistic function, broadcasting the text of Liberation Cell's second communiqué, a message at once picked up by every competing station and by all television newsrooms. Within minutes, it was going out in French and in English on international wire service teleprinters. Translated into English, it read:

Communiqué No. 2. October 6, 1970.

Mr. Cross's health is very good. Everyone, including his wife, can be reassured on that score. In addition, Mr. Cross has written to his wife and the letter has been placed in a mailbox at the corner of Sherbrooke and Victor Bourgereau Streets.

55

We ask that, as newsmen, you cooperate to break the wall of silence which the fascist police have erected around Operation Liberation by systematically stealing all the communiqués and our manifesto which were addressed to the various information media.

The ruling authorities do not seem to take the demands of the FLQ, which were outlined in the first communiqué, seriously. However, if they wish to save the life of Diplomat Cross, they must carry out the conditions we have established. It would be wiser to save Diplomat Cross's life by complying with our demands than by launching tear-filled appeals about the pills which J. Cross must take. Let it be quite clear that when the deadline has passed we shall not hesitate to kill Mr. Cross. Because the life and liberty of the political prisoners and the Lapalme guys are worth the lives of hundreds of diplomats who represent only the interests of the Anglo-Saxon and American "big bosses."

The ruling authorities will be solely responsible for the death of Mr. Cross.

We shall conquer

Front de Libération du Québec

N.B. <u>The contents of this second communiqué must be made public</u>.

5

In the theatre of political confrontation, television is the nth power. No one knew it better than he. A political enemy had said of him: "his version of parliamentary democracy can be summed up as 'I appear on television from time to time. I'm the show, you admire it. There's no discussion, no real exchange of views with different segments of the population.'" A damaging remark. He had struck back at that particular enemy, reversing Acton by saying that "lack of power corrupts absolutely." But *he* knew the power of television. It had made him Prime Minister. There were those who now compared him with the star of a top-rated weekly series: unknown to the public as a real man, so completely was he identified with his media-created character: the swinging Prime Minister, Pierre Elliott Trudeau.

He was aware of their strategy, these FLQ bandits. They were ordinary criminals whom the media tried to sanctify with a "political" tinge. And calling the ones in jail "political prisoners"! He would not dignify this squalid crime by treating it as a national crisis. He stayed offstage, advising, dissenting. In Ottawa, the national capital, he came and went quickly and inconspicuously in those first few days, ducking down back alleys to avoid the press-gallery reporters who had always hounded him with something of the same curious hero worship-hate which women's magazines once accorded Jacqueline Kennedy. However, on the third day of this affair, on his way to the morning session of Parliament he was, briefly, intercepted. Irked, he chose to be curt and evasive. He did, however, say two things to reporters which won him a rapt young audience on Rue des Récollets.

"You can't let a minority group impose its view on the majority by violence."

He was asked: "Is it true then, sir, that both the federal and the provincial governments will stick to their original decision not to yield to blackmail?"

"I don't intend bargaining on television in any way," he said.

When Jacques Lanctôt heard the Prime Minister's voice saying these words on a ten a.m. news broadcast, on that Wednesday, October 10, he at once assumed that the FLQ's all-important demand – television airing of their manifesto in prime time – had thus been denied them.

"You notice *he* brought it up," Jacques said. "The reporters didn't mention television. *He* did. He's read the manifesto, of course. And he's afraid of the truth!"

An hour later, Minister Choquette came on radio to appeal to the kidnappers. He asked them, in the course of a broadcast press conference, "to allow their respect for human life to overcome their political aspirations. They should realize that this manner of defending their cause can only bring about its eventual defeat."

"Spoken like a good village p-priest," C.T. said. "Giving us bad b-boys a warning in the confessional."

They listened, skeptically, to the Minister's statement that he would keep a special line open in his office and would stay there day and night in hopes they would contact him.

"Yes, my sons," C.T. said, doing his Jesuit imitation. "If you b-boys will please telephone my office and talk long enough for my *flics* to trace your call, we'll send a car down to get you and take you here to Gestapo headquarters to t-talk to me in p-person."

The others laughed, and laughed even more when Marc, hearing the Minister say that Mrs. Cross had received a letter from her husband last night which the kidnappers had placed in a mailbox, called out: "Got it last night? That was Special Delivery!"

"According to this letter," the Minister said, "the kidnappers seem to intend the deadline to be noon today, not eight-thirty this morning, as we had believed."

"Okay," Jacques said. "But it's now half an hour before noon. You'd better decide, Jérôme."

This time, there was no laughter. They had said it: "We shall not hesitate to kill Mr. Cross." It was one thing to say it, even to write it down in a communiqué, but now, in the next room, a living man waited. Singly, by drawing lots, or together, like some inept firing squad, they would have to go in there and end his life.

Marc shivered and bit on an antacid pill. He rose, bent over with the pain in his stomach, and went next door to relieve Yves on guard duty. He looked over at Cross who sat, silent, staring into his corner. What was their prisoner thinking? Was he afraid? Was he plotting some attempt to escape? He knew Cross had been listening to television last night when whatshisname – Heath – the British Prime Minister said the British government had full confidence in the Canadian government's decisions. Which surprised *me,* Marc thought. I was the one who said we should kidnap Cross because I thought the British would never stand by and let Trudeau call the shots.

Remember this summer when those two Jordanian irregulars tried to hijack a plane? The British got them. The girl, Lelia Khaled, was in jail in England. But the British let her go because the Jordanians hijacked a second plane, flew it to the desert, and threatened to kill the passengers. And some of the passengers were British. The British will fight a war for one Englishman, I said. I was wrong.

C.T. came in and picked up Marc's M-1. "You're w-wanted outside."

In the kitchen, Jacques Lanctôt was waiting. "It's noon."

Marc nodded. "Yes, I know."

"Robert Lemieux just said on radio that the government's playing cat and mouse with us. But that he still hoped we'd postpone the noon deadline. What do you think?"

"Robert is smart," Marc said. "Maybe he knows something we don't know."

Suddenly, Jacques laughed and hit Marc a playful punch in the ribs. "Jesus Christ! Why does every one of you think I'm itching to kill Cross?"

"I didn't say that."

"You didn't have to say it. Look, I know that if we kill Cross right now, we gain nothing. So let's give them another twenty-four hours. I'm working on a communiqué. When I've finished it I want you to get it on CKLM. We want to get it on Pierre Pascau's 'News Witness' show. Okay?"

"Okay," Marc said. He found himself smiling, almost carefree. He went back into the prisoner's room and signaled to C.T. that he was relieving him. When C.T. went out, Marc walked up to the prisoner, who sat, his back obediently presented to his captors, staring at television with the air of a bored churchgoer at an endless sermon. Marc bent close to the prisoner's ear. "Don't turn around," he said quietly. "I

60

just wanted to tell you that the ransom deadline has been extended."

In the double living room C.T. was reading through Jacques Lanctôt's new communiqué. "What's all this about a f-few dollars?"

"In England and in New York and Toronto they put in the headlines that we're holding Cross for $500,000 ransom in gold. They make it sound as if that's why we took him: to get money. But it's not money, goddammit! We just put that in with the other things."

"I see," said C.T. These communiqués were like poems to Lanctôt, C.T. decided. There was no point discussing them with him.

"It sounds all right to you, then?" Jacques Lanctôt asked.

"Yes. F-fine."

CKLM, a French-language radio station, is situated in a modest block of offices on the fifth floor of an unpretentious building on Ste. Catherine Street, a street that lost much of its importance as a shopping artery during the Expo 67 period when internationally known architects like I. M. Pei and planners like William Zeckendorf and Vincent Ponte completed their transformation of downtown Montreal from an American-style city, with the raiload terminals right in the center of town, to something which could be the prototype for the large international downtowns of our future: a central city of interconnecting underground streets and shopping plazas, of spotless, almost silent subway stations, huge office building complexes subterraneanly interconnected to modern hotels, and apartment buildings created by such architectural latter-day saints as Nervi and Mies van der Rohe. Ste. Catherine Street, with its old-fashioned hustling department stores, its ugly, overhanging neon signs, its narrow sidewalks and day-long clog of traffic, already seems, like radio itself, dated, a relic of a more provincial time.

Estelle LaFramboise, the receptionist at CKLM, sat, appropriately, in a thirties-style setting behind a desk on the fifth floor, sealed off from the adjoining studios by a door which was kept locked and could be opened only by authorized personnel. At one-thirty that afternoon, a man came out of the elevator opposite her desk, placed an envelope in front of her, and turned and stepped back into the elevator, which had not yet shut its doors. He was about fifty years old, short, stout, with gray hair. She thought he was a taxi driver, although she could not say why she thought it.

The envelope had been expected. Half an hour earlier, an anonymous telephone call had been made to Pierre Pascau, public affairs director of the station and the voluble host of an open-line show which had won high ratings on Des Récollets Street for its frankness. Pascau, a Mauritian, who had worked for Radio Luxembourg before coming to Canada in 1965, once publicly announced to the FLQ: "I don't judge. I am willing to serve as a link between you and the population of Quebec, so that we may at least understand what you want." A mustachioed young man, fluently bilingual, with an excitable radio style, Pascau was on the air with his show when Lanctôt's envelope was delivered to CKLM. His researcher, a bearded young fellow called Pierre Charbonneau, brought the envelope into the studio. Inside the envelope they found a communiqué, plus a note from Cross to his wife and a note from Cross to the authorities. Feverishly, Pascau examined this material. Ninety seconds later, Liberation Cell was on the air with its demands:

Communiqué No. 4. October 7, 1970. Delay 24 hours.

The Front de Libération du Québec has decided to grant a delay of 24 hours to the authorities to allow them to establish their good faith. This deadline will therefore expire Thursday, October 8 at 12 noon. As proof of good faith, we ask the authorities for:

1. Release of the complete text of the FLQ manifesto on Radio-Canada network stations. This program must be aired on radio and television between the hours of eight and eleven p.m. It should be read by a competent reporter (for example: C. J. Deverieux).

2. The immediate cessation of all searches, questionings, and arrests by repressive police forces.

We will consider any refusal to comply with these first demands as a proof of bad faith. We will then no longer have any choice.

As for us, be assured that we will not put the life of the diplomat J. Cross at stake over a few dollars.

We shall conquer

Front de Libération du Québec

Note: Attached to this communiqué are two letters by J. Cross. One to his wife and one to the authorities.

Cross's letter was handwritten. It read as though it had been dictated to him.

Tuesday
9.45 p.m.

1. I ask the authorities to respond favorably to the demands of the FLQ.

2. It will be faster and easier for everyone if all the FLQ communiqués are published in full.

3. Please assure that I am well and receiving the medicaments for my blood pressure.

4. I am being well treated but the FLQ are determined to achieve their demands.

J. R. Cross

Television. Only that morning the Prime Minister of Canada had broken his vatic silence to announce:

"I don't intend bargaining on television in any way."

They had replied that same afternoon by outlining their television program. The complete text of the FLQ manifesto to be aired on radio and television between eight and eleven p.m. and read by C. J. Deverieux, a commentator they admired.

Surely they would be refused. The Prime Minister had said that morning: "You can't let a minority group impose its view on the majority by violence."

Yet by evening the nation was told that a tiny minority would be permitted to air its view in prime time on national television. It had imposed its will by violence and threats of violence. Trudeau had done what he said he would not do. The announcement, made by Trudeau's Minister, Sharp, was aired, appropriately on the national television network.

64

I have seen the text of the latest communiqué from the abductors of Mr. Cross, together with a letter from Mr. Cross. Both the communiqué and the letter attached particular importance to the broadcasting of a certain manifesto or communiqué on radio and television over Radio-Canada. We are prepared to arrange for the broadcast, although we are not quite sure which document is involved. But we must have assurances that, without the imposition of unacceptable conditions, Mr. Cross will be delivered safe and sound.

I have already made clear that the set of seven conditions originally stipulated by the abductors is wholly unreasonable. What the government needs now is the precise basis on which it can be assured of Mr. Cross's safe release, and where and when. Otherwise there can be no dependable discussion, since the captors might hold on to Mr. Cross indefinitely. For this purpose and for the discussion of any other matters which might arise, the problem of arranging some acceptable means of communication with the abductors still remains. There are a variety of ways in which this could be done. But, as a first step, I invite those holding Mr. Cross to name some person with whom the authorities, or a person representing the authorities, can deal with confidence in making arrangements leading to Mr. Cross's early and safe release.

When this was heard on Des Récollets Street, the room erupted in excited, confused talk. "What does he mean, he doesn't know which document is involved, it's the manifesto, the manifesto! Yves, pass me those envelopes, the big ones, let's get some more copies out. Yes, tonight!"

Shortly before midnight Marc Carbonneau approached a taxi rank on Sherbrooke Street. Two cab drivers were waiting there. Marc gave each of them an envelope. One drove to the Radio-Canada studios on Dorchester Street and delivered the envelope addressed to French Network Public Affairs. At 12:15 a.m. the second cab driver delivered the second envelope to CKAC, a large French-language radio station. At CKAC, Pierre Robert, the news director, held a hurried conference with his reporters. After all, Trudeau's own Minister had announced that the contents of this very envelope would be aired tomorrow night on the government television network. So why not show a little journalistic enterprise and be first with the shocking news? Thus, at 12:30 a.m., on Thursday, October 8, 1970, at a time when the majority of people were in bed, the most subversive document ever made public in Canada was read straight, as news.

On Des Récollets Street they waited up to hear it. This, at last, was the dress rehearsal for their big show. For Jacques Lanctôt, it was surely one of the most gratifying moments of his life. These were his words, his insults, his grievances. And tomorrow evening, he, twenty-five years old, a junior college dropout, would be given the facilities of the most sophisticated propaganda equipment ever invented, to tell millions of his countrymen that, among other things, the Prime Minister of Canada was a *tapette*, which is French slang for homosexual.

6

Noon. Thursday, October 8. James Richard Cross sat in a darkened room. Blessedly, there was a moment's relief from the idiotic sound of the television set. Now it had been turned off and the guards he was never allowed to look at had gone out of the room to whisper in the corridor.

Suddenly, far, far away, factory whistles pierced the warm October air, clear across the great sprawl of the city, ululating like those air-raid sirens long ago in London, announcing the all clear, the end of danger when one knew the German bombers had been sighted recrossing the Channel, returning to Hitler's Reich. The sirens had always had a joyous sound to those who lived through that war. But for Cross, they could have recalled another, less cheerful omen, the mythical wail of the banshee in his native Ireland, that high cry of a female ghost which signals that some member of the family is about to die.

If, at this juncture, he were given to ironic speculation, he might reflect on the curious happenstance of his present fate. From the beginning he had had about him something of the understudy, the substitute; a second choice when the effort to kidnap the United States Consul General aborted. He was not even English, not even a true diplomat. He was Irish, a trade representative with no political duties. As a hostage, it must by now seem to him that he was not highly regarded. The Canadian government had, in fact, gambled with his life. Most ironic of all, at noon on this third day of his imprisonment, he would appear to have been spared, not for any amnesty of prisoners or princely ranson, but for something as curiously trivial as the promise of a television program to take place that same evening. Could it really be that he, a father, a husband, a British officer, a trained economist with a first-class honors degree, a senior official of Her Majesty's Department of Trade and Industry with a record of service in India, Malaysia, and London as well as in Canada, was being traded off, at this high point of his career, against a fifteen-minute television show?

But that was exactly what was happening. On Des Récollets Street his young captors were, at that moment, discussing whether or not the government would follow through on its promise before midnight.

"If only we could speak to someone like Robert Lemieux!" Louise said.

"His phone is being t-tapped, for sure."

They were silent, thinking of that. They had all read the morning newspaper stories. There had been raids before dawn both yesterday and today. Police squads armed with submachine guns and tear gas. Thirty people had been arrested, including three women. All were "FLQ sympathizers."

"For me, you know it's a question of Suzanne," Jacques Lanctôt said. "Those three women they arrested, one of them might be her. We've got to stop these raids!"

"We put it in the very first communiqué," Marc said, gently.

"Well, we'll put it in again. Those *flics* have got to be called off. We've got to make that clear!"

Marc nodded. "Yes," he said. Jacques Lanctôt's young wife, Suzanne, was seven months pregnant with her second child. Her boy, Boris-Manuel, was eighteen months old and was at present staying with a babysitter who did not know Jacques Lanctôt's whereabouts. Suzanne was living quietly with friends in the East End of the city, waiting for her husband's summons. He had written into the first communiqué that the wives and children of those "political prisoners" who wished to accompany them to Cuba or Algeria should be allowed to do so. He planned to take his own family – Suzanne, Boris, and the unborn child – to wherever this operation would lead them. Suzanne was to have come to Des Récollets Street yesterday but after they had successfully brought Cross to the house, Jacques felt afraid. Perhaps it was too risky? Perhaps she was being watched and followed by the police? Or was already arrested?

Marc agreed it was risky. That morning he had gone down to a barbecue chicken place some blocks from the hideout and had phoned Ti-Chrisse.

"One of the people the police arrested yesterday was Pierre Marcil. Another was Pierre Carrier," Ti-Chrisse told him. "Carrier was in that summer shack in Prevost when the cops raided it earlier in the summer. The shack where they found that plan to kidnap the U.S. Consul General. I thought you might be interested."

Marc was. There was only one conclusion to be drawn from these arrests and he drew it now, although he knew it would make Jacques Lanctôt even more nervous.

"The guy the police want is you," Marc told Jacques. "And not for jumping bail. Both those arrests are tied to you. And, starting with you, they're going to open up the file on all of us who were active last year with the Mouvement de Libération du Taxi. Remember, I was photographed with you, the two of us talking to reporters. From now on you're hot, man. You'd better stay right here in the house."

Jacques agreed. They talked again about the manifesto. "We've got to make sure they don't back down on reading it. And we've got to do something about the *flics*."

A new communiqué was drafted. C.T. was picked as courier. Shortly after one-thirty that afternoon, C.T. boarded a city transit bus, carrying a large brown envelope folded in three and addressed to Pierre Pascau of Radio CKLM. In the northeast end of the city Pie IX Boulevard intersects with a long sprawling street named Jean Talon. C.T. changed buses here and went several blocks west, alighting at the corner of De Gaspé Avenue. He entered a glassed-in public phone booth, phoned, gave a message, then hung up. A few moments later the phone rang, shrill and lonely in the silence of the booth. C.T. picked up the receiver. The time was 2:12 p.m.

"It's done," a voice said.

"W-was it Pascau?"

"Yes. They're sending someone."

"Good," C.T. said.

He stepped out of the phone booth, checking his watch. Ten minutes later he re-entered it. In the pages of the telephone directory he inserted the large, folded brown envelope. Coolly, he left the booth and crossed the street. He pretended interest in a store window and, three minutes later, saw a car stop on the corner. Two young men got out. One entered the phone booth and reclaimed the envelope.

When they had found the envelope, unaware that they were being watched by the kidnapper, the reporters staged their own small scene. One of them got a camera and photographed his fellow reporter "removing" the envelope from its hiding place. They then drove off. They were Claude Beausoleil and André Bernard, reporters for the French-language weekly *La Semaine,* who had been in CKLM's newsroom at the time a man, defined only by Pascau as "a lawyer," phoned and told him there was a package in a phone booth at Jean Talon and De Gaspé Streets. Pascau sent these reporters to reclaim it.

C.T. watched them go, satisfied that they were not police. He got on a bus, went back to Pie IX Boulevard, transferred to another bus, and went north. He returned to the Des Récollets address in less than half an hour.

An unknown and undistinguished young French Canadian riding a bus in a suburban street in a provincial city, in a country of the third rank. A handsome boy with a long mustache and a quick, cutting sense of humor. But anonymous, a face in the crowd. Yet as he reached Montreal North that afternoon, at 2:40 p.m., suddenly it seemed that the world waited for the message he had brought to it that day. At station CKLM, his communiqué was being scrambled over by reporters, photographers, and camera crews from Canada, England, the United States, and France. Dozens of photocopies were rushed off Xerox machines and handed out to other press and television newsmen, as, first with his scoop, Pascau went on the air. Then and only then, an aide called the police, who thus received the communiqué at second-hand. Furious at this, Paul-Emile Olivier, assistant Montreal Police director, publicly complained: "It seems some radio stations and other newsrooms have closer contacts with the FLQ than we do."

The police director had missed the point. Canada's police, unlike the more primitive police forces of South America, were in possession of many and sophisticated wiretap, bugging, and electronic tracing devices. To young men like C.T., Yves, and Jacques, brought up on Dick Tracy comics and B-movies, the telephone is always a trap; the police squad

71

car, screeching to a halt, is, in true movie fashion, only minutes away from the kidnapper in his phone booth. To these children of Canada's first TV generation, born in the early fifties when television programming came to the country, the electronic media were the natural conduit towards the public. Children of the first years of television commercials, they could conceive of no better method of getting their message across. Indeed, in this communiqué, they said as much:

```
Communiqué No. 5. October 8, 1970. Noon --
Deadline 12 hours.
    For the last time the FLQ warns the ruling
authorities. If, within 12 hours (midnight), the
ruling authorities have not:
    1. Proved their good faith by broadcasting our
political manifesto through Radio-Canada as
stipulated in Communiqué No. 4;
    2. Ordered the fascist police forces to put an
immediate stop to their searches, raids, arrests,
or torture;
the FLQ will be forced to liquidate the diplomat
J. Cross.
    Once these [two] conditions have been fulfilled,
the FLQ asks the authorities to specify in concrete
terms what they call "unreasonable" demands.
    As for the guarantees demanded by the ruling
authorities, they must exist amid good faith from
both sides.
    We repeat we will not put the life of J. Cross
at stake for a question of dollars. We will
release the diplomat Cross within 24 hours after
another condition has been met, namely the release
of the "consenting" political prisoners.
                    We shall conquer
            Front de Libération du Québec
Note: We reject the idea of a mediator. We will
continue to establish contact according to our own
methods, thus avoiding the traps being laid out
by the fascist police.
```

We reject the idea of a mediator, they had written in that significant note at the end of the communiqué. But, in fact, they had chosen their man. He was the man who, in his press conference the day before, had urged the government to nominate a mediator who would be acceptable to the abductors; someone, he suggested, like Claude Ryan, editor of the nationalist French-language Montreal daily newspaper *Le Devoir*. Or, he suggested, perhaps some religious leader because "incidents of this kind have been settled successfully in Latin America through the mediation of some high-ranking clergymen."

On Des Récollets Street, his press conference was listened to with close attention, although the mention of a clergyman drew loud, derisive cheers. It had to be a put-on, that remark. *We reject the idea of a mediator*, they had written in their communiqué. Yet, a few hours later, on the selfsame night the FLQ manifesto was to be read on national television, the third man in this strange drama was again center stage and had, in effect, become their spokesman. With an Aristotelian sense of logic he would make contact with them solely within the rules of this theater of fright, a wavering, unlinear contact which relied on the osmosis of that great information medium of our age: the televised press conference.

The man was Robert Lemieux, the New Left lawyer, a stage manager of impeccable theatricality who held his press conferences in the tavern of this same Nelson Hotel, a few steps away from the port of Montreal and the twisting old lanes in which the city's fur traders made early Canadian fortunes more than three hundred years ago. The hotel itself faces the Place Jacques Cartier, a charming old French square where farmers come to sell their flowers and vegetables from trucks in open-air market. Hotel and square both lie in the lee of Montreal's City Hall, a Belle Epoque extravagance, reminiscent of a Paris railroad station, that same City Hall from the main balcony of which, in 1967, General Charles de Gaulle called out: *"Vive le Québec Libre!"*

The Nelson Hotel, however, takes its tone, not from memories of an old man's dangerous rhetoric, but rather from the spirit of the odd statue which stands at the top of the square, its back to City Hall, its face to the port: the one-eyed adulterer, Lord Nelson himself. The hotel tavern that evening was, as always during a Lemieux happening, crowded with reporters, television cameramen, radio technicians, police spies, hippies, and a sizable contingent of young men who act as unofficial police for the star of the show. The tavern – normally a quiet nautical room with dark wood, sensible tables, captain's chairs, and advertisements for the Quebec government lottery and Dow and Molson ales – now was smoke-filled and clamorous with waiters rushing and stumbling in the cluttered aisles, with shouts of "*deux fois*" (meaning two-beers-a-man, delivered at once), with the pushing and jostling for position of the media contingent and, at a table, brightlit by floodlights, tense, laughing, moving instantly from French to equally fluent English, leaning into the barrage of table and hand mikes, Lemieux himself.

"More than fifty arrests, yes," he said, answering a question about police activity. "It seems to me that the government's refusal to call off these police raids officially means the authorities don't really want to negotiate. They're simply trying to buy time.

"Police operations are continuing at a rate that has never been seen in Montreal!" Lemieux shouted. "This is a new indication of the bad faith of the authorities."

On Des Récollets Street they listened as though Lemieux were on the other end of the telephone. What could they do if it were a doublecross?

"The two essential conditions for the release of Mr. Cross," Lemieux said, "are the liberation of the political prisoners and a moratorium on police activities."

"And the manifesto!" Jacques said.

Lemieux, obviously speaking to them and not to the press, said he thought the other demands, including the one for a $500,000 ransom, would be dropped by the kidnappers.

74

"Yes, sure, we told them that," Yves said.

Around Lemieux, his young men began hustling reporters aside, trying to still the yelled questions and give their man a moment of silence. Lemieux, leaning into the microphones, ended his conference with the terse, meaningful phrase: *"Ne lachez pas, les gars!"* (Hang in there, boys.)

"Hang in! Okay, let's hang in!" Jacques said.

Marc, who was with the prisoner in the other room, called out. "Hey, when does *our* show go on?"

"Ten-thirty," Jacques called back.

"I want to see it," Marc called.

Jacques went into the prisoner's room. "You can let him see it too," he said, pointing at Cross's back.

❊❊❊❊❊

At ten-thirty, when the announcer, seated at a table, holding their manifesto, appeared on the television screen, the first reaction of the kidnappers was anger. "We told them we w-wanted C. J. Deverieux," C.T. said. "He did a great job last year at the St. Jean B-Baptiste riots – he spoke up for our guys against the cops. Who is this d-dummy?"

"Shh!" the others cried, for the announcer had begun to read. In fact, the television network officials seemed to agree with C.T. and, anxious to avoid presenting the manifesto as news, chose, instead of Deverieux, a neutral-sounding news commentator, Gaétan Montreuil. It was, in American terms, the choice of a Walter Cronkite rather than a Mike Wallace. As

75

Montreuil began his reading, a subtitle was flashed on screen, and remained there throughout the telecast. It read TEXTE DE MANIFESTE FLQ. Read in a level, unemotional voice, the manifesto – crude, ill-written, abusive – was curiously moving and often effective, perhaps because its authors had rung in every real labor strike and grievance in Quebec since 1957, perhaps because, for the first time in the history of Canada, it was the angry, confused voice of the lumpenproletariat in the nation's most exploited region, the voice of the French defeat in a country which has traditionally papered over its racial differences with a thick paste of hypocrisy about a "biculturalism" which, in fact, does not exist. Translated into English, the following morning it would appear in newspapers throughout the other nine (English-speaking) provinces of Canada, a strange, distorting mirror held up to the Canadian face. As for its French-speaking Quebec audience, they listened that night with anything but boredom: disbelief that they were actually hearing these things said on television; shock at the naming of names and the vulgarity of the language. And yet, by a great many, perhaps by the majority, it was heard with secret amusement, a sense of vindication and revenge, for underneath the sour Mao dough of its revolutionary cliché was a certain leaven of truth.

The Front de Libération du Québec is not a messiah, nor a modern-day Robin Hood. It is a group of Quebec workers who have decided to do whatever must be done so that the people of Quebec will take control of their destiny.

The Front de Libération du Québec wants the total independence of Quebeckers, united in a free society, purged forever of the clique of voracious sharks, the patronizing "big bosses" and their henchmen who have made Quebec their hunting preserve for "cheap labor" and unscrupulous exploitation.

The Front de Libération du Québec is not a movement of aggression but the response to an aggression, organized by high finance and by the federal and provincial puppet governments.

76

The Front de Libération du Québec is self-financed by "voluntary taxes" taken from the same enterprises that exploit the workers (banks, finance companies, etc.). . . .

We once believed that perhaps it would be worthwhile to channel our energy and our impatience into the Parti Québecois, but the Liberal victory showed us clearly that what we call democracy in Quebec is nothing but the democracy of the rich. The Liberal Party's victory was nothing but the victory of the election riggers. As a result, the British parliamentary system is finished and the Front de Libération du Québec will never allow itself to be sidetracked by the pseudo elections which the Anglo-Saxon capitalists toss to the Quebec people every four years. A number of Quebeckers now realize what has happened and will now act on it. In the coming year Bourassa will have to face reality: 100,000 revolutionary workers, armed and organized.

Yes, there are reasons for the Liberal victory. Yes, there are reasons for poverty, unemployment, misery, and for the fact that you, Mr. Bergeron of Visitation Street, and you, Mr. Legendre of Laval, who earn $10,000 a year, will not feel free in our country of Quebec.

Yes, there are reasons and the guys who work at Lord know them, the fishermen of the Gaspé, the workers of the North Shore, the miners for the Iron Ore Co., Quebec Cartier Mining, and Noranda, also know the reasons. And the brave workers of Cabano whom they tried to fuck once again – they know the reasons. . . .

Yes, there are reasons why you, Mr. Tremblay, and you, Mr. Cloutier, who work in the construction industry at Saint-Jerome that you cannot pay for "Vaisseux d'Or" [Golden Vessels: a reference to a plush Montreal restaurant owned by Mayor Jean Drapeau], with all that beautiful classy music and all the pizazz as does Drapeau the aristocrat – who is so concerned with slums that he puts colored billboards in front of them to hide our misery from the tourists.

Yes, there are reasons why you, Mrs. Lemay, of Ste. Hyacinthe, you can't pay for little trips to Florida like all these dirty judges and members of parliament do with our money.

The brave workers for Vickers [Shipyards] and Davie Ship, who were thrown out without any reason being given, they know these reasons. And the Murdochville guys who were attacked for the sole and simple reason that they wanted to organize a union and who were forced by the dirty judges to pay $2,000,000 because they tried to exercise this basic right – they know justice and they know plenty of reasons.

77

Yes, there are reasons why you, Mr. Lachance of St. Marguerite Street, must go and drown your sorrows in that dog's beer – Molson's. And you, Lachance's son with your marijuana cigarettes. . . .

Yes, there are reasons why you, the people on welfare, are kept on it from generation to generation. There are lots of reasons and the Domtar workers at Windsor and at East Angus know them well. And the workers at Squibb and Ayers, and the guys at the Provincial Liquor Commission, and the boys from Seven-Up and Victoria Precision, and the blue-collar workers in Laval and Montreal and the Lapalme boys, they all know these reasons well.

And the Montreal policemen, who are the strong arms of the system, they should understand these reasons: they should have been able to see that we live in a terrorized society because, without their strength, without their violence, nothing could work.

We've had our fill of Canadian Federalism which penalizes the Quebec milk producers to satisfy the needs of the Anglo-Saxons of the Commonwealth; the system which keeps the gallant Montreal taxi drivers in a state of semi-slavery to protect the exclusive monopoly of the nauseating Murray Hill [Company] and of its owner-assassin Charles Herschorn and of his son Paul.

We've had our fill of a system which exercises a crazy policy of imports while turning the lowly paid textile shoe manufacturing industry workers out into the street in order to provide profits for a clutch of damned money makers driving around in Cadillacs:

We've had our fill of a system which rates the Quebec nation on the same level as other ethnic minorities in Canada.

We've had our fill, as have more and more Quebeckers, of a government which does a thousand and one acrobatic tricks to charm American millionaires into investing in Quebec, *La Belle Province*, where thousands of square miles of forests filled with game and lakes filled with fish are the exclusive preserve of these all-powerful twentieth-century lords:

We've had our fill of taxes which the Ottawa representative in Quebec wants to give to the English-speaking bosses to "encourage" them, if you please, to speak French, to do business in the French language; "Repeat after me: Cheap Labor: You say it in French as: *main d'oeuvre à bon marché*."

We've had our fill of promises of jobs and prosperity knowing that we will continue as dutiful servants and bootlickers of the big shots for just as long as places like Westmount, Town of Mount Royal, Hampstead, and Outremont continue to exist: for as long as all the fortresses of high finance on St. James's Street and Wall Street continue to exist, for as long as we Quebeckers fail to use every means to chase out, yes, even with guns and dynamite if needs be, these economic and political big bosses, who are ready to stoop to any lengths in order to fuck us up.

We live in a society of terrorized slaves, terrorized by the big owners, Steinberg, Clark, Smith, Neaple, Timmins, Geoffrion, J. L. Levesque, Herschorn, Desmarais, Kierans (in comparison with these big shots, Remi Popol, the girl chaser, Drapeau the dog, Bourassa the sidekick of the Simards, Trudeau the fag, are just peanuts!).

We live in a society terrorized by the capitalist Roman Catholic church, even though this seems to be diminishing (who owns the property on which the Stock Exchange stands?), by the payments to reimburse Household Finance; by the advertising of the grand masters of consumer goods like Eaton, Simpson, Morgan, Steinberg, and General Motors.

We are terrorized by those closed circles of science and culture, the universities, and by their monkey directors Gaudry and Dorais and by the sub-monkey Robert Shaw.

More and more of us now know and suffer under this terrorist society and the day is coming when all the Westmounts of Quebec will disappear off the map.

Production workers, miners, lumberjacks, service workers, teachers, students, unemployed workers, take what belongs to you – your work, your determination, and your freedom. And you, the workers at General Electric, you're the ones who make your factories run, only you are capable of production; without you, General Electric is nothing!

Workers of Quebec, start today to take back what belongs to you; take for yourselves what is yours. Only you know your factories, your machines, your hotels, your universities, your unions. Don't wait for an organizational miracle!

Make you own revolution in your own districts, in your places of work. And if you don't do it yourselves, other usurpers, technocrats and others, will replace the iron hand of the cigar smokers we now know, and everything will have to be done all over again. You alone are capable of building a free society.

We must fight, not one by one, but uniting, using every means we possess to achieve victory, just as the Patriots of 1837-38 did (those whom our Holy Mother the Church went out of her way to excommunicate, as part of her sell-out to British interests).

From the four corners of Quebec, those whom they dared to call "lousy French" and "alcoholics" will plunge into the fight against those who bludgeoned liberty and justice. We will put all these professional thugs and crooks out of commission: the bankers, the businessmen, the judges and sell-out politicians.

We are the workers of Quebec and we will stop at nothing. We want to change this slave society of ours into a free society, functioning by itself and for itself, a society open to the world.

Our struggle can only be victorious. An awakening people cannot long remain in misery and error.

> Long live Free Quebec!
> Long live our comrades who are political prisoners!
> Long live the Quebec revolution!
> Long live the Quebec Liberation Front!

"*Vive le* FLQ, *vive le* FLQ!*" Louise shouted, jumping up with a clenched fist signal. The back living room on Des Récollets Street erupted suddenly into a group of overgrown children, running around, punching each other, embracing, and letting out yells of: "Eeeo – oooww, "EEEEE – ooo-ooow."

"This broadcast has been read for humanitarian reasons, with a view to save, if possible, the life of James Richard Cross."

But nobody on Des Récollets was listening to this announcement. Nobody, that is, except the prisoner, who sat in his usual place, facing the television set in the darkened back room, blinkered, forbidden to turn around. The manifesto had taken thirteen minutes to read and with opening and closing announcements had lasted exactly fifteen minutes. The passing of time, which drags for a man immobilized, in darkness, imprisoned against his will, must for Cross that evening have seemed swift and alarming. What would have happened to him had the manifesto not been televised? What might still happen if these young, volatile revolutionaries decided that the police manhunt had not been called off? What if their other conditions were not met in the next several hours?

Twenty-five minutes later, while the national television news was on and everyone on Des Récollets was watching it, the doorbell rang. It was not a preconceived signal. It simply rang twice.

At once, both television sets were switched off. The kitchen light went out. Yves Langlois, who was guarding Cross, turned his M-1 on his prisoner's back. Marc Carbonneau, holding the other M-1, took up a position in the doorway of the right front room, covering Jacques, who, his Beretta pistol at the ready, stood behind the front door. The door was booby-trapped with powerfrac dynamite, set to blow. Louise waited beside the mechanism, her hand on the de-fusing device.

"Who is it?" Louise asked in French.

"*Moi. Suzanne.*"

Louise's face opened in a smile, but Jacques signaled her to wait. Perhaps there was somone else, a cop, right behind the door. C.T. had gone down to the garage to peer out at the street. Now he stamped his foot to sound an all clear. Jacques nodded. Cautiously, Louise opened the door. Suzanne Lanctôt, young, pretty, pregnant, came into the hall. "I'm sorry," she said. "But there was no way to phone."

"Christ!" Jacques said. "Were you followed?" He embraced her.

"I heard the television. The manifesto! I know I should have waited, but, anyway. I changed from bus to subway and then went to the Berri de Montigny stop and went up and down and around and came out. And took another bus. I'm sure it's all right."

"How's the kid?"

"Fine. I'm going to see him tomorrow."

"No," Jacques said. "Now you're here, you're going to stay a while. We're six now."

"Six who made a revolution," Marc said, grinning. "The Battle of Algiers, eh, Jacques?"

"The Battle of Quebec," Jacques said. "I told you we'd make it some day."

7

Four or five days, they told each other, a week at most. By then the government would certainly give in. Then they would deliver Cross, privately, to someone like the Cuban consul in Montreal, with instructions that he was to be released only when a plane carrying the twenty-three "political prisoners" touched down in Cuba or Algeria. They themselves would slip away into the East End, to continue the struggle in Quebec. Which was why they wore masks at all times in the presence of their prisoner.

If the handing over of Cross could not be accomplished without their being compromised, they were, of course, prepared to go into exile with the freed "political prisoners." Either way, as they planned it, the operation would be completed by the weekend. Therefore, they had bought only a minimum of furniture for the apartment on Des Récollets. Two tables, six kitchen chairs, three lamp fixtures to light the rooms; linen, radio and television sets. Coming upon them in the early morning after the arrival of Suzanne as they lay sleeping or on guard in the various rooms of the apartment, they seemed to C.T. like guerrillas bivouacking in an abandoned building. He found it hard to believe that this was happening, not in some foreign land, but in Montreal where they had lived all their lives.

Returning that Friday morning with the newspapers (seven of them, purchased at two different locations so as not to arouse suspicion), C.T. re-entered the apartment quietly, using his key, not wanting to wake the Lanctôts, who lay together in a double sleeping bag in the front bedroom. He glanced in at them as he went by, remembering the sounds he had heard as he came off guard duty last night – giggles, whisperings, jokes about disturbing the baby inside Suzanne, and then, as he himself undressed next door for sleep, the unmistakable, prolonged sounds of lovemaking. Excited despite himself, he had tried to slip, naked, into Louise's sleeping bag, but Louise (pretending to be asleep, or really asleep: he never knew) resolutely pulled the covers close about her and turned her back, leaving him naked and alone on the bare floor of the room.

Now, looking in at the Lanctôts, he saw that Suzanne was nude in their sleeping bag. She lay on her side, one arm shielding her face, her breast uplifted, its full brown nipple staring at him like a warning eye. He lingered, looking, until, with a start, Jacques Lanctôt turned over on his back, groaning in some fitful dream. Guiltily, C.T. drew back and went on into the kitchen. The newspapers under his arm were all about Jacques. The *Gazette* headline was typical: KIDNAP MANHUNT KEYED TO MISSING CITY CABBIE. Most of the papers identified Jacques Lanctôt by name and age. The stories said there were four other suspects. Jacques will have to leave Canada, C.T. thought. And then, suddenly: *Our first plan was a dream. We will all be forced to leave Canada. Perhaps we will never be able to return.*

Jacques Lanctôt slept. He did not yet know that today his name was written on the front pages of newspapers all over

North America and even in faraway Europe, did not know that from this day forth he had lost his anonymity and, in losing it, would lose himself. He dreamed of his father, with whom he had quarreled; he had not seen his father in seven years. In his dream his father sat on a sofa at home, showing him a scrapbook filled with yellowing press clippings of the Leader, telling how the Leader went out to fight the system. The Leader: Adrien Arcand, French Canadian, a tall man, a former journalist with the narrow mustache and plastered-down dark hair of a twenties matinee singer; Arcand who admired Moseley and the Führer, who had founded his own National Unity Party of Canada, drilling his men in a uniform of blackshirts and black riding boots under swastika banners, until the red Jewish atheists of Moscow and the international Jewish cabal conspired to arrest and intern him for five long wartime years. Arcand who returned thin and ill and old at the end of the war; Arcand who, in the very year Jacques Lanctôt was born, regrouped the party to fight the Jews again. But the Jews, Arcand said, the filthy Jews owned everything in Canada: they controlled the press here, just as they did in America. It was well known. The Jews, his father's generation believed, were the real enemy of Canada. They needed a flaming torch, an Arcand, to purge the land of those swine.

At fifteen, Jacques had admired his father, admired him because his father had not, like Pierre Vallières' father, lived as a dumb ox, not daring to revolt against the Anglo-Saxon bosses and their French Canadian valet, the old Dictator Duplessis who sold Quebec's forests, minerals, and people cheap to the Anglo-Saxon companies, all the while protesting he was saving the province from communism and helping preserve the old French Canadian ways. No, Jacques' father was a rebel in his day. But his father had joined the wrong rebellion, he had been blinded by Arcand. Jacques knew it was not the Jews who were to blame, they were an easy target, scapegoats used by Duplessis and the Church. The real enemy was capitalism

84

itself. But Jacques' father's fight was rooted in another decade, in Arcand's manifesto. "We must rescue Canada from the red clutches of Moscow and International Jewry," that manifesto said. His father believed that Jacques had become "radicalized" because the Quebec police, in cells, kicked and beat the boy. His father did not understand. *Et mon père ne comprendra jamais.*

Jacques Lanctôt slept. At that moment, Yves was getting off a bus in the north end of the city, at the intersecion of Pie IX Boulevard and the Boulevard St. Joseph. He looked for the address Marc had given him. 4055 St. Joseph Boulevard East. It was a modest building, near the intersection, ugly and newish, the upper storeys red brick, the lower storey of imitation gray flagstones. Nervously, Yves looked up and down the boulevard, then pushed open a chrome-and-glass door and stood in the small entrance hall of the building. The basement rooms were occupied by a notary: CLAUDE GIRARD, NOTAIRE; and by a chartered account firm: LOUIS PHILIPPE HÊTU, COMPTABLE AGRÉE – the upper floors were apartments. Between the outer and inner doors of the entrance hall was a small, gray-green carpet. Yves, as instructed by Marc, lifted this carpet up and slipped a brown envelope, folded in three, under it. He replaced the carpet and, unseen, left the building.

The envelope contained Communiqué Number 6, written at eight a.m. that morning. It also contained a letter from Cross, dated 8:30 a.m. The purpose of Cross's handwritten note was to assure the authorities that he had not been killed at eight a.m. as threatened. It read:

Vendredi,
8.30 a.m.

The headlines in the *Journal de Montréal* this morning are
    Première Concession
    Radio Canada a cédé
    [First Concession: Radio Canada gives in]
Please tell my wife and daughter that I am well.

J. R. Cross

The communiqué itself contained the first compromises made by the kidnappers. It dropped the ransom demand, the demand for the reinstatement of the striking postal employees, and for the reinstatement of the striking postal employees, and for publication of the name and photograph of the police informer. It announced that it was temporarily suspending its threats to execute Cross, following the broadcast of the manifesto on Radio-Canada. It listed as "the last two conditions" which must be fulfilled to save Cross's life as (1) liberation of the "political prisoners" and their transport to Algeria or Cuba and (2) the cessation of all searches and arrests by the police. It promised to free Cross in twenty-four hours following the return of the journalist observers who would accompany the "political prisoners" to Cuba.

The envelope containing the communiqué and Cross's letter was addressed to Pierre Pascau, CKLM Radio Station. But when he left the building Yves did not phone Pascau. He and the others were afraid the police might have a phone tap on the station to intercept any communiqué.

So Yves went to a nearby phone booth and called, not CKLM, but the weekly newspaper La Semaine. When a reporter came on the line, Yves said: "There is a message from the FLQ for Pierre Pascau of CKLM. It is under the rug in the entrance hall at 4055 St. Joseph Boulevard East." And hung up.

He returned, by bus, to Des Récollets Street. In negotiations carried out between the authorities and the kidnappers, a paranoid fear of betrayal was present at all times, and on both sides. This was to be one of the bad days. At La Semaine, Yves' phone call was regarded as a crank message. No one went to claim the envelope. As a result, the morning passed in silence. By one p.m. the Quebec and federal authorities grew increasingly uneasy when no new communiqué was fed to the media by the kidnappers. The newspapers had headlined that the police manhunt was still in progress. Perhaps the kidnappers had interpreted this as a refusal to deal with them and had killed their prisoner? The tension was great. There were consultations with the British High Commissioner's office. At 2:45 p.m. that day, Friday, October 9, five days after Cross's abduction, Quebec Justice Minister Jérôme Choquette tried to contact the kidnappers in the only way he knew: through the media. A message from the Minister was read on all Montreal radio stations. It asked that the kidnappers send a handwritten letter from Cross which would include the following sentence: "It is now five days since I left and I want you to know, darling, that I miss you every minute."

In the kitchen at Des Récollets, Marc, Jacques, Louise and Suzanne sat around, discussing this reply in a spirit of gloom. "They've suppressed our communiqué," Louise said. "They don't care if we kill Cross."

"We said we'd give them twenty-four hours," Marc said. "They're counting on that. Maybe they have some lead to us, maybe they hope to track us down by tonight."

There was a sick silence in the room. They were ready to die, yes. Ready to fight, to dynamite themselves, to die without surrendering as the FLN had in the battle of Algiers. But to wait, doing nothing, until the police came up the street, to wait, not knowing what their enemies were planning?

"Let's try again," Marc said. "Maybe we can get another communiqué through."

"They'll intercept it," Louise said gloomily.

"Let's try, goddammit," Marc said. "Come on, Jacques. Let's write a communiqué."

"And another letter from Cross," Suzanne said. "We've got to prove he's still alive. Make him write a letter with the sentence Choquette asked for."

At 8:50 that night, the silence was broken. Pierre Pascau went on the air with the new communiqué. He also read a copy of Communiqué Number 6, the one Yves had left under the rug on St. Joseph Boulevard that morning. The news communiqué gave Cross a twenty-four hour lease on life. In it, the FLQ complained that the authorities were trying to gain time by refusing to release the contents of the previous communiqué. Unless the "political prisoners" were released before six p.m. Saturday, the new communiqué promised that Cross would never be found.

The new letter, written by Cross on a ruled sheet of notebook paper, read:

3 p.m.
Vendredi

I have heard the message from the Minister of Justice on the radio and hereby repeat it.
   "It is now 5 days since I left and I want you to know, darling, that I miss you every minute."
Please give my love to my wife and daughter. I hope to see them soon.

J. R. Cross

In Montreal North, they sat on their air mattresses listening in silence. Relief that their communiqués had not been suppressed mingled with the new responsibility of what had been said. This day and these communiqués had turned the situation

88

from one of simple crisis into a time bomb. And, had they known it, a new and terrible factor had entered into their scheme. But they did not know it: nor did the government, nor did anyone else except for four young men also listening to this news in a rented bungalow on the other side of the Saint Lawrence River.

At nine-thirty, half an hour after Pascau read the communiqués, the federal government again entered the bargaining ring. From the East Block operations center in Ottawa a spokesman for Pierre Elliott Trudeau issued a terse announcement: "The kidnappers of Mr. Cross must give us a clear answer to the question: where and when will Mr. Cross be released? The reply must constitute some form of guarantee."

"What answer can we give them without screwing ourselves?" Marc asked the others.

"It's not up to us to give them a guarantee," Yves said. "It's up to them to get an airplane on the runway and get the prisoners on it."

"So we'll leave it up to them?" Jacques said. "We sit tight. Are all agreed?"

They were all agreed.

8

C.T.

Jacques Cosette-Trudel.

He considered himself to be different. On that Saturday while they guarded the prisoner, made meals, and worried about the police, the others spent every free moment listening to the news on radio and television. He sat all afternoon in the kitchen, reading Che Guevara's speeches. He was calm: but it was the sick calm of a young man who has accepted the worst. If nothing happens at six tonight, he asked himself, if, as I know, Trudeau denies us what we want, can my wife and her brother and Suzanne, and Yves, and Marc, become Che's "cool, calculated killing machines . . . with confirmed ideological foundations . . . motivated by revolutionary love"?

Of course not. There has always been an element of self-deception in our position. I knew it two summers ago at the Maison du Pêcheur, Paul Rose's camp in the Gaspé. Jacques getting all worked up, telling those Toronto kids from The

90

Company of Young Canadians that they'll never understand French Canadians because we're a people conquered hundreds of years ago by the English, a race which lost its land and its dignity all at once, a people whose only heroes are failed revolutionaries. But is that true, or is it, perhaps, a "romantic fallacy"? Would a guy like Jacques believe that, if some old-line Quebec politician said it? No. But Pierre Vallières wrote it down and that made it gospel. What if Jacques Lanctôt hadn't read *Soul on Ice,* or Fanon, or that book by Malcolm X, all of those books I gave him?

Sometimes I think we've read too much and watched too many films. I suppose, in a way, everyone invents his life. We invented this story, didn't we? And now must act it out. But what do we know of other lives, what do we know of the thought processes of our enemies who are twice as old as we? How can a taxi driver like Marc Carbonneau put himself inside the skull of a Trudeau, a millionaire who never had to work, a dreamer who went to see Mao, a man who, when he wanted to become Prime Minister, could make it happen? And how can Trudeau understand the life of a guy like Marc, the scraping up for taxi payments, losing your cab to finance companies, having a wife and four kids somewhere that you left, not because you hated them but because you wanted to fight people like Trudeau?

Trudeau has not given in to us. He is ignoring us. He will not give in.

And we will not kill Cross. From the first, this has been play-acting, hasn't it? Could I go in there and kill Cross and then go to bed with Louise a week later? Am I Che's "cool, calculated killing machine"? Or am I, as I suspect, someone who has begun to act out a daydream?

"You're very quiet," Jacques Lanctôt said, coming into the kitchen, reaching into the refrigerator for the lemon-lime drink he consumed in quantity.

"I'm reading."

Jacques stood at the kitchen window. Far away on the boulevard, an ambulance siren. Or a police car. It came. It went. It was quiet again. "What do you think?" Jacques asked.

"I think they'll s-say no."

Jacques said nothing. He went out of the kitchen.

A few minutes later Louise came in looking hopeful. She went to C.T. and kissed him on his left ear. "Choquette's giving a TV press conference at five on Radio-Canada. They just announced it."

"Five? And the deadline's at s-six. I wonder."

"You wonder what?"

"Nothing," he said. Choquette. Not even the Premier of the province, let alone the Prime Minister of the country. When they send the Justice Minister up to bat, it's to punish us. It will be no. He will say no.

❊❊❊❊❊

Yet at four o'clock, an hour before Choquette was due to speak, ineluctably, there were signs of optimism and rumors of hope. The networks announced that this would be the first large-scale press conference given by the authorities since the kidnapping occurred. Facilities had been set up for reporters to question the Minister. The press of six countries had gathered at the television studios for the conference. Broadcaster Pierre Pascau and the FLQ's lawyer Robert Lemieux said they would be willing to go as monitors on the flight to Cuba.

Five o'clock came and went. The Minister was delayed. At five-thirty, Choquette, looking haggard from four fitful nights on his office couch, appeared at the studios with a police motorcycle escort. He strode to the waiting cameras and mikes, without greeting the assembled reporters, and in a strained, emotional voice read a prepared statement, first in French, then in English. It was obvious that he and Robert Bourassa, the young Premier of Quebec, had labored over what they would say. It was a plea from French Canadians to French Canadians and was aimed directly at the kidnappers.

"I understand that those who have kidnapped Mr. Cross acted in the name of a certain ideal of society," the Minister said:

But they cannot impose this ideal on the majority of their fellow citizens by violence or murder which would, in effect, discredit their point of view. While the authorities will not accede to undue or dangerous pressure, they do realize that there are areas of discontent in our society and that injustice does exist.

I think that the kidnappers of Mr. Cross are adult enough to admit that there can be a divergence of viewpoints. They are free to express their point of view by word and deed, as long as they do not resort to violence or the death of an innocent person.

The Quebec government is a government dedicated to reform. It is deeply concerned with social justice, especially for its needy citizens.

Therefore we ask you to believe in our good faith and respect our desire to honestly examine these injustices in our society. What mechanism, what institution should we set up? The government is making a real effort to listen to each group of citizens. The importance we place in citizens committees is a proof of our interest in reform.

We intend to confer with all groups who are interested in useful reforms, to improve our institutions and to work with individuals and groups so that social evolution will come about within the state.

It would completely negate these efforts to act now in a way which would destroy the social order which we are in the process of building. That is why we cannot wipe out the offenses committed by those whom you call political prisoners. There is a parole procedure which applies to all prisoners and it will be followed.

Similarly, we cannot dismiss or wipe out the actions of those accused who are now before the courts, because, again, this would mean the destruction of that social order which we must build. But we will consider these acts with clemency, a clemency which will be influenced by your behavior, behavior which should now put an end to this terrorism.

Thus, in order to save the life of Mr. Cross, the federal government informs us that it is prepared to offer you safe conduct to a foreign country. If, on the other hand, you choose to refuse this offer of safe conduct, I can assure you that when you come before the courts, your cases will be considered with all possible clemency in view of your humanitarian gesture in sparing Mr. Cross's life. On this, I give you my word.

I ask you, therefore, for a total gesture of good faith: release Mr. Cross at once.

Over and above all individual considerations, we must build a society of justice and liberty. Gentlemen, you have a part to play in this endeavor, if you so choose.

When he had finished his speech, the Minister looked into the television cameras, looked blindly into the unknown, looked at the kidnappers who sat, silent, watching on two screens in Des Récollets Street; looked blindly at James Richard Cross whose death warrant this speech might be. The Minister seemed exhausted. With a wave, he dismissed the babble of questions which at once welled up among the ranks of seated reporters in the studio. He turned and walked out, stepping into a waiting elevator. It was exactly four minutes past six as he walked stiffly across the lower lobby of the Radio-Canada building, going toward his police escort and his limousine, his face lit by dead photoflash as photographers scurried ahead of him, snatching their shots.

In the back room of Des Récollets there was a sudden silence. Yves and Jacques Lanctôt were with the prisoner. Yves turned down the sound of the television.

"Monsieur?" the prisoner said. He faced the wall, his cowl obscuring his features. But now he was sitting up, straight and tense.

"Yes?" Jacques said.

"May I ask what you are going to do with me?"

There was a silence. "Well," said Jacques, "I suppose we'll hold you for a few days – just to taunt the police – you know? Then we'll let you go."

"I see."

As though drugged, Yves got up again and turned up the television set. Commentators were trying to sum up what Choquette had said. It was five past six.

They had issued their ultimatum: no more communiqués, no more delays. And now, in Ottawa, the federal government, Trudeau's government, had finally spoken. They were to be given nothing except their lives. If they accepted they would have achieved only one end: the reading of their manifesto on television. Time was up. Like candidates in an examination they must now answer the question. Would they accept to go to Cuba? Or what? For Jacques had said it. They could not kill Cross.

Minutes passed. Witless, the television news continued. And then, at 6:23 p.m., a sudden, shocked, excited voice on CKLM, another shocked voice on television. "Pierre Laporte, Quebec Minister of Labor and Immigration, has been kidnapped in front of his house by armed men."

Jacques, Yves, Marc, Suzanne, C.T., and Louise. They congregated in the prisoner's room, staring at each other, wonderingly, bemused, excited, filled with conjectures, close to tears. Suddenly, the revolution they had dreamed of seemed about to happen. They were no longer just six. They were no longer alone.

Pierre Laporte drove home at four-fifty. The Cabinet meetings were over and he, like the other provincial ministers, waited for Jérôme Choquette to announce the government's decision. He kept his car radio on as he drove off the Island of Montreal, across the huge gray-green span of Jacques Cartier Bridge. Below him was the Saint Lawrence River leading up to the Seaway locks. Laporte, who lived in the suburb of St. Lambert with his wife and two children, would be home in a few minutes.

His house was on Robitaille Street, a quiet street, only four blocks long, with residences on one side only. On the far side of the street was a pencil line of small trees and, beyond that, the quiet of a suburban park. Laporte's house, a largish suburban structure, with gray stone walls and a graceful wooden roof, was handsome, a catalogue house from some builders' brochure which one might see in any middle-class suburb in the United States. All was open and American: no fences, well-kept lawns, neat shrubs, a suburb where one knows the next-door neighbours but not the people four doors away.

Laporte was forty-nine years old, a confident politician who had spent most of his life in the front hall of power, first as a newspaperman covering the Quebec Legislature when it was a circus under the ringmastership of the old boss Duplessis; later as an up-and-comer in the new Liberal regime, a moderate rebel who at one time flirted with the idea of a special status for this French-speaking part of Canada, but who now was firmly in the federal camp. What had made him seem liberal fifteen years ago made him, today, conservative to the young nationalists of the Parti Québecois and anathema to the extremists of the FLQ. Like Hubert Humphrey, Laporte had recently been bypassed in the big lottery of power: Bourassa, a younger, less experienced man, had been chosen to lead the Liberal Party and become Premier of Quebec. Like Humphrey, Laporte was, at this stage of his career, a winning loser.

At four minutes to five, Laporte parked his car at the side of his house and hurried in to turn on the television set. His wife was in her room, getting ready to go out to a dinner engagement.

At five-fifteen his car was observed as it sat in the driveway beside his house. The young men who saw it drove away at high speed. Their car was a dark blue Chevrolet with black vinyl top.

At five-thirty, Laporte finally saw his colleague Jérôme Choquette on television, delivering the government's refusal to the kidnappers of James Cross. When the televised speech ended, Laporte got up and went outside to take the air for a few minutes. As he stepped out on the lawn, the time was two minutes past six.

Five miles away, a young man switched off the radio in a rented bungalow and looked at the three other men who had sat with him, listening to the Choquette broadcast. "That's it,

97

then. I told you they'd never give in for a guy like Cross."

They looked at their watches, then got up and put on trench coats. Two wore light trench coats, two wore dark ones. They went outside and got into the dark-blue Chevy, Quebec license 9J-2420. They put a twelve-gauge shotgun under the front seat and replaced the seat cushion. In the front of the car, beneath their feet, they placed two M-1 semiautomatic rifles. The time was two minutes past six.

At that moment, five miles away, Laporte's nephew Claude, an eighteen-year-old junior college student who had also been listening to the Choquette speech, switched off the television set in the living room of his family's house in Berkeley Avenue, just around the corner from Laporte's house. He took up a football, went out, walked down the block, and saw his uncle standing on the front lawn, looking at the evening sky. Claude's father, Roland, had died three months ago. His uncle was like a father to him now. Claude called out and threw the football. His uncle caught and returned the pass.

Inside Laporte's house the telephone rang. Mrs. Laporte, hurrying to get ready, answered. Was Mr. Laporte at home? Yes, he was but he'd just gone out on the lawn. He was about to leave. The caller said he would call later.

The caller was in a place called Mike's Restaurant in nearby Longueuil. He went out and got into the back seat of the dark-blue Chevy. The caller was five feet seven inches tall, with the pale face and staring eyes of a Raskolnikov. He was twenty-three years old but, at the moment, seemed older because he was wearing a gray wig and a false mustache. He was an unemployed laborer named Francis Simard. The driver who sat beside him in the front seat was Jacques Rose, an unemployed laborer who wore a dark trench coat and a gray wig. In reality he was also twenty-three years old, with the clean, open good looks of the young ranch hand in a television commercial. In the back seat of the car was Jacques' older brother, a powerful young man, twenty-seven years old, weighing two hundred pounds, six feet tall, his right eye filmed over by a cataract. He wore a white trench coat, his dark curling hair was covered by a blond wig and a navy tuque. His given name was Paul; he was a former teacher of disturbed children. Sitting on his right, dressed in a light trench coat and wearing an army cap, was Bernard Lortie, nineteen, a student, with large, liquid brown eyes, handsome fawnlike features, and a quiet manner. The car took off again, went left on Tiffin Avenue, then down Berkeley to the corner of Robitaille Street. Laporte's house was the corner house, and it must have seemed to his abductors, when they first caught sight of him on the front lawn, that he was waiting for them, dressed for the evening, playing catch with his nephew until they came.

The Chevy stopped quietly, half a block from the house. One of Laporte's neighbors came up behind it and tried to pass. But the Chevy, parked in the middle of the small street, did not budge. The neighbor honked his horn, but Jacques Rose looked around and shook his fist at the interrupter. The neighbor, alone in his car, seeing four men in the other car, did not want an argument. He backed up and took the next street.

The Chevy moved again. As it rolled towards the intersection, its occupants watched the scene ahead, the man and the youth playing catch, the football sailing high, caught, sailing high again. Inside the Chevy, Bern Lortie pulled down a cloth flap with eyepieces, which he had fitted into his army cap. The others pulled down their tuques as masks. Eyeholes were cut in the wool. Lortie took the sawed-off twelve-gauge shotgun from under the seat.

The Chevy turned the corner onto Robitaille. There is a statue of the Virgin Mary, a life-size wayside shrine, across the street, directly opposite the Minister's house. But the Virgin, her hands outstretched in love and supplication, does not face the house. Her back was turned to Laporte as the kidnappers' car moved up towards the verge of his well-cut lawn. Young Claude threw a low pass and the ball skidded along the ground. As Pierre Laporte bent to pick it up, Jacques Rose jammed on the brakes. The tires squealed. Paul Rose, a large, menacing figure, got out of the back seat of the car. Lortie also got out, holding the twelve-gauge shotgun. Paul Rose went up to the Minister, pointed the M-1 at him and said: "This isn't a joke. Get in the car, and make it fast." Laporte stood, confused. Paul Rose took him by the arm and moved him towards the car.

At that moment, Mrs. Laporte appeared at the front of the house to say she was ready to go off to dinner, perhaps to apologize for being late. Paul Rose pushed the Minister into the back seat of the car and the car accelerated, turned south on Mortlake, right on Tiffin, then out onto Taschereau Boulevard. Only a few hundred yards, but already gone as far as another city. In these discreet streets there is no community of workmen, or village of small tradesmen, or road of farm families, no place where a stranger would be seen as in a village. As soon as the car started, Laporte, sitting in the middle of the back seat, was told by Paul Rose to stretch out on the floor. He obeyed. Simard and Rose were obliged to put their feet up on the back of the front seat to leave room for the big, prone body. They told the Minister to shut his eyes and not to look at them. He obeyed. They drove without incident, reaching the intersection of Taschereau Boulevard and St. Paul Street. There, they went through the prisoner's pockets, not to steal, but to find something which would identify him. They found, among his credit cards, his identity card as a member of the Quebec National Assembly. Simard put this card in his pocket and, as previously arranged, got out of the car. He returned to Montreal alone, by taxi, carrying a communiqué which they had all four helped compose. His job was to deliver it to a Montreal radio station.

100

The Chevy drove along the boulevard onto Chambly Road, past shopping centers and rural frame houses, and signs which said CHIROPRACTICIEN, TAVERNE, REPAS, BIÈRE, and again into that gut of road entrails which winds about the edges of a city. On this road, passing the St. Hubert traffic circle and crossing the railroad tracks, suddenly, a police car approached them and as it passed, alarmingly, its red light lit up. "Look straight ahead," Paul Rose told the boys who were sitting in the front seat. "They must have received the call." The police car passed. The kidnappers drove on, going into another non-place, the Canadian Armed Forces Base at St. Hubert, a great military camp of federal architecture, with quarters for Married Forces and Military Police Posts and hangars for jets and helicopters, a place of On and Off Limits, a military staging ground. Only four miles from where they had found Laporte playing with a football on his front lawn, Jacques Rose turned the blue Chevy up a side road, leaving behind the big Base signs which read:

H.Q. MOBILE COMMAND
QUARTIER-GÉNÉRAL HEADQUARTERS

And there, at the very end of the military terrain, was a three-storey hangar, near a curve in the road at which were clustered the small signposts of private flying clubs: AERO CLUB DE MONTREAL, WON-DEL AVIATION LTD. Beside the hangar was a parking lot and, beyond the lot, a field with a parked row of light planes. The Chevy passed this lot, going on up that quiet road, taking the second turning on the left. This street is named Armstrong, a street which is not a street, a camping place for federal base workers and other working-class transients, a street of bungalows like summer shacks, glorified with temporary winter insulation and floor heat, with, among them, a few trailer homes grounded forever in this waste lot. A migrant street where the dogs bark at everyone because they know no one. There, to a six-room bungalow

101

with a garage stuck up against it, with baby-blue paint trim and the peeling white slats of a bungalow in a southern California shacktown, they brought Pierre Laporte.

Bernard Lortie got out and opened the garage door. The Chevy drove in. Paul Rose raised the Minister up and told him to sit on the back seat and keep his eyes shut. Jacques and Paul Rose covered his eyes with wadded Kleenex tissues and strips of green tape. Then led him through a hole, cut two months before in the wall of the garage, giving it direct access into the bungalow. They took him into a bedroom, handcuffed him and chained him to the bedposts. There in 5630 Armstrong Street in St. Hubert, his captors went to ground. There, exactly a week later, they would sit and stare through field glasses across the empty fields down the road, to that lonely three-storey hangar and the row of light planes and the parking lot with its sign: WON-DEL AVIATION LTD. Only five miles from the comfort, the normalcy of Pierre Laporte's home. A short way, a long way: for Pierre Laporte and for those who had brought him here, there would never, ever, be any way back.

�֍ �֍ ✖ ✖ ✖ ✖

On Des Récollets Street that evening, Jacques and Suzanne Lanctôt, Yves Langlois, Marc Carbonneau, C.T., and Louise Cosette-Trudel were caught up as in a fever. Whether they guarded the prisoner or sat in the other room with television and radios, they were barely able to speak to each other so busy were they, like the rest of Canada, listening to each rumor and opinion, trying like everyone else to determine what had happened, what would happen, and why.

When they had kidnapped Cross they had sat in the eye of the storm, caught in the calm of dead center. But even the outside commotion was different from what was happening tonight. The kidnapping of Cross had been a crisis, yes, but a crisis of the sort that is part of the flux of the world's day.

Tonight, that had changed. It was as though this new kidnapping was no longer a news story but a catastrophe. On television, on all networks, in English and in French, normal programming was suspended, all staff was recalled to duty. Even on the American channels, this news seemed to have pre-empted the rest of the world's business. Radio stations across Canada were on instant alert, their switchboards jammed with callers waiting to orate, to be reassured, or to cry for vengeance. Newspapers put out special editions. And, all evening long, on television, a procession of commentators, reporters, and public figures pondered, puzzled, and followed every last rumor. Like a village disaster, it was, to Canada's citizens, the only news in the world that night.

"The Rose brothers did it," C.T. said and looked at Jacques Lanctôt. "What do you think?"

In September, Jacques and Suzanne and the baby had spent

two weeks at 5630 Armstrong Street. The Cosette-Trudels had been there at the same time. There had been talk about forming two cells. One a kidnap cell, and one to raise funds. But it was just talk.

"That's how revolutions start," Jacques said. "One cell breeds another."

"The Roses and Francis?" Louise said.

"And Bern Lortie," C.T. said.

"But they were going to Texas," Suzanne said. "I remember, Claire went with them and they took their mother. They went in her car."

"That's right," Jacques said. "Paul talked about some contacts in Texas."

"Know what I think?" Marc said. "I think they were down in Texas and they heard about this. And Paul Rose said, 'I thought they were supposed to kidnap a Yank. This isn't good enough.' So Mister Smartass comes back and captures a bigger fish than we did. Which is fine. It backs us up."

"But Jesus Christ!" Jacques said angrily. "How can you start off on a thing like this with no plan – I mean, those guys were always broke! Every finance company in town was after them!"

"Maybe they got some money in Texas."

"Goddammit," Jacques said. "I don't like it. If it isn't planned, they'll just screw up."

"Well, we'll find out soon."

"How?"

Marc smiled and pointed to the TV set. "How does anybody find out anything these days? Watch this channel."

It had not been planned. It had grown like a seed dropped in wilderness, had drawn back its unlikely conspirators from another obscure and unexplained wild-goose chase on the flatlands of Texas. On September 20, a little over two weeks before James Cross was kidnapped, Mrs. Rosa Rose was having supper with her daughters, Lise, Claire, and Suzanne, in the kitchen of Lise's house on Dorion Street in a working-class area of Montreal. Mrs. Rose was one of a generation of French Canadian working-class women that Pierre Vallières has written about: mothers who "live for half a loaf of bread," conditioned to their husbands and sons being out of work, to finance-company bailiffs waiting to take back the living-room suite, to sickness, to children needing new shoes and spectacles, to an examination of every move, every situation, with the nagging fear that perhaps it may be a change for the worse. She worried about her eldest sons, Jacques and Paul. She knew they had a lot of debts. She knew both were without work, that they were rebels, angry men, willing to demonstrate in the streets, shout at the police, go to jail. But she loved them. She loved all her children.

On that night in September, both Paul and Jacques showed up at Lise's house. Paul said he had been given a cheque for $600 from the Canadian National Railroad in payment for work he had done there some time ago. Mrs. Rose did not ask how this pay could be so much. She loved Paul. Both boys said they wanted to use this money to get out of Montreal, to run from their debts, perhaps to find new jobs down in Texas. They wanted her to come with them, at least to look around. They wanted to take her car. It would be a vacation for her. And for their little sister, Claire.

Mrs. Rose was glad to go. They left Montreal on September 23, at about 6:30 in the evening. When Paul and Jacques showed up they had a friend with them, a pale-faced boy with staring eyes. His name was Francis Simard. They drove south, heading towards Texas. Mrs. Rose did not know the United

States well. They drove a long way, stopping quite often. They tried to buy revolvers, but for some reason she did not understand, nobody would sell them revolvers. When she asked why they wanted revolvers, they said they would need them in Texas. Everybody wore guns there. They reached Texas and drove on to Dallas. While they were in Dallas, they heard on the radio that James Cross had been kidnapped by the FLQ in Montreal. That was on Monday, October 5. They heard it in the evening and, at once, the boys decided to go back to Montreal. Paul was astonished at the news of this kidnapping. He thought it a mistake. "Isn't that stupid? Isn't that awful?" he said. "They know damn well the government will never give in to save a guy like that."

They were in a hurry now. They took turns driving. She was dead tired, but they only stopped to eat and, once, near New York, they bought two mounts for carbine barrels. The mounts cost $30 apiece. She did not ask them why they wanted the mounts now, since they were no longer going to Texas. Driving all night, they arrived in Montreal on the morning of October 8, three days after Cross had been kidnapped. She wanted to go home at once, but the boys were hungry. They all ate breakfast at the Woolco. Then Jacques drove her and Claire to the Towers Shopping Centre, turned over the car to her, gave her twenty American dollars for expenses, kissed them both, and said goodbye.

When he had left his mother and sister, Jacques Rose picked up a blue Chevy with black vinyl top. It was a 1968 model and had false license plates, which was why they had not taken it to Texas. He went to get Paul and Francis, then all three went to a motel on Taschereau Boulevard in suburban Longueuil. They stayed there for a day. Francis Simard went over to the house on Armstrong Street in St. Hubert to see if it had been raided in their absence, or if it was being watched by police. It was clear.

Next day, Friday, October 9, they returned to the bungalow on Armstrong Street. The three of them sat around discussing the Cross kidnapping. If the government did not give in to-morrow night on Cross, they decided they would kidnap Pierre Laporte. They knew where he lived and had checked his movements before they went to Texas. He was conveniently close; so if a roadblock were thrown up and an alarm went out at once, they would not have to take him very far.

That afternoon they got on a bus and went into Montreal. On Notre Dame Street, in a pawnshop, they bought two M-1 rifles to fit the mounts. They went to a theatrical costumers and bought a blond wig, two gray wigs, a false mustache, and makeup. In a second pawnshop they bought two pairs of hand-cuffs. Then Jacques Rose phoned Bern Lortie, who was living in a pad on the South Shore with some young friends. Bern had agreed that summer to be their backup man if they formed a cell. To kidnap Laporte they needed four people. Lortie joined them that night in their bungalow in St. Hubert.

The next day, a Saturday, they tried on their makeup and discussed their plan. They wrote a communiqué and argued over drafts. When they had decided what it would say, Paul Rose drafted it, while Jacques Rose and Francis Simard took the blue Chevy and drove over to Longueuil. When they came back in the car it was after five. They all sat in the bungalow, waiting for Minister Choquette to speak. They grew very nerv-out. Finally, at five-thirty he was announced. His speech was a refusal to provide a plane to send the "political prisoners" to Cuba. At two minutes to six, they put the guns in the Chevy, donned the wigs, mustaches, and trench coats, and drove out of the garage. At six-eighteen, Pierre Laporte was in their hands.

10

Daniel McGinnis is a young man who could escape notice standing in a store window filled with well-dressed male mannequins. But at five minutes past eight on that Sunday morning he was uncharacteristically unshaven, rumpled, and weary, having just put in twelve hours as anchorman on the French-language radio station CKAC. It had been a night of rumor, devoted mostly to telling and retelling how Labor Minister Pierre Laporte had been kidnapped from his home by masked men of the FLQ. So, that Sunday morning, as McGinnis drove home in one of the station's radio cars, he was irritated, to say the least, when the car intercom began to crackle, calling him urgently to come in.

McGinnis picked up the mike. Five minutes later, he pulled his radio car to a halt, less than three blocks from the studios where he worked. As he got out of the car and ran into the Peel Street subway station at the Metcalf Street entrance, his fellow reporter, Norman Malthais, a bearded older man, was slamming his own radio car to a halt at a second entrance.

They met, both running, at a trashcan at the foot of a mobile stairway near the Metcalf Street entrance. There were not many commuters around at that hour on a Sunday morning.

"I was just going home," Malthais said, grinning at McGinnis. "I heard them call and figured I was closer."

"Go ahead," McGinnis said. "Be my guest."

They both laughed. Malthais bent down, gingerly, and looked in the wastepaper basket. He sifted the trash and came up with an envelope. It was addressed to Radio Station CKAC.

At once they got in their radio cars and drove the three blocks back to their place of work. There was no question that this might be a hoax. While the communiqué was written on different stationery from that used by Liberation Cell – this stationery had no logo of a *habitant* and used the patriot French Canadian colors (red-green-white) in a band across the top of each page, on which were imprinted the large letters FLQ – there was, clipped to the communiqué, an unmistakable proof. It was a Quebec National Assembly identity card bearing the photograph and signature of Pierre Laporte.

As soon as they had made photostats of the communiqué to pass on to other information media, McGinnis went on the air. As he began to speak, the station called the police.

On Des Récollets Street, Liberation Cell was at morning breakfast of eggs, peanut butter sandwiches, and instant coffee when C.T. came running in from the other room, motioning them to listen.

"*Voici le communiqué,*" said the familiar voice of Daniel McGinnis, as he began to read:

FLQ
Because of the stubbornness of the ruling
authorities in refusing to comply with the FLQ
demands and according to Plan 3, established
beforehand to provide for the contingency of such
a refusal, the Chenier* Financing Cell has
kidnapped the Minister of Unemployment and
Assimilation of Quebeckers, Pierre Laporte.
   The Minister will be executed Sunday night at
10 p.m., if between now and then the ruling
authorities have not acceded to the seven demands
issued on the kidnapping of Mr. Cross.
   All partial fulfillment of the demands will be
considered as a refusal. In the meantime Liberation
Cell will outline the technical procedures to be
carried out for the overall completion of this
operation.

We will conquer.

FLQ

---

*Dr. Jean Olivier Chenier (1806-1837), a leader of the unsuccessful revolt by French Canadians against British rule, was killed in battle against British troops at St. Eustache, Quebec.

"Those stupid bastards!" Jacques Lanctôt said. "They want *all* the conditions reinstated. And before ten o'clock tonight. *Now* what are we going to do?"

But the question was rhetorical. By unspoken agreement, they moved their chairs from the kitchen into the living room. Like other Canadians that Sunday morning, they sat by the television and radios. And waited.

Shortly after ten a.m., the radio announced that police had gone to the Hotel Nelson and arrested Robert Lemieux, the lawyer who had acted as their unofficial spokesman. He was charged with obstructing police officers in the discharge of their duties. His files were seized.

"*They* kidnapped Robert."

"Now, the only way we have left to speak to the authorities is through publicity – the media," Marc said.

"It's still the best way," Jacques said.

At eleven a.m. on that Sunday morning the modest radio studios of CKAC on Mansfield Street were like the scene of a presidential press conference. Three U.S. television networks, a French TV network, and a Belgian one all had set up crews there. The halls and office were crowded by Canadian, American, and British newspapermen, awaiting developments. A call came through for Daniel McGinnis. To McGinnis the caller sounded young, confident, and well-educated. He said there was a message from the FLQ under a piece of paper at the south end of Phillips Square, two blocks away from the radio station. Jacques Peyrac, the reporter who had picked up the first Cross communiqué a week earlier, went to get this note.

Phillips Square is one of the main squares of Montreal, flanked by some of the tallest buildings in Canada and adjoined by the baroque domes of St. James Basilica. Its center is a park, a place for Sunday strollers. Peyrac searched but did not find the letter. As he searched he was observed by the mysterious telephone caller. After ten minutes he abandoned his search and returned to the radio station. But before he managed to re-enter the station – it was only two blocks from the square – the caller had again phoned McGinnis. "Your reporter missed the communiqué. It's on the south side near the bus stop. Under a piece of cardboard. There's a communiqué and a letter from Laporte."

Peyrac went back to the south side of the square, but, again, did not find the message. He started back. The caller was on the phone ahead of him. This time, McGinnis listened to the instructions and went himself. He found the communiqué under a piece of cardboard near a trash can. It was not, however, on printed FLQ stationery. It was handprinted. The purported letter from Laporte, written with a ballpoint pen, could also be a forgery.

McGinnis returned to the studio and went on the air. He broadcast the communiqué, in part, and also read the letter. He told his audience he had reservations because the communiqué was not on FLQ stationery and was not typed.

This handwritten second communiqué read:

Communiqué: Second and Last

   This is the last communication between the Chenier Financing Cell and the ruling authorities. The Liberation Cell (that is, the one which carried out the kidnapping of James Cross) should send you a communiqué summing up the situation.
   We repeat: if by 10 p.m. tonight the two governments have not favorably met the seven conditions set by the FLQ, Minister Pierre Laporte will be executed.
   Pierre Laporte will be released in the 24 hours following the carrying out in full (that is, the seven conditions) of Operation Liberation's demands.
   The least hesitation by the ruling authorities will be FATAL for the minister. It is already a very large concession on our part to be obliged

to return him alive and in good condition. You
must not ask too much of us.

We will conquer,

Front de Libération du Québec

The handwritten note, in French, from Pierre Laporte was
addressed to his wife.

12 October 1970
7 a.m.

Darling,
I am well, in good health, and have had a good night. I
insist that you and the children do not take things in such a
way as to endanger your health.
I think of the three of you constantly and this helps me bear
up.
It is important that the authorities act.

My love to everyone,
Pierre

At ten minutes past five that afternoon, the anonymous young
caller again telephoned Daniel McGinnis at CKAC. "Chenier
Cell has drawn up a third communiqué to authenticate the
second one, the one you were worried about," the caller said.
"It will be typewritten and will be on normal FLQ stationery.
There will be a note from Laporte and we've put in his credit
cards. And Mrs. Laporte will be able to recognize the handwriting. She should have recognized the handwriting on
Laporte's first note. We've left this communiqué and the note
and the credit cards in a trashcan on Maisonneuve Boulevard
between University and Union Streets." The caller did not
sound hurried: he talked for over three minutes, time enough
for his call to be traced, had the police been on the line. Again,
the place he mentioned was only a few blocks from the radio
station.
McGinnis sent for the communiqué. It was in the trashcan as indicated, under a piece of paper. In addition to several

113

of Laporte's credit cards it contained his driver's license. It announced that the kidnappers of Laporte had not had any news from Liberation Cell. It asked Liberation Cell to issue an eighth communiqué telling whether Cross was still alive, and clarifying the conditions for the operation. It said that if Liberation Cell had executed Cross, Chenier Cell would still carry on the operation and would issue a further communiqué "when the governments have made known their decision or indecision."

❧❧❧❧❧

"Listen to them," Marc said, on Des Récollets. "What sort of communiqué do they want us to put out? What are they talking about?"

"They think we've already killed Cross."

"Listen, listen. They're reading Laporte's letter."

McGinnis read, in French:

Mr. Robert Bourassa,
My dear Robert,

1. I am convinced that I am writing the most important letter of my life.

2. For the moment I am in perfect health. I am well treated; even with courtesy.

3. I insist that the police cease all searches to find me. If they succeed, this would develop into a murderous shoot-out from which I certainly would not emerge alive. This is absolutely crucial.

114

4. In effect, you have the power to decide on my life. If it were only a matter of that and, if this sacrifice produced good results, one might consider it. But we are faced with a well-organized escalation, which will not end until the liberation of the political prisoners. After me it will be a third, then a fourth and a fifth. If all politicians are guarded, they will strike at other groups in society. Therefore act at once and avoid a bloodbath and a useless panic.

5. You know my own situation which should be considered. I had two brothers: they are both dead. I am all alone as the head of a large family which consists of my mother, my sisters, my own wife, and my children, as well as the children of my brother Roland, whose guardian I am. My death would cause irreparable distress, for you know the close ties which unite the members of my family. It isn't just I who am involved, but a dozen people. I think you understand.

6. If the freeing of the political prisoners is organized and carried out satisfactorily, I am sure that my personal safety will be assured, mine and the safety of those who might follow me.

7. This could be done quickly. I don't see why by taking more time you would continue to make me die little by little in the place in which I am being held. Decide – my life or my death. I count on you and I thank you.

Regards,
Pierre Laporte

P.S. I repeat, stop the searches. And don't let the police decide to go on with them without your knowledge. The success of this search would be a death warrant for me.

PL

Reporters waited all evening outside the Quebec Premier's heavily guarded hotel suite as he conferred with his Cabinet and others. At eight p.m., the Canadian Broadcasting Corporation sent over a portable videotape unit which was set up in the Premier's suite. News commentators on radio gave this as evidence that Bourassa would appear on television before the ten p.m. deadline. The word was also out that this would be an important announcement.

In this speech Bourassa would hold the power of life or death over his Cabinet Minister. He was not the sort of man who one would have thought would find himself in such a situation. He was thirty-seven, the son of a French Canadian bookkeeper, bookish, brainy, the most brilliant student of his year when he graduated in law from the University of Montreal; he had been a Rhodes Scholar, had studied law at Harvard, and had married the daughter of a politically powerful French Canadian millionaire shipbuilder who had launched him precipitately into politics. A year ago he had been elected as the youngest Premier ever to rule Quebec. He was a natural technocrat who believed in solving the province's problems through economic self-sufficiency and in government by a team of competent managers. Despite his Anglo-Saxon education, he was not, like Trudeau and Choquette, fluently bilingual. Nor was he a skilled politician. The man he had defeated for leadership of the Quebec Liberal Party and for the job of candidate as Premier was the man who now, handcuffed and blindfolded, awaited the life or death sentence of his speech: Pierre Laporte.

Bourassa appeared on television just five minutes before the deadline. His statement, rambling, evasive, but desperately seeking the right words, was, to his listeners on Des Récollets, a sign that perhaps, just perhaps, there was a chance that they might win. In his speech he said: "I am too proud to be a Quebecker not to tell you that I am determined, and the government which I head is determined, to surmount this crisis. On the one hand," he continued,

the Front de Libération du Québec has released a communiqué demanding the total and unconditional acceptance of their seven commands. On the other hand the Minister of Labor has sent me a letter which deals only with two of these demands – the cessation of police search and the liberation of political prisoners.

Is it necessary to say that we want to save the lives of Mr. Laporte and Mr. Cross? Fate, in a rare example of its cruelty, has chosen them as the fulcrum on which this situation turns and it is because we really wish to save the lives of Mr.

Laporte and Mr. Cross that we want, before we discuss the demands that have been made, to have some machinery which would guarantee, to use the example mentioned by Mr. Laporte, that the release of political prisoners would result in the certain safety of the lives of the two hostages.

Ordinary common sense obliges us to ask for this condition. That's why we ask the kidnappers to establish communication with us. How on earth can we give in to demands without knowing that the other side will cooperate?

"They want to negotiate!"

"We've made it!"

On Des Récollets Street there was a sudden elation, a release of the week's tension. Louise put her arms around C.T.'s neck and kissed him. "Oh, God, if only we can get away with no trouble!"

"Right," Marc said. "Screw Chenier Cell. We're not going back to the seven original demands. That just means delays and doublecross and maybe weeks of dickering."

"Let's stick to what we asked for in Communiqué Number 6," Jacques said. "Let's get the political prisoners free and out of the country."

"We s-started this show," C.T. said. "We're running it. Not those Ch-Chenier lunatics."

"Let's get it written up in a new communiqué. And tell Yves to tell Cross we need a new letter from him."

In sudden excitement Jacques went into the kitchen and put a fresh sheet of FLQ stationery in the typewriter. "C.T.? Come in here, I want you to help with this."

But when he looked up, expectantly, he saw, in the kitchen doorway, not C.T. but Suzanne, pregnant, looking at him strangely. There were tears in her eyes.

"What's the matter? Aren't you pleased?"

"Are we really going to go to Cuba?"

"Or Algeria. Whichever place will take us."

"*La Presse* and *Montréal Matin* say there are right-wing groups being formed to shoot us. To kill us!"

"Newspapers say a lot of things. It sells copies."

"But they *are* forming right-wing groups! You said it yourself. I heard you saying to Marc that you were worried."

"Well, let *me* worry, then. Relax."

"What if they shoot us on the way to the airport? What if they shoot Boris?"

"Nobody's going to shoot a little kid."

"How do you know? I want to see him." She began to weep, in earnest.

"Well, okay. We'll arrange it."

"I want to go tonight."

He looked at her for a long moment. "All right," he said. "Yves is going downtown with the communiqué. You can go with him. He'll drop you off first."

"I'll come back in the morning."

"No," Jacques said. "Go to Marie's house. I'll have somebody telephone you there tomorrow morning."

"Are you mad at me?"

"No, no," he said. "Now cheer up. Let's hope it's Algeria. They speak French there."

118

Yves took her with him that night. He and Suzanne traveled together by bus and subway to the big towntown interchange at Berri de Montigny. There, he put her on a train for Longueuil, across the river. Afterwards, he was supposed to go to the north end of the city to drop his communiqué. But he had something he wanted to do. A private thing.

First, he telephoned. When she said yes, he went off and made his silly purchase. When he picked her up outside the Dutch Maid Espresso, she was still wearing her ridiculous Dutch milkmaid's cap and the blue-and-white dirndl skirt. Over them she wore a man's khaki army trench coat which she had bought at the Salvation Army Shop. He handed her the cupcake with three candles in it, then lit the candles, standing there in the street.

"*Mon ami Pierrot*," she said. "You remembered. *C'est gentil, ça.*"

"Twenty-one is a very big birthday."

"We had a party at lunch time. The chef made a *quiche*. I would have invited you if I'd known where you were. Where *have* you been, Pierre?"

"Out of town. Let me walk you home."

She took his arm. She was a tall girl with dark hair which fell to her waist. He thought her beautiful. He still remembered their first time in bed together, last summer, when he came back from Europe and went up to the Gaspé to hippie heaven, as they called the Maison du Pêcheur. She was a Gaspésienne and at that time was working as a maid in a local hotel. She used to hang around the Maison du Pêcheur after work. He said his name was Pierre Seguin. She asked him if he were FLQ.

He laughed and shook his head. It was the right move. Later, when she took him up to her attic room in the hotel where she worked, she told him that was her test for revolutionaries. "If a boy is serious about the revolution, why should he try to impress a person he doesn't know?" she said. "And you *are* serious. I know. You're FLQ."

She was naked when she said it, curled up at the end of her narrow bed under the sloping roof, her chin propped on her bare knee. She was, he thought, the most beautiful girl he had ever seen. He was in love with her.

"No," he said. "I'm not FLQ."

"Word of honor?"

"Yes."

"Oh." She seemed downcast.

"Sorry," he said. "I guess I'm in bed with you under false pretenses."

She sighed, then stretched out on her stomach. He looked at her long, tanned back, at the white line of her small buttocks where her bikini had been. "You see," she said, "I want to join the FLQ. I thought you were one of them."

"It would have been easy to lie to you."

"I know." She turned and held out her arms. *"Embrasse moi,"* she said. *"Mon ami, Pierrot."*

In the fall, when he came to Montreal, he found this job for her at the Dutch Maid Espresso. She was glad to come to Montreal, glad to see him. But now it was as a friend, not *the* friend he had wanted to be. And, ironically, in Montreal he joined with Marc Carbonneau and Jacques Lanctôt in this operation. You didn't become FLQ by paying dues and getting a party card. But of course he could not tell her that. He had thought of her often in these last days. He knew today was her birthday. And now, as he walked her home at eleven at night, it occurred to him that if he told her what he was now, he would seem a hero in her eyes.

"What's that you've got?" she asked, pointing to the plastic sales envelope he carried. "Are you working now?"

"No. Studying," he said.

She lived in a top-floor flat, only two streets away from the espresso bar where she worked. "Would you like to come up for a while?" she said suddenly as they turned into her street.

He looked at her, hesitated. "I have an errand."
"My roommate won't be home until one."
He turned, caught her, and kissed her.

It was after one when he reached the drop Marc had indicated, at the intersection of Beaubien and 10th Avenue in the north end of the city. He dialed CKLM. We even have different radio stations, he thought. Chenier has CKAC.

As he waited for the number, he noticed the tavern and the local French-fried-potato place across the way. Both had signs in that unconsciously comic French which the Anglos made fun of. LE TAVERNE DONALD DUCK. And the French-fried place was JOE LE ROI DE LA PATATE (Joe the Potato King).

"CKLM," said a woman's voice.

"*Je veux parler à M. Pierre Pascau, s'il vous plaît.*"

When he had finished, Yves placed a brown envelope, folded in three, as usual, in the pages of the phone book in the booth.

The communiqué was broadcast by CKLM radio at ten minutes past two that Monday morning, October 12. It was a time when most people were asleep and, indeed, as Liberation Cell found out later, this communiqué was not heard by the Chenier Cell kidnappers. In their message Jacques and C.T. had tried to sound reasonable, to contradict the "killer" tone used by the Laporte kidnappers, to end the game of deadlines,

121

and above all to warn their unknown allies against what they now feared: the killing of Pierre Laporte. The communiqué, Number 8, asked simply for fulfillment of two conditions: first, the freeing of "political prisoners" and their safe conduct with wives and children to Cuba or Algeria, and second, the cessation of all police activities. It promised to release both Cross and Laporte within twenty-four hours of the return from Cuba of "observers" accompanying the "political prisoners." It said that while the FLQ could not announce where Cross and Laporte would be freed, the authorities would be advised "within minutes" of their freeing. Lastly, the message said it would trust to the good faith of the authorities and would not set a deadline, hoping that the conditions would be speedily met. It enclosed a letter from Cross, as proof that he was still alive.

Across the St. Lawrence River, on Armstrong Street, the kidnappers of Pierre Laporte did not hear these broadcasts. But, earlier, they had listened to the government. As soon as the Premier's speech was over, they ordered *their* prisoner to write a letter. They then drafted an impatient, menacing communiqué. On the following morning, Paul Rose, the former part-time teacher, left the Armstrong Street hideout to deliver both letter and communiqué. He took a taxi into the central area of Montreal and left the messages in a wastepaper basket in the Place Des Arts subway station. He then phoned CKAC. At 10:30 a.m. that morning, letter and communiqué were broadcast. It would be difficult to say which set of listeners heard them with greater disquiet: the kidnappers of James Cross or the government of Quebec. The letter was hand-written in French:

My dear Robert,
I have just heard your speech. Thank you. I expected no less from you. While eating quite frugally, I had the impression this evening of taking my last meal.

122

As for the arrangements for carrying out the conditions, I am told that you are already aware of these. The best thing would be for the political prisoners to leave Monday in the evening, during the night, or on Tuesday morning. The other things should be done concurrently. My good friend the Hon. Jean-Pierre Côté should be told that the affair of the Lapalme employees is of primary importance. Maybe we could help by placing a certain number of them in the Workmen's Compensation Board or at the Minimum Wage Board in Quebec, or in Montreal, if they want.

The FLQ people want Mr. Robert Lemieux to handle the arrangements, negotiations, etc. They are willing to give him full power of attorney from his prison cell if need be. You can appoint whoever you want to represent you. Would you be good enough as soon as you get this letter to telephone Françoise to reassure her and give her and the children all my best. You, quite rightly, asked for guarantees for the release of Mr. Cross and myself. You are right. I am ready, unconditionally, to accept the word of my abductors and I ask you to do the same.

Thank you again. My thanks to all who have contributed to this reasonable decision which you announced with strength and dignity. I hope to be free and back at work in 24 hours.

Regards,
Pierre Laporte

P.S. You can tell the handwriting expert that this letter is really in my handwriting.

The Minister's social security card was pinned to this letter. With the letter was a menacing communiqué which announced that Chenier Cell refused to negotiate. It insisted that the six conditions not complied with be each and every one granted. These were: reinstatement of the postal workers; payment of $500,000 in gold bullion; release of the "political prisoners" from jail; provision of an aircraft to fly them to Cuba or Algeria; publication of the name and photograph of the FLQ informer; cessation of all police manhunts. It reiterated that Chenier Cell had had no contact with Liberation Cell and did not know if Cross were alive.

By midmorning when these messages were broadcast, Paul

Rose discovered that Liberation Cell had already replied to Bourassa and that Cross *was* still alive. Rose took a taxi and rushed back across the river to the Armstrong Street hideout. A new communiqué must be drafted. It must be on FLQ stationery and they, who held Laporte, the ace in the hole, must stiffen the resistance of those weaklings at Liberation Cell. "All or nothing" was the motto of the new abductors.

The next communiqué was brought back to Montreal by Rose. He placed it in a telephone directory in a public phone booth only a few blocks away from CKLM, the radio station used by Liberation Cell. It was the first time the Laporte kidnappers had used CKLM. Foreign television and wire service reporters rushed from CKAC radio down the street, up to this new lucky dip in the information treasure hunt. Photocopies were passed around and at 4:30 p.m. that afternoon, the tripartite bargaining between the two kidnap cells and the Quebec government was resumed in normal fashion – through the news media.

On Des Récollets Street, Liberation Cell listened to its new allies' demands with a mixture of rage and fear. The Roses were now suggesting two separate deals, one for their prisoner, one for Cross. This was their communiqué.

Following publication of the 8th communiqué of Liberation Cell and the last communiqué from Chenier Cell, this is the situation.

1. The safe release of Mr. Cross depends on fulfillment of the following two conditions: liberation of political prisoners and cessation of police activities.

2. The release of Pierre Laporte depends on the complete observance of all six original conditions of the FLQ.

From this position, then, there are three possible developments.

1. That the government refuses the demands, or delays carrying them out, or takes too long to answer. If this happens, both hostages will be executed.

2. That the government decides to accept two conditions (liberation of political prisoners and cessation of police activites). In this case James Cross will be freed during the 24 hours following the return of the three observers and the execution of

Pierre Laporte will be cancelled, unless the police find the place where Pierre Laporte is being held. *But the Minister of Unemployment and Assimilation of the Quebec people will not be freed.*

3. That the government decides to meet the six original FLQ demands. In this case, Pierre Laporte and James Cross will be freed safe and sound within 24 hours following the successful completion of Operation Liberation.

This communiqué is the last from Chenier Cell before the execution or liberation of Pierre Laporte. The situation is clear. Any obstinacy, any delay, will be considered as a tacit refusal.

Jacques Lanctôt and Marc Carbonneau studied this latest demand. "They want to be heroes," Jacques said.

"Screw them!" Marc was furious. "They can't even think straight. Do they really expect the federal government to let the prisoners go to Cuba and not even get Laporte freed as part of the bargain? How do they think Quebeckers will feel if they know that the English diplomat went free and the French Canadian Minister is still kidnapped? It doesn't make sense."

But to their surprise, the Quebec government did not seem to agree. An announcement at 7:15 that evening, from Bourassa's suite, stated that the government had appointed a negotiator to confer with Robert Lemieux, the FLQ's lawyer. The negotiator was a thirty-three-year-old Montreal lawyer, a political unknown, Pierre Demers. That night he visited Lemieux, in prison.

The provincial government of Quebec seemed ready to negotiate. In the federal capital, however, there was a subtle and dangerous shift of mood. It was all but unnoticed that first evening. Four hundred combat troops were moved into Ottawa to help the RCMP guard federal buildings and federal politicians. It seemed, simply, a precaution. In reality it had more significance. For the man in shadow, Pierre Elliott Trudeau, a man whose intransigence exactly matched that of the Laporte abductors, was, unwittingly, about to show his hand.

11

"I am the Prime Minister of Canada."

Ten years ago that sentence would have seemed the stuff of a Walter Mitty daydream. At that time he was a university professor, writing articles for *Cité Libre*, the Quebec version of a Parisian Left Bank magazine. But, astonishingly, at forty-eight, an age when most dreamers might find their when-I-grow-up fantasy impossible to sustain, he had turned it into fact. Pierre Elliott Trudeau had become Prime Minister of Canada.

At first, he was a great success. He was young-looking, despite his thinning, carefully combed hair. So young-looking that in his official parliamentary biography he could pretend to be two years younger than he actually was. He had the ugly good looks of the day: the pitted skin and battered boyishness which is the hallmark of this age of Yves Montand and Jean-Paul Belmondo. Trudeau does not look like a Prime Minister. He looks like, and is, a French actor who can stare into a television camera as he would into a woman's eyes. It was television which made him the leader of his party and his country, as surely as it downfaced his old-fashioned oratorical opponents. The new style in acting is the actor who runs counter to type, the heavy who looks like a hero. Trudeau was counter-cast. He has been counter-cast all his life.

To begin with, he is a French Canadian, but very rich. His father, Charlie Trudeau, put together one of the largest chains of gasoline service stations on Montreal Island, sold out at the right moment to Imperial Oil, went into stocks and real estate, bought an amusement park and a piece of a ball club, and wound up five million dollars flush.

So Pierre Elliott Trudeau did not need to work. Not ever. In the posh classical college he attended in Montreal he ran with a crowd known simply as *les snobs*. It was just a game, playing snob. He was fond of games. As a French Canadian he did not think it right to fight in an imperialistic Second World War. He did get into uniform, though: one wartime summer he dressed up in a German officer's uniform and drove around Laurentian summer houses on his big 1,200-cc Harley Davidson bike, stopping to ask in guttural tones for *"wasser."* He was fond of jokes.

He had always been bright in school, and in university. He went on to Harvard. After Harvard, he moved to London University where he studied economics. In 1948 he got tired of that and went on the sort of extended grand tour a rich boy might make if he were influenced by the novels of André Malraux. He grew a beard, carried a knapsack, and some-times, in the Far East, wore a turban. He bummed his way across occupied Germany and, with faked papers, entered Communist countries like Hungary, Poland, and Yugoslavia. He swam the Hellespont because he was there. In Palestine, according to his own colorful account, he feigned lunacy when picked up by Arab guerrillas. He did this by spouting French

127

Canadian *patois* and passages from Corneille. The Arabs respect madmen. They let him go. He is a good actor.

He moved on to Pakistan and India. He often stayed in monasteries. He met with Parsee sect leaders and meditated with Buddhist monks. He got as far as Shanghai before he sailed home to Canada. In Quebec, on his return, he helped found the magazine *Cité Libre* and wrote political articles which won him the enmity of Premier Duplessis. Because of it he was denied a professorship at the University of Montreal. However, he studied there and became the university ski champion. He learned scuba diving with Jacques-Yves Cousteau. He paddled a canoe 400 miles down the Coppermine River to the Arctic Ocean. He went to Moscow to an economic conference. For a time, this resulted in his being denied a visa to enter the United States. He went on to China with a group of Canadian intellectuals and talked with Chairman Mao and Premier Chou En-lai in Peking. "It was a moving experience," he said. "These mature men, these old men with beards, today represent the triumph of an idea, an idea which has shaken the entire world and changed the profound course of history."

Back in Canada, he grew a beard himself. It was a time when Duplessis was putting down striking asbestos miners with his Quebec Provincial Police. Bearded and hip, Trudeau counseled union leaders and addressed mass meetings of strikers. The men liked him. They were amused at his appearance. They called him "St. Joseph."

In the federal capital, Ottawa, he was offered the job of an economic adviser to the Privy Council of Canada. He took it. But when Duplessis died and a new, more liberal regime came into power back home in Quebec, the men of this "quiet revolution" at once offered him the professorship denied him by the old regime. And so he joined the Faculty of Law at the University of Montreal. In 1965 he decided on politics,

128

and ran as a Liberal for a seat in Parliament. He was elected. He went back to Ottawa, now as a politician. At once he was singled out by Lester Pearson, the Liberal Prime Minister. He became one of Pearson's aides. In 1967, he advanced several squares on the political chess board. He became Minister of Justice and Attorney General of Canada.

He was a new face, he had a new style, and he was copy. He drove around the capital in a blue Mercedes sports car, wore a green leather raincoat, a Cardin hat, and took to strolling into the House of Commons in ascot and sandals. He could be seen sniffing a flower as he sat on the government front bench. Sometimes he greeted people by making a small *namaste* bow in the Indian fashion, hands joined together and touching his brow. He was not married, but he dated pretty girls and kissed them publicly. Women found him attractive. He went around with fashion models and actresses. (Later, as Prime Minister, he had a number of well-publicized dates with Barbra Streisand. In 1971 he would marry a girl twenty-two years his junior.) He worked hard at politics. He was noticed for his legislation, which included liberalization of the laws on divorce, abortion, and homosexuality. He said: "The State has no business in the bedrooms of the Nation." He hired bright assistants, used computers, and built a staff. In 1968 he ran for the leadership of the Liberal Party. Three years before, he had not even been a Member of Parliament. In those years of "charisma" he was touted as a Canadian J.F.K. He was that, and more. He won handily. As the Liberal Party was the party in power, this meant that he became Prime Minister. Four months later, he consolidated his position by going to the polls in a general election. He won a big mandate. He had political clout.

An intellectual had come to power; other nations were intrigued. He was better read than John Kennedy and his own writings were literate and informed. As a federalist, he was wary of internal dissensions. "I am less worried about what is over the Berlin Wall than about what might happen in Chicago or New York or in our great Canadian cities," he said prophetically, two years before the idea of a kidnapping had entered Jacques Lanctôt's mind. As Prime Minister he did not favor a special status for Quebec. He was hostile to the Separatist Parti Québecois. He had seen it begin as a cloud no bigger than the vaporings left after one of those old Duplessis speeches extolling the separate destiny of French Canada. He had seen it jump from nowhere to twenty-four per cent of the popular vote in less than two years. He knew it as his future threat. And English Canada knew that he knew, knew that he, better than any other leader, could keep a rein on Quebec. If he was not wholly successful as Prime Minister and party leader, he had always seemed strong in this. He would bring Quebec back into the fold. He was the man in shadow, for it was important that the provincial government of Robert Bourassa should seem independent. French Canadians running French Canada, with no interference from Anglo-Saxon Ottawa. But everyone knew. Trudeau called the plays.

Pierre Laporte was kidnapped on the night of Saturday, October 10. On Sunday, October 11, the government of Quebec set in operation what may have been the biggest manhunt in history. Thousands of city, provincial, and federal police were assigned to sixteen-hour shifts. They failed to turn up a single clue. Meanwhile, in Montreal, the Front d'Action Politique (FRAP), a loose grouping of radical elements which had joined to combat Mayor Jean Drapeau's Civic Party in municipal elections two weeks hence, had announced, obliquely, its passive support for some of the aims of the FLQ. Trudeau listened to reports from Quebec. Then, on Monday, October 12, while the populace was busy with the turkey and trimmings of the American-style holiday which

130

is Canadian Thanksgiving Day, the Prime Minister quietly ordered 400 combat troops to enter the capital to guard politicians, diplomats, and public buildings. Obviously he had wind of something, or had some plan.

That supposition seems to have occurred to the leader of the Conservative Opposition in Parliament. On the day after the troops moved into Ottawa, Tuesday, October 13, Robert Stanfield, a cool fellow-Harvardman, rose from the Opposition front bench to put a discreet question to the Prime Minister. Was there any further information the Prime Minister could give the house at this time in regard to the kidnapping case?

The Prime Minister rose. He thanked the Leader of the Opposition for his understanding way of putting the question. There was complete agreement, he said, between the government of Canada and the government of the province of Quebec on the position taken by Premier Bourassa of Quebec. A mechanism must be established for the release of Mr. Cross and Mr. Laporte.

Then, the Prime Minister's tone altered. There was in his voice a tinge of anger, an anger he had concealed all week.

"I might add," he said, "that on the general topic [the kidnappings] I can only express an opinion. I do sometimes wish that the media, the radio, the television, and the press, would exercise a bit more restraint in talking about these problems. It is a mistake, I think, to give them [the FLQ] the publicity which is the thing they hope for most. I also think it is a mistake to encourage the use of the term 'political prisoners' for men who are bandits."

After lunch he returned to the House for the afternoon session. He may have been irritated by the manifesto, that scurrilous farrago which the government, of which he was Prime Minister, had agreed to promulgate to the Canadian people on television. He himself had been quite unknown a few years ago and look what exposure by television had done for him! The comparison would seem ridiculous to some people but to a man like himself there could be no under-estimating television. Publicity could make heroes of these criminals!

His temper was his secret wound: he tried to keep it in check. (Out west, the year before, he had suddenly reached for and ripped up a placard which had been held up to taunt him all week. It was held by a girl demonstrator. The incident got into the newspapers. Another time when a young demonstrator annoyed him he had grabbed hold of the boy's hat and squashed it down around his ears. There was a protest about that. A columnist made a story about it.) Now, as the Prime Minister came to the door of the Parliament, he was waylaid suddenly by two reporters, backed up by mobile TV cameras, microphones, the lot. One of them was Tim Ralfe, national affairs reporter for the government-controlled Canadian Broadcasting Corporation. Ralfe's voice was tight with hostility. That morning he had heard the news media attacked by Trudeau. The troops the Prime Minister had called into Ottawa were pushing reporters and photographers around. So Ralfe and Peter Reilly, a reporter for an Ottawa television station, had decided to confront the Prime Minister. There was, at once, some heated and confused give-and-take about the deployment of troops. Ralfe, completely forgetting whom he was talking to, lost his temper and talked wildly about a police state. Reilly, seeking to cool the discussion, cut in and asked the Prime Minister if, in view of his statement to Parliament that morning, he thought the press had been "less than responsible" in its coverage of the story so far.

"Not *less than responsible*," Trudeau corrected him. "I was saying that they should perhaps use more restraint, which you're not doing now. You're going to make a big news item out of this, I'm sure."

"With great respect," Reilly said, "it *is* a big news item."

The Prime Minister's voice rose: "The main thing the FLQ is trying to gain from this is a hell of a lot of publicity for the movement. And I'm suggesting that the more recognition you give to them, the greater the victory is, and *I'm* not interested in giving them a victory."

By this time, all tempers were lost. Neither reporter thought to ask the Prime Minister why, if he thought this, he had given the kidnappers one of the most extraordinary publicity bonuses of all time: prime time on television to air their point of view. Trudeau complained again about the term "political prisoners" being used for the men in jail whom the FLQ wanted freed and sent to Cuba. "They're not political prisoners," he said. "They're outlaws! They're criminal prisoners. They're not political prisoners, they're bandits – that's why they're in jail!"

Ralfe then came back into the argument complaining that the massive use of army troops to protect the government made this event seem like a war. Ralfe said *he* believed in a free society, not in a society with troops at the ready, even if that meant that government ministers would be kidnapped.

Trudeau caught his breath. There, facing him, recording, photographing all this, was a television mobile unit. This was not a private squabble with reporters. Uncalculated anger is to the politician as unlimited alcohol is to the drunk. Ultimately it will destroy him. He tried again. It was the duty of the government to protect important people against being used as tools for political blackmail, he said. He tried to sound calm. But, infuriatingly, Ralfe would not give up. Back he came with his question – that one had to choose between living in a free society or an armed camp. At that moment, Pierre Elliott Trudeau, the man who could charm his country by staring into a television camera, found himself unmanned, raging, undone by his secret wound. Turning to the pitiless electronic eye, he snapped: "Well, there's a lot of bleeding hearts around here that just don't like to see people with helmets and guns! All I can say is 'go on and bleed!' But it's more important to keep law and order in society than to be worried about weak-kneed people who don't like the looks of an army."

"At any cost?" asked the infuriating Ralfe. "How far would you go with that, how far would you extend that?"

The Prime Minister glared at him. "Just watch me," said Pierre Elliott Trudeau.

12

She was looking directly at C.T., but not listening to him, trying to will him to look at her. He was talking to her brother. Marc Carbonneau sat, facing her but staring past her at the television screen. Yves was in the back room with the diplomat. Sometimes, she thought, it's as though I weren't here at all, as though I weren't a woman, as though our marriage was something that happened and is over. What sort of life can C.T. and I have in Algeria? Visiting with Suzanne and Jacques, cooking suppers of whatever it is they eat there? Will we ever have any sort of normal life again?

She thought of all the things that happened today. Was it any wonder C.T. and Jacques and Marc now had the look of mad people: as, probably, she had herself. How could any of them help feeling like lunatics when everything they had heard today on television and radio and read in the newspapers was about them! About me! *La petite Louise*, they used to call me. "*La p'tite sotte*," Sister Marie Claire used to say. Stupid old nun, what will she say when she hears that that little fool, little Louise Lanctôt, is the terrible FLQ the Prime Minister is screaming about there on television; that the provincial Cabinet is meeting about tonight; that the army has been called in to protect the ministers against; that Robert Lemieux and Demers, the government negotiator, met about this afternoon and could not agree on and are meeting about now while the whole country waits to hear what happens – and – listen – here is Robert again. Talking to *us*.

It was 11:30, on that same night, Tuesday, October 13, the night of the day Pierre Elliott Trudeau had been betrayed by his temper. During the first of two press conferences held on that Tuesday in the bar of the Hotel Nelson, Lemieux had been flanked by Pierre Vallières, their hero, the man who wrote the book which was their testament. On Lemieux's right hand was Michel Chartrand, another hero, a New Left labor leader and lay saint of Quebec's youthful protestors. Their world, exemplified by Vallières, its philosopher, and Chartrand, its champion, had now ranged itself publicly against the enemy in Ottawa and the enemy in Quebec. Lemieux had been released from jail that morning so that he could speak for them. In the first meeting, Demers, the government negotiator, had suggested that one member of each cell – Liberation and Chernier – be imprisoned as hostages, until the two kidnap victims were released. The government would promise a safe conduct to these two hostages, allowing them to join the "political prisoners" later in Algeria or Cuba. Lemieux turned this down. And now, after a second meeting, here was Lemieux again, late at night, back in his lair in the Nelson Hotel, in an atmosphere of furious excitement, shouts, an atmosphere of crisis and betrayal.

Two hundred reporters, photographers, and others were jammed into the small hotel ballroom, drinking beer, pushing and shoving each other, with microphones, TV and newsreel

136

cameras, portable sound units. And there was Lemieux in the center of the lights and the noise, long-haired, earnest, leaning into a battery of microphones, surrounded by young men who were there to protect him; Robert Lemieux, talking not to the press, not to the public, but to Louise and her husband and her brother, to Marc and to Yves – and, of course, to those others who held Laporte.

"I am speaking to those who gave me the mandate to negotiate for them," Lemieux said, in French. "You have given me a mandate to discuss the methods of putting the six demands into effect, but you have left open the preliminary question of a guarantee for the safe return of the hostages –"

"Could you tell us that in English?" a voice kept interrupting, the voice of Ronald Golden, a Reuters correspondent from New York.

"According to the mandate you gave me I cannot discuss this preliminary question — "

"In English please!"

Around Robert Lemieux the young men grew angry and nervous, knowing as they did that Lemieux was trying to speak directly to both cells of the FLQ, that this was no ordinary press conference, but a channel, the only channel which he could use to make contact.

In rage, they began to push and shove at Golden.

"Shut up, fool!"

"Speak French, damn Englishman!"

But Golden would not be silenced. The young men caught hold of him. Television light poles crashed to the floor. Reporters jumped up on tables for a better view of the scuffle as Golden was pushed, half carried, to the door and thrown out. Lemieux continued speaking in French.

"I declare that in view of the government's refusal to negotiate with me under the terms of my mandate, I cannot

137

continue these negotiatôns without receiving a new mandate."

"Oh no, Robert! Hang in there!" Louise cried. "You asked *us* to hang in, so please hang in!"

"But what can he do?" her brother asked. "It's not us, it's those Chenier Cell screwballs with their six demands! They're going to screw up the whole thing."

The conference was over. They were now without a negotiator. And without knowing what the Laporte kidnappers would do, they could not send out a communiqué asking Robert Lemieux to forget the six demands and concentrate, as they had asked, on freeing the political prisoners and getting all of them out of the country. Louise felt her head ache as though she had a migraine coming on. Until two days ago she had not even dared to hope. And now, when it had seemed that, at last, the authorities were ready to negotiate, they were right back where they had started. Trapped in this house with Cross.

As though in confirmation, shortly after midnight, Premier Bourassa of Quebec came on the air with a statement. The government would not consider releasing the twenty-three prisoners without first settling on a means by which the hostages would be returned alive. It was what both sides had feared: a stalemate.

"All right," Marc said. "There's no other way. We've got to contact Chenier."

"I'll go," C.T. said. "I'm the c-courier now."

She felt herself tremble. Not C.T.! "But what if the police are watching them at Armstrong Street?" she said. "You can't go there. It's too dangerous!"

"I can ph-ph-phone," C.T. said. "We can meet some p-place downtown. The Berri de Montigny subway, for instance." He grinned at her. "Stop worrying."

"Okay," Jacques Lanctôt said. "But phone back here and we'll talk before you make any deals. Okay?"

"Okay."

13

Last week, before they kidnapped the Minister, a man called Krankenberg appeared at the bungalow at 5630 Armstrong Street in St. Hubert. He said he was the South Shore administrator for the landlord. He said the rent was overdue.

Krankenberg might come back this week. The prisoner was chained and blindfolded in the back room. So on Tuesday, October 13, Paul Rose telephoned for a taxi and went over to Longueuil. There he took the subway across the river to Montreal. He was in downtown Montreal, paying the rent at two in the afternoon, just at about the time government troops were moving into Ottawa to protect officials against him, at a time when, all about him, in Montreal, the greatest manhunt in Canadian history was in progress to try to flush him out.

When he had paid the rent he was short of money. He was saving their remaining cash to stay mobile by using taxis. Yesterday when they said they had no food in the house, except for a loaf of bread, the prisoner had offered them money. He had $60 in cash. They had used some of the money to buy barbecue chicken from a take-out place.

Now, Paul Rose came out of the rental office, wondering where he could get more cash. A big burly man, his right eye filmed over by a cataract, a man who might be noticed in a crowd. Suddenly he stopped, in tension. The blue Volkswagen was parked a block and a half away on the far side of the street. He had first seen it in downtown Montreal on Sunday, just after he delivered the third communiqué to CKAC. He thought he saw it a second time, on Monday, when he got out of the taxi at the Longueuil subway station. He had not been sure it was the same vw but, now, there was no mistake. Two men inside. *Flics.* He realized he could not go back to Armstrong Street.

Keep calm. The point is, the *flics* are following hundreds of people this week. They don't know I did anything. They probably have a tail on me as a person who's made trouble in the past, a person who was Separatist and might be FLQ and lead them to something. All right. I'll lead them around a bit.

He took the subway and went back across the river to Longueuil. He found the vw again, waiting in the next street as he walked away from the subway. They sure traveled fast. He went to Mama Venne's house on Ste. Alexandre Street. He had not seen her for a long time and the Vennes had no idea of what he was mixed up in: Mama and her husband had worked with him, a year or so ago, organizing for the Parti Québecois. Mama was upstairs in bed. She had heart trouble. The kids were downstairs, watching television. He phoned Fernand at his office and Fernand said he would be home around suppertime. Then Paul helped the kids with their homework and sat with them watching the third game of the Baltimore-Cincinnati World Series on television. At suppertime Fernand came home and Paul asked if he could borrow a jacket and a change of shirt. Afterwards they ate supper and watched the television news. He told the Vennes he had financial troubles, which was nothing new to any of them. Fernand couldn't help. He would have if he could. So, after supper, Paul asked if they could give him a lift into Montreal as he was broke and there was a finance company after him and he thought they were waiting outside, tailing him. He asked René, the fourteen-year-old kid, to get on his bike and go to Briggs and St. James Streets and see if there was a blue Volkswagen there. The kid got on his bike, cycled off, and came back. "Yes. And there are two men in it."

The kid would be staying home. The *flics* might come to the door. He took the kid aside and said: "Look, if someone asks for me, say I've been here three weeks to a month. Okay? You see, I'm having trouble with this finance company."

"Okay," the kid said.

The *flics* were so discreet it was easy. He went out the back, with the Vennes, and drove off unseen in Fernand's car. The blue Volkswagen remained parked at Briggs and St. James Streets. The Vennes drove him across the river and dropped him at the corner of Pie IX Boulevard and Ontario Street. He went into one of those big gloomy taverns and sat with a bunch of workingmen watching television all evening. Saw the whole damn thing, the news, the Lemieux press conferences, the whole mixup. At eleven-thirty when the tavern emptied out, he had come to a conclusion. He must get in touch with those others, wherever they were. He went out of the tavern. There was no blue Volkswagen. He went into a public phone booth and phoned Armstrong Street. His brother Jacques answered.

"C.T. called," Jacques said. "He's waiting for you now at the Frontenac line at Berri de Montigny subway station."

"Okay," Paul Rose said. He walked down to Papineau Street. C.T. was only one subway station away. They met in the quiet, modern corridors of the Metro, walked and talked, two young men waiting for a late train home. Then C.T. went to a phone booth and reported to Jacques Lanctôt. He leaned out of the telephone bubble and asked Paul Rose to take the receiver. Stood around, aware that Paul and Jacques were arguing. Paul came out of the bubble, pointed to the receiver hanging there. "He wants you again," Paul said, and walked away up the platform.

C.T. picked up the receiver. "Did you hear what that bastard said?" Jacques Lanctôt's voice was filled with half-suppressed rage. "I've told him we're against killing Cross or anyone else."

"And what does *he* say?"

"He says if the government doesn't release the political prisoners, the FLQ will not intervene in Mr. Laporte's favor to stay the execution pronounced against him by the authorities."

"What in Christ's name does that mean?"

"Ask him!" Jacques said, bitterly.

So C.T. hung up and walked up the track towards Paul Rose. The big, burly figure stood staring down at the subway rails, brooding. C.T. stood beside him. "What does this mean, you won't intervene, et cetera?"

Rose turned. One eye was bright with anger: the other filmed and dull. "You know what it means," he said. "It's agreed now. Go home."

C.T. turned away. He felt sick. Execution. Just a word for murder.

"*Nous vaincrons*," Paul Rose said.

He nodded. He walked on. He did not look back at Rose.

He reached Des Récollets after two. He and Jacques worked until five, writing and rewriting what was to be the first and only joint FLQ communiqué. It was found next morning by a CKLM reporter under a strip of dirty gray carpet in a cheap apartment house in a middle-class residential section. Broadcast at 10:15 a.m., it announced that the FLQ refused to surrender a member of each cell as hostage. It said: "We renew Mr. Lemieux's mandate as to the carrying out of our conditions and give him carte blanche to negotiate these conditions." It announced that the FLQ would issue a new communiqué following the Wednesday negotiations between the mediators and, at that time, would set up a last deadline for meeting the FLQ's demands.

Carte blanche. Jacques had been explicit. Within an hour after the broadcast of the communiqué they heard on the news that Robert Lemieux had ended his boycott and was meeting with Demers, the government negotiator. "My mandate has been renewed by the FLQ and something new has been added," Lemieux said. "I will now be able to discuss the conditions themselves with the government."

It was Wednesday, October 14. James Richard Cross had spent nine days handcuffed and cowled in a dark room. Pierre Laporte had spent four days chained, handcuffed, and blindfolded in another anonymous room. Suddenly, it seemed possible that they would be set free. Suddenly, as C.T. said to the others, that afternoon in the kitchen on Des Récollets, "for the f-first time it seems we've done it right. It's going to w-work."

"And the manifesto," Louise said. "Did you read about the students at the University of Montreal? Nearly all the kids they interviewed said we were right, because the manifesto takes the part of the workers and maybe the only way to get the people of Quebec interested in the problem is to do what we did."

"Goddamn!" Jacques said. "If the only thing we got out of this was the manifesto made public on television, then we didn't fail."

That night they received unexpected further support. A group of ten of the most influential leaders in the province met and signed a joint statement urging the provincial Premier to act independently of the federal government and release the twenty-three "political prisoners" in exchange for the safety of Cross and Laporte. The signatories included the heads of the two largest and moderate Quebec labor unions, the head of the separatist Parti Québecois, the editor of the influential daily newspaper *Le Devoir*, the president of the Quebec Teachers' Corporation, and the head of an insurance firm.

"The kids, the big shots, the Separatists, the unions, damn nearly everybody!" Jacques Lanctôt exulted. "Okay, you goddamn ruling authorities, there's the voice of your people. Let's open up the jails. Algeria, here we come!"

They would never see Algeria. The Algerian government had indicated to the government of Canada that it was unwilling to accept the twenty-three "political prisoners" and the kidnappers of Cross and Laporte. In Cuba, while Fidel Castro was not eager, he had not refused sanctuary. He had always maintained diplomatic relations with, and traded with Canada, even in the hard years after the Bay of Pigs. He would accommodate the Canadian government if it wished to make a deal. The Cuban Ambassador in Ottawa was ready to act as go-between.

So, if they were to go at all, it would have to be Cuba.

14

But he had no intention of letting them go.

When he was a young man, in the days when Montreal's streetcars connected to overhead current wires by trolley bars, as a prank he would lean out of the rear window and pull the trolley off the wire. If this irritated some other male passenger enough to protest, young Pierre Trudeau would invite the man to step off the streetcar and finish the argument in a back alley "between men." He knew how to fight.

Between men. But Bourassa had no *machismo*: he was a new boy in politics, a technocrat, a friend of Laporte's, who waffled and, irritatingly, gave the impression that he was ready to negotiate with these criminals. Still, in the complex struggle of politics, he could be bent. Bourassa was a Liberal, and Trudeau was head of the Liberal Party. Federal power could be invoked, if Bourassa proved unable to control this big unruly province. And certainly, in the last day or two, what with these student strikes and teach-ins, what with left-wing labor leaders like Michel Chartrand making inflammatory speeches – saying that the executive committee of his union *"supports unequivocally* all the objectives of the FLQ manifesto read on Radio-Canada, last Thursday October 8" – and even the big moderate Quebec unions offering "pressing support to negotiations" and with people like the editor of *Le Devoir* agreeing with René Lévesque, the Separatist leader, that the kidnappings were "primarily a Quebec affair," and urging the Quebec government to release the twenty-three prisoners – well then, goddamit, what you had was a potentially seditious situation!

For these kidnappings were not primarily a Quebec affair. They were a federal affair. *His* affair. The world was watching Canada to see how he would handle this crisis. He had taken a stand. He was not, and never had been, a man to back off from a fight. Only two days ago he had been seen by millions of people in North America, on CBS, and millions more in Europe, on BBC and French National Television, taking a very strong line, saying that he would not let these terrorists dictate to him. There was no question of backing down now.

Not that it was easy to get a consensus. He had never worked harder, not even during the elections. This was Parliament and Parliament was not in his pocket. In Ottawa, there were people like old John Diefenbaker, the former Conservative Prime Minister, all turkey wattles and outrage, rising up in the House against him, asking if it were true that he was contemplating hauling the old, British-inspired War Measures Act out of mothballs.

He was: but could not say it just yet. The Act had just the muscle he needed, the right to empower the police *to arrest anyone they wished without warrant or permit, to search anyone's house, to detain without charge for up to 21 days and without trial for 90 days; to suppress information, to forbid publication.* And do other things as well. Stanfield, the Leader of the Opposition, lunged up from the front benches to demand that before any such act be used, it be submitted to Parliament for approval. As if sedition and kidnapping and a threat to government could be dealt with as though it were a Housing Bill! "It's obvious," he said, acidly, answering Stanfield, "that if urgent action is required at some time in the middle of the night, we cannot ask Parliament to approve it first."

"You have no power to do it except through Parliament!" shouted Diefenbaker.

Oh yes? Well, perhaps the time had come for a little jawboning in caucus, time to remind opponents and government members alike that if we give in now, who'll be next? That was his point. He had no intention of handing over any criminals in exchange for Cross and Laporte. Which was unfortunate because although he had to say it, to make his point, wouldn't you know, it leaked out and the damned reporters at once rushed with it to the provincial Premier's office in Quebec City, where Bourassa, dithering and swithering, caught off guard and close to panic, said he would have to read the transcript of the remarks before he commented on the Prime Minister's statements. And came close to an admission that it was the intention of the provincial government to make some sort of trade.

No deal. *He* had other plans for these bandits. He had just been forced to cancel his state visit to Russia, arranged months ahead, something which would have entailed world-wide publicity. Premier Kosygin had sent him "a very understanding reply" the other day when he mentioned that he might have to delay his trip. It was inevitable that some wag would say he bet the Russians understood. It was their sort of problem.

He worked, he phoned, he cajoled, he used party muscle. But nothing was settled that day, Wednesday, October 14.

148

That evening, he had further telephone conversations with Bourassa in Quebec City. Of course what worried Bourassa was the kidnappers' reaction when they were told there would be no deal. If anything happened to Laporte, Bourassa would be blamed. Bourassa wanted to deal. The mildest suggestion Bourassa came up with was that they recommend parole for five of the prisoners now in jail and safe conduct for the kidnappers to go to Cuba in a government transport plane. These five prisoners were already eligible for parole, Bourassa argued. So it wasn't much of a compromise.

A compromise is a compromise, Pierre Elliott Trudeau felt. Still, Bourassa was in a difficult spot. He was a close friend of Laporte's. Laporte had appealed to him in that emotional letter. Yes, it was hard on Bourassa.

On Thursday, the following day, when there was no settlement, when Lemieux and Demers were still fencing, there was, at least from *his* point of view, a strengthening of the situation. Bourassa agreed to ask for federal troops "to assure the security of the [Quebec] population."

Right. That was more like it. Big Hercules C-130 troop- and vehicle-carrying aircraft were given the go-ahead. Helicopters moved in for shuttle duties. Combat troops, jeeps, truck convoys, ambulances, supply vehicles. The Quebec government announced that the "energy of the police forces had been considerably overtaxed." And that the federal troops had been called in to protect persons and places "as a last resort."

Quebec made its official request for help at two p.m. Most Canadians were busy with the World Series on television that afternoon. The Baltimore Orioles and the Cincinnati Reds were in the final innings of the fifth and eventually decisive game as helicopters landed combat troops in downtown Montreal. Meantime, Pierre Elliott Trudeau had been having a full day in the capital. He met the Cabinet in an early morning session, then moved to private meetings with leaders of three Opposition parties. Then went to Parliament, where he announced cancellation of his Russian trip. He was on the phone to Bourassa in Quebec. He met privately with Diefenbaker. He spoke by telephone to Toronto where former Liberal Prime Minister Lester B. Pearson was staying. All of these meetings and talks were fence-building courtesies. To send in troops requested by a provincial Premier – the Premier of Quebec in this case – he did not need to roll out the big gun – the War Measures Act – or to clear the action with Parliament. But he had a much bigger move in mind. It was a day for meetings, hand claspings, for politics pure and subtle.

Night: Thursday, October 15. Shortly after nine p.m. it was announced that, following consultation with the federal government, Premier Bourassa of Quebec would "recommend" parole for five of the men now in prison for FLQ activities. He would not guarantee this parole but would recommend it to the parole board, which could, of course, turn down the recommendation. Furthermore, safe passage to a foreign country would be guaranteed the kidnappers of James Cross and Pierre Laporte. This was the provincial government's final decision, Bourassa said. He asked the kidnappers for a reply within six hours. That meant by three a.m. next morning.

In Ottawa, at the time of the announcement, Pierre Elliott Trudeau was on Parliament Hill, meeting with members of Opposition parties. It was now in the open. "Emergency Powers." He assured the Opposition that the government would not use these powers if the FLQ acceded to Bourassa's terms. But made it clear that neither he nor Bourassa expected FLQ acceptance.

(In fact, his government had already put into motion the means of securing the War Measures Act. The Mayor of Montreal and the Chairman of Montreal's Executive Committee had, at federal suggestion, written letters requesting that the federal government invoke emergency powers. Their letters, prepared in advance, were dated on that day, Thursday, October 15. A letter from Premier Bourassa, also requested, was postdated for the following day, Friday, October 16.)

Shortly after Bourassa's offer to the FLQ, Lemieux, the FLQ's lawyer, angry and histrionic, called a press conference. "My mandate is over," he told reporters. "The six conditions of the FLQ have been completely refused. I am almost 100 per cent certain that this hard line was imposed on the provincial government by Prime Minister Trudeau."

Shortly afterwards Lemieux hurried over to the Paul Sauvé Arena, a French Canadian sports center in the East End of Montreal. There, something was happening which fitted perfectly into the Prime Minister's game plan. Three hundred plainclothes policemen sat in the auditorium, watching, as a crowd which grew to fifteen hundred students cheered speeches made by Lemieux and other radical figures in support of the FLQ demands. Pierre Vallières, the movement's theoretician, said: "The government claims the FLQ is a small band of criminals. But *you* are the FLQ, you and all the popular groups that fight for the liberation of Quebec. We must organize the fight for liberation in each district, in each plant, in each office, everywhere."

"FLQ! FLQ! FLQ!" the students chanted. But the speakers warned that any street demonstrations would be playing into the government's hands. Thus warned, the meeting dispersed peacefully at eleven p.m. Minutes later the telephone rang in the Prime Minister's Ottawa office. Staff members received news of this latest development and reported it to Trudeau. From his point of view it was perfect. He had instigated these emergency powers long before the meeting occurred. But no one, later, seemed to notice this discrepancy. In subsequent debates on his actions he would use this meeting as prior proof of "an apprehended insurrection."

151

He stayed late in Parliament. He did not leave until 12:30 a.m. But, by the time he went home to bed, his plan was becoming fact. Something was afoot and the media people sensed it. Television networks, which normally closed down at midnight, stayed on the air, rehashing the day's events, filling in with movies and spot announcements. Something was due to break in Ottawa.

On Des Récollets Street they also stayed up late that night. The deadline was three a.m. They had heard nothing from the Chenier group, but knew they were ready to kill Laporte. *They* had expected a compromise: instead Bourassa had taken a hard line. It was beyond the blinkers of their comprehension and they talked about it, endlessly, as the clock moved towards three.

Marc Carbonneau saw it in orthodox Marxist terms. "I'll tell you why Trudeau turned us down. It's because they're afraid that, if they give in, this sort of thing will spread from South America to North America. And all those people in the States will be doing it – the Weathermen, the Panthers. I'll bet you the government in Washington has told Trudeau: be careful, don't give in, you'll create a precedent. Yes, the word came from Washington, that's for sure."

"If it had been Pearson or Stanfield, or any other Prime Minister, anybody but Trudeau, they would have negotiated, they'd have let the prisoners go free," Jacques Lanctôt said. "But Trudeau knows the support our manifesto brought us. He's afraid of a revolution in Quebec."

The truth was, the kidnappers' Marxist rhetoric could not comprehend the complexities of the situation: they could no more have imagined the bargaining, the maneuvering, the jawboning necessary to secure the extraordinary measures now afoot than could Trudeau understand what it was like to be young, enraged, impotent. They would never understand him: he would never think to comprehend them. They, not

152

he, had misjudged the situation. He knew there was no mass sedition in Quebec. He had not consulted Washington: he had not consulted anyone. He was not afraid. He was the man he had always been: the tough in the back alley, his blood up, eager to fight.

The Bourassa deadline expired at three o'clock in the morning. A few minutes before three, a courier carrying letters from the Premier of Quebec, the Mayor of Montreal, and the Chairman of the Montreal Executive Committee arrived on cue at Parliament Hill. The Prime Minister was home in bed. Instead the courier was met by four Cabinet ministers who proceeded with the paperwork necessary for a proclamation of emergency powers. The ministerial team, headed by the Solicitor General of Canada, completed its work before four a.m. Their final step was to dispatch a courier of their own to Government House where the Governor General, that figurehead who is the Queen's Representative in Canada, signed his approval, making it law.

Word had become deed. At four a.m., the French-language television network came out of a late-night coma of movies and music and suddenly went live. At 5:17 when most of the nation was asleep, the networks announced that the most repressive wartime powers ever invoked in a democracy were now the peacetime law of Canada.

15

They all said he was crazy. "For Christ's sake, Jacques," Marc told him. "Two hundred and forty people have been arrested since five o'clock this morning. Robert Lemieux, Pierre Vallières, Michel Chartrand, Gaston Miron, the poet, Dr. Mongeau – every single person who ever said a word for the FLQ, man or woman, has been thrown into jail. I mean this is *it,* man. And you want to go out and sit in Lafontaine Park."

Of course they were right. It was foolish. But he had not seen Suzanne since she left here on Sunday night. He had promised if there was no solution by Friday he would go to the park to meet her. The woman who was babysitting with little Boris would bring the kid to a certain part of the park. Suzanne would pick the kid up there and join him at four near the University pavilion.

So this morning, after they heard news of the raids, he went out and telephoned Marie. Suzanne was expecting him, Marie said. No, there had been no raid on Marie's place. Not yet.

"I'll be there," he told Marie. He went back to Des Récollets and told the others. At that time they did not realize how widespread these raids were. All over Quebec, the ten a.m. newscast said.

"I quote," said C.T. *"Violence can b-by itself pr-produce a revolutionary situation.* That's what Mao says. Counter-revolutionary measures produce repression of the p-populace, which can invoke a p-popular uprising. Let's face it. This is what we wanted. Right?"

Well, yes. But it was frightening. Something called the Police Act had been enforced yesterday in preparation for the big weapon – the War Measures Act. But even under this Police Act, according to this morning's newspapers, Maurice St. Pierre, Quebec's police chief, was now, after Trudeau, the most powerful man in Canada. St. Pierre could arrest, detain, do God-knows-what. *"Calice!"* Marc Carbonneau swore. Just think of it. They've put him in charge of 1,700 men – seventeen hundred men against ten – us and the Chenier Cell! Five thousand combat troops flown in from New Brunswick and from the West. Paratroopers! The Toronto *Globe and Mail* says half of Canada's infantry troops are now in the province of Quebec! And twelve thousand cops – Mounties, Provincials, and city police. Twelve thousand! And today's the day Jacques Lanctôt decides to go and visit in the park!"

Raids. No warrants. Doors smashed down. Two hundred and fifty people pulled out of bed, dragged down to police headquarters, stuffed in cells, no bail, no charges, no lawyers. People like Pauline Julien the nightclub singer, who sang songs about free Quebec. Up to five years in prison if you were a member of the FLQ or were found to have helped them in any way. Broadcasting, televising, or printing any communiqué or message from the FLQ forbidden under threat of jail. Arrest of anyone carrying political slogans or leaflets.

"Censorship," C.T. said. "That's w-why Trudeau used this

Act, that's the real reason he p-put up this scare about an 'apprehended insurrection' being planned in Quebec. Remember, three days ago he said: 'The main thing that the FLQ is t-trying to gain from this is a hell of a lot of p-p-publicity. . . . The more recognition you give them, the greater the victory is, and I'm not interested in g-giving them a victory.' "

"He's invented a revolution to keep us off television and the air," Jacques said. "What a laugh!"

"It's not so funny," Marc said. "If we can't send any communiqués, if no one *knows* what we do, then what does it matter *what* we do? If everyone who could speak for us is in jail and if everybody else is afraid because they can be arrested just like that, then what do we do with Cross? What will Chenier Cell do with Laporte?"

They sat in silence. "There's a lot of p-p-people are against this Act," C.T. said. "*La Presse* says that the Opposition p-party leaders are hinting it's a fake, a p-p-put-up job. Maybe the people of Canada won't stand still for this."

"*Calice!*" Marc said. "They'll stand still for anything! And the Opposition leaders complaining, that's just the goddamn capitalist smoke screen! They all agreed to it, didn't they?

"Sure they did," Jacques said. "I told you. They got their orders from Washington."

Jacques left the house at three. It was a cold day so he wore his topcoat. He did not put on the false mustache Marc offered him. "You're a stupid bastard!" Marc said, as he went out of the door. Marc had left his own wife and kids: he often said he loved them but that he was married to the revolution. Still, goddamit, this was different: Suzanne was seven-and-a-half months pregnant, she had to worry about that in addition to everything else. If Jacques didn't show up today she could worry herself sick, maybe even into a miscarriage.

He took a bus out west and picked up the Number 2 subway line. The city seemed much as usual. There were no soldiers in this part of town. He decided the soldiers were in the city to protect the big bosses in Westmount, not to protect the ordinary people you met on Berri Street. This part of the city was unusually quiet; it seemed more like a Sunday than a Friday afternoon. A lot of people must be at home, watching television, waiting for news of more arrests or maybe even this insurrection that Trudeau was talking about.

On the subway, he stood at the rear of the car, wearing his large hexagonal sunglasses, facing the window, his back to the other passengers. It was good to be out on the streets again: to be away from that room with Cross in his corner and you in yours, where everything that happens, happens on television or radio. It was exhilarating to remember that he, Jacques Lanctôt, had started all this. He had made Canada jump.

He stood at the southwest corner of Lafontaine Park, waiting. The bank clock down the street said five minutes to four. A cold wind, a first hint of the winter to come, shook the trees, sent leaves in fitful, aimless scurryings along the park paths. He looked down towards the Université de Québec's Lafontaine Pavilion where, twelve days ago, they had dropped their first communiqué. The college seemed empty: the newspapers said that most of the junior colleges were out on strike in solidarity with the FLQ. Which sounded great in print, but the truth was he had no faith in these college kids and their strikes, strikes to them were just an excuse to tell the college to go and eat shit.

As if to prove his point that students are not serious, two boys, shaven-skulled, wearing some pink salve on their foreheads and dressed in Buddhist robes, went hurrying past, incongrous in their cloth overcoats. Hare Krishna chanters; he had seen their sort before on street corners collecting for some nut religion, goddamn college snots, he wanted to go and kick them in their runty asses. Sometimes his rages alarmed him. Sometimes, uneasy, he thought of his father's generation and

157

their rages: of Arcand beating up on the Jews. He had inherited that rage, but could he kill? In war, perhaps, in a demo against cops. But what about in a room, the way the Roses and Francis might do it?

The street was quiet, the park paths empty. Then, little Boris appeared, with the drunken stumbling run of the eighteen-month-old, with Suzanne, very pregnant, some steps behind the kid. At first he drew back, waiting to see if there were *flics* behind her, but now, seeing her close, there was almost no risk he wouldn't take. He went out and saw her face change completely, losing its strained look in a big smile, but then, when he held her, she wept; wept as though this were a death. He held her, then bent down and squatted by the baby. He looked back up at her. "What are you crying for?"

"No, it's nothing."

"What is it?" he said again. "Is something wrong?"

"You're here," she said. "That's why. I thought you wouldn't come."

"But I said I'd come."

"Oh God! When are we going to get away from all this?"

"Soon," he said. "Very soon." He kissed the baby again. The baby put a fat little fist in his face. His son. This baby will speak Spanish, he thought. If I am lucky. And the baby not yet born, will it be a Cuban citizen?

"How have you been?" he asked her.

"Scared."

Hunkered down beside the baby, he held up a red india-rubber ball. The fat little fist reached out for it.

They had not taken off the blindfold since morning. His eyes hurt: his eyeballs felt swollen and painful. Earlier, they had allowed him to walk around for about two minutes after feeding him some more of that stale, disgusting fried chicken for breakfast. He had asked for tea, but they had no more teabags. Before they went out to buy the chicken, with money he offered them, they had nothing but bread in the house.

Pierre Laporte, Minister of Labor and Immigration for the province of Quebec, lay on a bed, his legs and wrists shackled, blindfolded, restless, in pain. Whatever was happening today, they were more interested than ever in the television and radio. They never turned it off. He heard snatches: something about troops, and Trudeau was to speak tonight on national television "on the crisis," and he had heard one of them say there were a couple of hundred people arrested this morning in police raids. The worrying thing was that, if the police broke in here, everybody would be shot dead. These kids, whoever they were, were madmen, filled with a lunatic rage. From the beginning he had known they were not bluffing. That was why he wrote the letter to Robert Bourassa. They would shoot him as quickly as they would a cat.

"Lie still, goddamit," said his unseen guard. "You're making me nervous."

The shackles around his ankles were connected by a chain to handcuffs on his wrists. The leg shackle was locked to the bedpost; when he moved, the chain rattled, the bedpost shook. "It's my legs," he said. "I have bad pain in them today because I can't move them. Can't you tie me up some other way?"

The guard got up and went out. After a moment, two of them came in. They took the shackles off his leg. His arms were now free, except for the handcuffs. His legs were free. "Get the dog leash," one of them said. They put a single chain around his leg and attached the other end to the foot of the bed. "That way, you can sit up and move your legs," one said. "But don't get any ideas."

He heard the guard sit down again, heard his body creak on the chair. The other one went out. After a moment he heard his guard get up, very, very cautiously. Sometimes they left the room, in a stealthy way so as not to let him know they had gone. Usually he could hear the floorboard creak as they crossed the threshold. The board creaked now. Whatever was happening today on television, they couldn't stay away from it. He suspected the police might be closing in. After waiting perhaps a minute, he decided to experiment. A dog leash would be about three feet long and, as this one was wrapped around his ankle, he estimated that would give him, say, two feet to maneuver in. He had seen the window when they took the blindfold off. The blind was kept down. The window was on his left, about six feet from the bed.

It was good to sit up for a change. He tried to hear what the television was saying, or was that the radio?

Then he heard it, coming very quickly, coming this way, a police siren, loud, LOUDER. He rose up. If they started shooting he would be killed! He did not have time to think. He lurched: he was a big man and the bed moved with him. He bent, grabbed up the pillow on which his head had rested. The window was in front of him now, he was sure. With a lunge, holding the pillow to protect his face, he threw himself at the window, felt the glass cut his wrists, his chest, felt the chain jerk his leg, holding him, felt the window, Oh Christ – the lower pane was covered by a wire mosquito screen. Panting, he raised his hands and tore the taped blindfold from his eyes. At first he could not see, but then, getting his bearings again, he undid the dog leash from his ankle and, free to move now, put the pillow in front of his face and tried to leap up and hurl himself through the upper pane of the window. But it was impossible: he crashed through the pane glass and lay, half in, half out, bleeding, trapped. He let go of the pillow and it fell down to the walk outside. The siren died. He heard them behind him, cursing. One of them lifted him back off the jagged broken pane, pulling him back into the room.

"Did they see him?"

"No. Fucking miracle. It's a fire or something down the street. They're down there now."

"What are they doing. Yes, it's a fire, all right. Holy Mother. He threw his pillow out onto the street! It's all covered with blood!"

"Francis, run round the side of the house and get that fucking pillow! Quick!"

One of them ran out. They lifted him onto the couch and he felt wet in his trousers. There was a cut on his belly, bleeding, but that was nothing, it was his wrists, they were the worst, the left one was spouting blood so fast it frightened him. "Stop the bleeding," he said, thickly. "Make a tourniquet!" But they did not seem to understand. They were picking glass out of his cuts. One made a cold compress for his stomach and undid his trousers to put it on. Another cut a green towel and a blue-and-white bedsheet into long strips to bandage him.

"Up higher on my arm," he said, wavering between fainting and consciousness. Wrap them tight. Tight! Don't be afraid. I'll tell you when it hurts."

They did what he said. He did not know why, but he began to weep. "It won't do," he said. "For God's sake, take me to a hospital!"

"How can we do that? The police are after us."

"I'm still bleeding."

"No," they said. "We can't. There are police patrols all over the place."

"Put his blindfold on again," one said. The other shoved wads of Kleenex against his eyeballs and wound on the hateful green tapes. Then they tied him again, shackles and cuffs. They had trouble getting the cuffs on over his bandaged wrists. "Take me to a hospital," he said, again. He wept.

"Shut up," the guard said. He heard the others go out. They turned the radio up. The door shut. He could hear only a jumble of radio noise.

After a while, despite the pain from the tight bandages, suddenly, mercifully, he fell asleep.

Yesterday, while Francine was out, he had spent the afternoon dyeing his hair. The dye had been auburn but now as he stepped out onto Queen Mary Road at six p.m., even, at dusk, in street lighting, his hair seemed unnatural. He put on a tuque, then took it off. It was not cold enough to wear a tuque. He walked away from the Gaston Apartments, passing the Wax Museum with its advertisements for wax effigies of presidents Lyndon B. Johnson, John F. Kennedy, and Charles de Gaulle. MUSEE HISTORIQUE CANADIEN (DE CIRE).

He took a bus to the nearest subway. It had been arranged that he meet Bern Lortie at 6:30 p.m. at the Berri de Montigny station. He had not been back to the Armstrong Street hideout since Tuesday when the Vennes helped him give that blue Volkswagen the slip. On the way to Berri de Montigny, he kept checking to see if there was a new tail on him. He believed he had been clean since Tuesday.

He stood near a newsstand at the Berri de Montigny station, a big brooding figure in a torn green woollen sweater and dark slacks, clean-shaven, with his new, too-auburn hair. Bern came up and stood about twenty feet away, as though waiting for a train. The drill was if one of them suspected he were being followed he would buy a newspaper and move off. They stood, waiting, for almost a minute. Neither went to the newsstand. Bern walked up to Paul and they strolled down the platform together, the slight young man and the big burly one, casual, chatting. Paul Rose stared ahead, his face impassive, his good eye bright with anger. "I can't believe it!" he said. And then: "How much blood did he lose?"

"I don't know. A lot."

He looked at Bern. "Here," he said, handing him a twenty-dollar bill and an address. "Go and stay with these people until I get in touch with you. I'm clear now, there are no *flics* following me. I'm going back to Armstrong Street."

"Don't you want me to come with you?"

"No. Do what I say. We'll get in touch with you."

Paul Rose then took the subway to Longueuil. At 7:30 p.m. he was back in the bungalow, looking at the prisoner's wounds. Trudeau was due to speak at eight, that night, Friday, October 16.

He did not speak at eight. Tapes had been prepared in English and French so that there could be simultaneous transmission in both languages. But something was wrong with the wording on the English tape. He did not appear on television until 10:20 p.m.

He was conservatively dressed. French-language network

executives who had watched him perform on other occasions noticed that tonight he was strikingly different. It was, as one said, "as though he were acting this speech. He wasn't arrogant, as he usually is, with the television people. He read his stuff carefully and when he came to the part about the FLQ, spoke without his usual anger against them. He was cool and relaxed." It was, they agreed, "his best performance."

On Des Récollets Street, C.T., watching, pointed out something the commentators had missed. For the first time since the kidnapping this was an official speech by the Prime Minister of Canada, not an interview, not impromptu comment. And it was the first speech by the Establishment which was not addressed to them, the kidnappers. It was a justification to Canada and to the world of the use of the War Measures Act.

"Should governments give in to this crude blackmail," the Prime Minister said, "we would be facing the breakdown of the legal system and its replacement by the law of the jungle.

"It is the responsibility of the government to deny the demands of the kidnappers. The safety of these hostages is, without question, the responsibility of the kidnappers."

The threat posed by the terrorists, he said, "is out of proportion to their numbers. This follows from the fact that they act stealthily and because they are known to have a considerable amount of dynamite in their possession."

He told Canadians that the "political prisoners" whose release the FLQ sought were murderers, bombers, armed robbers, criminals. He said the kidnappers did not care anything for their victims. "The kidnappers' purposes would be equally well served by having in their grip you or me, or perhaps some child."

He apologized to the people of Canada for the use of the War Measures Act. "These are strong powers and I find them as distasteful as I am sure you do. They are necessary, however, to permit the police to deal with persons who advocate or promote the violent overthrow of our democratic system. . . . " The government "is acting to make clear to kidnappers, revolutionaries, and assassins that, in this country, laws are made and changed by the elected representatives of all Canadians – not by a handful of self-selected dictators. Those who gain power by terror, rule through terror. The government is acting, therefore, to protect your life and your liberty."

⚜⚜⚜⚜⚜

"It's me," C.T. said into the receiver. "Is Paul there?"

On Queen Mary Road, he heard her hesitate. "No, he's not here. He went back."

"When?"

"About six, I think. I was out when he left. You saw the big show? Trudeau?"

"Yes."

"What are you going to do?" She said it, then caught her breath. "I'm sorry. Maybe I shouldn't ask that."

He could see her, in his mind, probably curled up on the old green sofa, her thick blonde hair caught in a rubber band at the nape of her neck, wearing a sweater and one of those long quilted skirts she affected: he remembered her habit of staring at you fixedly, like a child caught out in a lie.

"Yes," he said. "*Don't* ask."

"I was to tell you. Francis called."

"When?"

"After the broadcast. He said to tell you Trudeau has given us our answer. We're not going to intervene, he said."

"Is that all he said?"

"Yes. Did I get it right?"

"Yes."

"Did you want me to tell Francis something, when he calls again?"

Wait, he thought, tell them to wait, tell them maybe something will change, maybe something will. . . . But Francis Simard's pale hawk face came into his mind, Francis Simard's eyes, the eyes of Raskolnikov. And Paul Rose. He thought of Paul Rose the other night, staring down the subway tracks in the Metro station. *The* FLQ *will not intervene in Mr. Laporte's favor to stay the execution pronounced against him by the authorities.* "What does that mean?" he had asked Paul. "You know what it means," Paul Rose said.

"Hello?" She sounded worried. "Are you still there?"

"Sorry. I was thinking."

"So what will I tell them?"

"Nothing," he said. "Just say we'll call tomorrow."

16

About four, he supposed it was four, but he had not been given anything to eat all day, had not been hungry but sick and in pain, sleeping fitfully, hearing the radio, if it was a radio – about four in the afternoon he had asked if they would take the blindfold off and let him go to the bathroom. The guard took the tapes off and he saw it was still light. His stomach was empty: he did not really have to go to the bathroom, but the guard let him wash his face and neck, then changed the bloody bandage on his left wrist and the compress on his abdomen. At that time, coming back into the bedroom before the guard put the blindfold back on, he saw two young men in the other room, sitting by the television. One was, he thought, the big one who had come up to him on the lawn . . . how long ago?

"How long have I been here?"

But the guard did not answer. The guard blindfolded him and shackled him onto the bed as before. He thought the guard went out of the room, soon after that. He heard the floorboard creak. Then thought he heard a doorbell ring, but was not sure. He was asleep when they came in. It was just after the six o'clock news. There was no news on the six o'clock news. More than four hundred persons were in jails across the province of Quebec. There had been more than 500 police raids. Additional military reserves had been flown into Montreal and into the city of Sherbrooke. There was, the television announcer said, no further word from the kidnappers. The government would continue its firm line. The War Measures Act would, unless revoked, be in force for six months, until April 1971.

They did not wait for the rest of the news but left the television sound on loud. They came into the bedroom. He woke. He started up on the bed. They did not speak to him; they did not tell him it was the end. Two of them held him as, blindfolded, he struggled. The third caught hold of the thin gold chain which he wore around his neck. There was a small religious medal on the end of the chain. Perhaps they did not mean to kill him as they did: perhaps they meant to smother him. But as he lunged for his life, the chain tightened and, thin as it was, its tempered links held. His face contorted and they saw that the chain would do it. Two held him down. The third stood behind him, young, strong, desperate, twisting and tightening the chain.

At 6:18 p.m., Pierre Laporte, Deputy Premier of Quebec, Minister of Labor and Immigration, died by strangulation. One of them noticed the time. It was exactly a week, to the minute, since they had come down Robitaille Street and taken him from the front lawn of his home. He was forty-nine years old. One of his murderers was twenty-seven, the other two were twenty-three years old. They wrapped his corpse in a brown-and-orange blanket. They carried it through the bungalow, through the hole in the wall which led into the garage.

They bundled it into the trunk of the dark-blue Chevy, license 9J-2420. Paul and Jacques Rose got into the front seat of the Chevy. Francis Simard opened up the garage door. It was already dark. The Chevy drove out. The Chevy's headlights lit the road. Simard got into the white Chevelle which was parked outside. They left, going south on De la Savanne Road, then west. At the corner near the three-storey hangar, the white Chevelle stopped. The blue Chevy drove into the parking lot, facing the row of light planes, under the signs which said AERO CLUB DE MONTREAL and WON-DEL AVIATION LTD.

It was Saturday night: there were not many cars in the lot. The Chevy drove to the far corner and stopped. The Rose brothers got out and walked back across the Won-Del lot in the evening dusk. They got into the white Chevelle driven by Francis Simard. They went towards Boucherville, a village on the South Shore, then doubled back towards Longueuil. At the intersection of Jacques Cartier and Tremblay Roads, in a quiet spot, they threw out the two M-1 rifles they had bought a week ago and also a bag containing wigs, tuques, and false mustaches. They drove on a few streets, then stopped the car and abandoned it. They went on foot to Lemoyne Street where they took a bus across the river to Montreal. At seven o'clock they were in downtown Montreal. Paul Rose went into a phone booth and called radio station CKAC.

"Pierre Laporte has been executed. His body is in the trunk of a car which is in a parking lot near St. Hubert Armed Forces base. The car is a blue Chevrolet, license 9J-2420. It's in the Won-Del Aviation parking lot."

Then they took a second bus and went to the Gaston Apartments on Queen Mary Road. Their friends were there. At CKAC there had been several crackpot calls that day. This was treated as another. No one checked it out.

At 8:30 p.m. they called again. Their message was listened to. No action was taken.

They waited another hour. At 9:30 they called a third time. Michel St. Louis, a young radio reporter who had just come on duty, took this call and thought he recognized the voice of the caller. It was the same voice which had called a week ago to announce the abduction of Laporte. The caller said that if St. Louis would go to the hall of the Port Royal Theatre in the Place Des Arts and look under the fourth book in a bookcase in the theater's entrance, "it is there."

"What's there?" St. Louis asked.

"Something."

"What?"

"I don't have time to speak any longer," the caller said and hung up.

St. Louis did not know what to do. The War Measures Act was in force. The president of the government-controlled Canadian Broadcasting Corporation had just publicly announced that his network would from now on use "restraint" in reporting these kidnapping events and had said: "I think we have to show a different sense of responsibility when it happens here than we do when it happens in Guatemala, Uruguay, or Brazil."

At CKAC no official decision had been taken. Still St. Louis and Pierre Robert, his news director, faced the threat of up to five years in prison for publishing FLQ viewpoints. St. Louis took a chance. He went to the Place Des Arts. The Port Royal Theatre was dark that night but the advertised play was, ironically, Eugène Ionesco's *Jeux de Massacre* (Games of Massacre). The empty theater hallway contained a bookcase with books and magazines. In the fourth book he found the communiqué.

He returned to the radio station. Pierre Robert, Daniel McGinnis, and Norman Malthais, already experts on FLQ communiqués, studied this one. It was handlettered, using the same block script as the second communiqué delivered to the station, the Sunday before, by Laporte's kidnappers. Under-

neath the message was a rough map of the area around the
St. Hubert base, showing the private parking lot. The message
read:

```
Faced with the arrogance of the federal
government and of its servant Bourassa, faced
with their obvious bad faith, the FLQ has decided
to act.
    Pierre Laporte, Minister of Unemployment and
Assimilation, has been executed at 6:18 this
evening by Dieppe Cell (Royal 22nd)*. You will find
the body in the trunk of a blue Chevrolet
9J-2420) at St. Hubert base.
```

We shall conquer.

FLQ

```
P.S. The exploiters of the Quebec people had better
     act properly.
```

St. Louis did not broadcast this message. He and two other
reporters went to St. Hubert. They found the Chevy, as indicated. They looked inside the car, and noticed that the trunk
sagged as though there were something heavy in it. They
called the police, who examined the car, then called for an
army bomb squad. The time was 11:30 p.m.

C.T. let himself in with his latchkey. The others were listening
to another special news announcement from Premier Bourassa.
If the kidnappers would surrender themselves and their two
hostages to the Cuban consul on St. Helen's Island (the site

---

*An ironic reference to a French Canadian regiment, many of whose members died in
the ill-fated Dieppe raid in World War II.

of Montreal's *Man and His World*, a permanent exhibition grounds which, a few years ago, had been built for Expo 67), a waiting Armed Forces helicopter would ferry them to a Canadian transport plane at Montreal International Airport. The hostages would remain in the custody of the Cuban consul until the kidnappers' plane landed safely in Cuba. As a further guarantee to safety, the government had declared pavilion buildings where the Cuban consul waited a temporary extenison of the Cuban consulate with full diplomatic immunity.

They were all in the prisoner's room. Cross was watching too. C.T. signaled Jacques and Marc and Louise and led them into the kitchen.

"It's funny," Jacques Lanctôt said. "Trudeau doesn't want to do a thing, but Bourassa still hopes we'll make a deal."

They were walking into the kitchen as he said it, all of them nervous, all waiting for C.T. to speak. He had gone down to Rue Martial and had called the Queen Mary Road apartment.

"It's t-too late," C.T. said. "Laporte is dead."

At twelve midnight the radio began to tell what was happening at St. Hubert Armed Forces Base. Army and police were carrying out a joint operation. Two bomb squad officers were moving towards the blue Chevy in the parking lot, behind a large protective bomb shield. One officer, using a long steel-tipped, spear-type rod, began hacking away at the locking mechanism of the trunk. After twenty minutes' work, he stopped and pried open one corner of the trunk lid.

Television cameras, floodlights, police, radio units. There was a sudden silence in the Won-Del lot. The officer raised his hand spotlight and flashed it into the trunk. He turned and ran back to the waiting bomb disposal group, some fifty yards in the rear. He whispered, then returned and pried the entire back lid open.

On Des Récollets Street, James Richard Cross heard the announcer's words in French. *"Il y a le corps d'un homme dans la malle!"* (There is the body of a man in the trunk.) He did not, of course, turn around to look at his captors. None of them spoke. Because they already knew? Yes, they already knew. He did not speak to them. They did not speak to him.

His fellow kidnap victim had been murdered. The excitable voice, speaking in a French which he sometimes had difficulty in understanding, said something about the body being shot through the heart, the wrists bleeding, bandaged. A brutal, sadistic mangling, it seemed. And then, in what was the worst night of James Cross's life, on the Canadian Broadcasting Corporation national network, from the Toronto newsroom, three hundred and fifty miles from Quebec, a flustered news reporter announced that Cross's body had been found in the Quebec town of Rawdon. Correction. No, it hadn't. Further correction. Yes, it had.

His death: announced on television as he sat watching, handcuffed, a prisoner. Knowing that his wife, on Redpath Crescent, would be hearing that his body, like poor Laporte's, had been found, a bloody corpse.

For his captors too, it was a terrible night. Yves Langlois summed it up. "They'll never let the political prisoners go now. Never. The whole country will turn against us. There's no question of counter-terror or repression any more. Everybody will say the War Measures Act was the right thing for Trudeau to do. Trudeau has won."

17

Everywhere on the airwaves that Sunday morning they heard it like a knell. Mourning music. No commercials. Just mourning music. Everywhere, everywhere. No news at all. *They* tried to make news. They must show that they were not killers, that Cross was still alive, that, somehow, a channel should be kept open to negotiate.

And so they made Cross write a letter saying he was still alive, saying "early this morning I have seen my death announced on television. This was terrible." And telling how he had written a letter to his wife yesterday, the day of the murder, a letter left in a church, which had never been picked up, although two radio stations had been informed of its whereabouts.

Cross wrote, as always, under dictation, but in the small part about his wife he seemed to speak in his own voice. How terrible it must have been for Barbara Cross to sit and watch television last night, hearing that his body had been found, only minutes after the discovery of poor Laporte, whom, apparently, they had beaten and tortured. But, as the letter went on, the dictation resumed, asking that the Red Cross or the Cuban consulate act as intermediary to exchange him for the jailed FLQ prisoners. The last line of the letter had a strangely doomed note: "Everything can be done without violence. I hope this can be accepted."

"Everything can be done without violence," Jacques Lanctôt dictated. He was sweating and nervous and it was a prayer, a prayer offered up in contrition against the sin those others had committed last night. But the sin was mortal. They knew it. Trudeau knew it. Two days ago, like Pilate, Trudeau had washed his hands, refusing to choose between life and death for the hostages. Last night he had received his reward, absolved by murder as though he had never been in danger of censure. For the kidnappers, there would be no forgiveness. They might try to justify what had been done with talk of fascist police raids and the War Measures Act, and reminders to each other of the hundreds of innocent people now jailed without cause. *Mais, maintenant, il faut le Tougher. Le Tougher* is a French Canadian coinage, another dogsbody word adopted from English. It means to endure, to survive the blows. It describes a condition which French Canadians have been forced to cultivate. From now on, the kidnappers must tough it out alone.

So, that morning, they wrote a communiqué which they enclosed with Cross's note to the authorities. It was never broadcast, never televised, never printed in any newspaper. When CKLM received it, together with the note from Cross, they broadcast only the note. Seconds after the broadcast, the police were on the phone. There was no longer any spluttering indignation. The tone was cold. That broadcast had just broken the law. No copy of Mr. Cross's note was to be given to any other media. The note was not to be broadcast again.

175

As for the communiqué which they had received and had not broadcast, the police would be over to pick it up at once. And remember. Your actions have just contravened the War Measures Act. Is that clear, *monsieur*?

Clear. The FLQ had lost the battle of the airwaves. The airwaves were now the territory of the federal and provincial governments. That afternoon, when it was announced that Premier Bourassa wanted to broadcast from his hotel suite, the CBC rushed a portable videotape unit to the hotel. It was a courtesy, sending the unit. It was treated as a right. Reporters and cameramen were searched before being allowed to enter the suite. Bourassa, pale and silent, his mind filled with thoughts of the death of his Deputy Premier and political rival, did not even look up as the media people entered. He, who normally played the affable politician, read his speech, ignored all civilities, and afterwards had his men show the press out. That same day he would have to face Laporte's widow and Laporte's two children. His speech was brief, filled with anger and grief.

The Premier of Quebec did not return to the capital in Quebec City but remained in his hotel suite in Montreal. Later that afternoon the Prime Minister of Canada also came to Montreal. He was there to confer with Bourassa and Mayor Jean Drapeau about the Laporte funeral. Possibly, in the history of Canada there had never been an event which claimed such world-wide attention as this. If Laporte were buried with the highest ceremonial honors, it would make two points: it would honor the victim and condemn the FLQ.

Pierre Elliott Trudeau had proclaimed the War Measures Act. Having assumed extraordinary emergency powers, he continued to act as though there was an extraordinary danger abroad in the realm. He who normally traveled with as little ceremony as a congressman taking the Washington-to-New York shuttle now flew into Montreal by army helicopter, escorted by eight green Sikorsky troop helicopters which waited to guard him as he conferred with the Mayor and the provincial Premier in City Hall. Everything he did on that day was visible, planned, and symbolic. He led a delegation of federal, state, and civic figures to the nearby Criminal Courthouse where Laporte's body lay in state. Soldiers and police were everywhere visible around him, shielding him from harm. Afterwards he was spirited out of a back door in the courthouse, taken to his helicopter and lifted into the sky. Back in Ottawa that night, he again appeared on national television. Symbolism was used to introduce him to the television audience. Cameras opened on a shot of the Peace Tower, familiar to Canadians as their symbol of Government. The clock sonorously struck eleven. At 11:01, the cameras cut from the clock on the Peace Tower to the Prime Minister, seated at his desk. He spoke for three minutes. Of the murdered minister, he said:

> His record of struggle and accomplishment sounds like a trumpet in comparison to the whines of self-pity and screams of hatred which have poured forth from the FLQ. Yet this was the man the FLQ murdered in cold blood.
>
> We must expect that these vicious men may attempt again to shake our will in the days ahead. I speak for all of you when I say that any such attempt shall fail.
>
> The FLQ has sown the seeds of its own destruction. It has revealed that it has no mandate but terror, no policies but violence and no solutions but murder. Savagery is alien to Canadians; it always will be, for, collectively, we will not tolerate it.

The master of television finished his speech. He had prepared the next act. The nation would move on to a great funeral.

The next day, Monday, C.T. came into Des Récollets with the morning papers. He brought them straight to Marc Carbonneau. One by one he slid them across the kitchen table. One by one Marc picked them up. In almost every morning newspaper, he saw his photograph, full face, next to the bearded photograph of Paul Rose. The headlines in all newspapers were similar.

TWO HUNTED AFTER LAPORTE SLAIN

"They f-found the St. Hubert house," C.T. said.

"How?"

"Don't know. But they f-found Paul Rose's f-fingerprints there. They know it's where Laporte was held."

"But why me?" Marc said. "I haven't been there in months."

"They connected Rose to the Maison du Pêcheur," Jacques Lanctôt said, reading. " 'Rose in hippie haven,' it says here."

"But why *me*?"

"They have police bulletins out," Jacques Lanctôt said. "Your description, Paul Rose's, and mine. It says here that warrants are out for all three of us across Canada and in the States."

"But why me? Why, all of a sudden, me?"

No one could tell him why.

❧❧❧❧❧❧

The afternoon papers carried pictures and stories about the house at 5630 Armstrong Street. A neighbor had called police

178

late Saturday night, saying he had seen "funny things" going on there lately. Other neighbors said they thought the house was a brothel. Some said regular groups used to meet there sometimes at noon, sometimes at two p.m., sometimes at four p.m.

"What were the Roses d-doing? Giving classes?" C.T. asked.

The newspaper also said Laporte had been shot in the head.

"Did he say they shot him, when you t-talked to him?"

"No. He just said Laporte was dead."

❅❅❅❅❅

When the evening editions came in, C.T. read out a story to the others. "Listen to this! Bourassa is *still* offering C-Cuba:

Premier Bourassa said the road leading to the former Canadian Pavilion at the *Man and His World* Exhibition grounds in Montreal will be cleared and left unguarded by police and the army. The bridge across to the pavilion, which is on an island, will also be left unguarded. When the kidnappers arrive at the pavilion they would turn Mr. Cross over to the Cuban consul who is waiting there, every day, until further notice. The Cuban consul would then ask the kidnappers to hand over their arms. In the hour following their arrival at the pavilion, the kidnappers, accompanied by the consul, would be conducted to an airport where they would be placed on a Canadian government Yukon transport plane which is already on standby for this purpose. A limited number of Canadian government officials and officials of the Cuban government would accompany the abductors to Cuba.

179

> On arrival in Cuba, the government there would authorize its consul in Montreal to turn Mr. Cross over to the Canadian authorities. Travel documents have been prepared and would be given to the passengers.
>
> Premier Bourassa said this arrangement is acceptable to federal officials and to Cuba.

"There you have it," Jacques said. "The script for our cop-out. *If* we want it."

"Would that offer include the Roses and Francis Simard?"

"I don't know. If they think Paul Rose murdered Laporte how can they let him leave the country?"

"They think *I* killed Laporte," Marc said. "Me and Paul Rose. That rules me out too."

"They don't know anything about you, they're just guessing," Jacques said.

"Maybe we should contact Chenier Cell to find out what's going on."

"You mean on Queen Mary Road?"

"Yes."

"No," Jacques said. "Let's wait till after the funeral."

❉ ❉ ❉ ❉ ❉ ❉

The widow refused a state funeral. She refused to let her husband's body be laid out in the National Assembly. She asked for a private funeral.

180

Her husband was buried in Notre Dame Church in the heart of Montreal, the Canadian equivalent of St. Patrick's Cathedral or Westminster Abbey. A cardinal, an archbishop, and a bishop officiated at the ceremony. Senators, members of Parliament, Opposition leaders, the Cabinet, foreign diplomats, all were present. The event was covered by television and shown on the evening news throughout the world.

"Why are they doing this?" Louise asked, as she sat with the others on that Tuesday afternoon, watching as the television cameras picked out the rooftops of the Champ de Mars, the old square surrounding the church. On every roof were the red berets and glinting rifle barrels of paratroopers. Helicopters wheeled, monitoring the crowd. An announcer said police dogs had been used to search the church before the ceremony. Bomb squads had gone through the sewers under surrounding streets. Combat troops, machine guns at the ready, covered the exit of official mourners from their limousines. A double phalanx of fifty plainclothes policemen lined the steps leading to the front door of the church. Herds of police motorcycles stood corralled in side streets. Military troop and weapons carriers moved everywhere. "It doesn't make sense," Louise said. "Something must be going on."

"It's like they expect a revolution," Marc said. "Maybe they *do* know something. Maybe our manifesto really started something."

C.T. was watching in the prisoner's room. He said to Cross, "I bet there's never been a f-funeral like this anywhere in North America. What do you think?"

But Cross did not speak. Since Saturday night he had made it clear he no longer felt like talking to them. He drooped his cowled head and stared at the television set.

The service was over. Awkward as wooden soldiers, the undertaker's men moved down the steps with the flag-draped

181

coffin. The flag of Quebec: the fleur-de-lis. A corner of the flag, tugged by the wind, flipped back over the polished wood. A hand drew it back into place. The coffin slid onto the support rails of the big Cadillac hearse and was locked into position. The hearse moved off on Pierre Laporte's last automobile ride, the journey to the grave.

18

"No, Monsieur is not here. Madame? Madame has stepped out. Who is it is calling please?"

"I would like to leave a message. When will she be back?"

"Maybe soon," the old woman's voice said.

"Will you tell her Pierre called. And ask her to ring – ah – " he bent and read off the number of the pay phone booth.

The old voice repeated the number. "Pierre, you said? Pierre who?"

"She'll know," Yves Langlois said.

He left the pay booth and strolled over to the coffee bar across the aisle. He was in a subway exit off Craig Street. He had called Marcel twice yesterday but had no answer. On Wednesday, three days ago, a child had answered and said his father was away. Now, they could not wait much longer: their money was running out.

But if Marcel's wife did not call back in five minutes he decided he would move on. It was too risky, waiting around:

suppose the police had a tap on Marcel's phone? He was jumpy, yes, who wouldn't be? It had been a terrible week.

The phone started ringing. He ran back to the booth.

"Pierre?"

She knew him as Pierre Seguin. Nearly everybody did. He did not want his family mixed up in this. The FLQ was his choice, not theirs.

"Yes, Pauline," he said. "I want to get in touch with Marcel."

"Didn't you know? He's in jail."

"I'm sorry."

"They came on Sunday morning. We were in bed. I haven't been able to get in touch with him. Nobody has. I don't even know where he is."

"That's awful."

"Pierre, did you call about money?"

"It's all right, it doesn't matter now."

"Listen," she said. "There's someone who can help, he's a saint. I know you laugh when I talk about saints, but he *is* a saint. Doctor Montel. Charles Montel. He runs a clinic for poor people on Desarts Street. Go and see him this afternoon. I'll phone him now. I'll tell him you're a friend of Marcel's."

He thanked her and hung up. He had heard of Dr. Montel, one of those physicians like Dr. Mongeau or Dr. Ferron who really devoted their lives to helping the poor and the sick. But how could he tell Dr. Montel what they wanted? And why?

There was a stout woman with a boil on her nose. And an old man whose left hand shook. But mostly it was children, noisy, crying, pulling the torn magazines off the little bamboo table, climbing over the worn green velveteen of the sofa and chairs. Their mothers attended on them: young, most of them, younger than he, with the gray skin of convicts and slum dwellers. The girl opposite him had two children under two and was a child herself. He noticed her bad false teeth.

When the doctor opened the door of his surgery and looked out into the waiting room, Yves was surprised. The doctor was handsome and young: his white coat was frayed but spotless: he looked like a doctor on television.

"Are you Pierre Seguin?"

"Yes."

"Please."

The surgery stank of some antiseptic. The equipment was old. The doctor stood by an examination table with steel stirrups. How many thousands of women had climbed up there? Yves wondered.

The doctor looked at him.

"You heard about Marcel?"

"Yes. I didn't know."

"It's very bad," the doctor said. "The figures they've released admit that about 390 people are still being held. The Justice Department refuses to release the names of those who are in prison. You know and I know that these people aren't FLQ. They may be for an independent Quebec, some of them may be union people and some — " he shrugged. "Some are just people who help the poor. It's not the arrests, it's the distrust. I don't know where it will end, do you?"

"No."

"A terrible business," the doctor said. "Killing Laporte. Those guys must be maniacs. Strangled with the chain of his St. Christopher medal or some such. It's disgusting."

"Yes," Yves said.

The doctor went over to his old writing desk, littered with papers and government health forms. He sat down in a creaky swivel chair and opened his desk drawer. "Let's see," he said. "It should be here, somewhere." But stopped searching and looked at Yves. "I don't know what *your* feelings are," the doctor said. "I know I find it hard to be hopeful. I was going to do what I could to help that new Civic Party in the municipal elections tomorrow. But it's a waste of time, now. The kidnapping and the murder of Laporte has ruined any chance at – what do the English call it? – due process, the ballot. No. That fraud of a mayor will win in a landslide."

"That's true," Yves said. "But he would have won anyway. Maybe it's too late to change things by the old ways."

"But what is the FLQ's program?" the doctor asked. Assassination is not a program. Do they really think that the people of Quebec will rise up and take power?"

"It's happened in other places," Yves said.

"And if we throw the rascals out," the doctor said, and laughed, "what will we offer the people instead? A real plan?"

Yves did not answer. He began to distrust this doctor.

"Ah," the doctor said. "I wish I knew the answer." He reached into the drawer and, pulling aside a stack of forms, produced a brown envelope. "There is two hundred dollars in here, I believe," he said. "That's what Marcel told me. He asked me to keep it for an emergency. Pauline says I should give it to you."

"Thank you."

"Thank *you*," the doctor said. "I'm glad to get rid of it. I never lock this desk."

They went together to the door. Outside in the waiting room, faces veered up, hopeful, waiting their turns. Thin young faces, old shaking heads, the nose with the pus-filled boil, the bored faces of children. The doctor looked at his

186

patients. "Not that I'm against the manifesto," he said. "You know that, don't you? but the other . . . ah!" He shook his head. "Think about it," he said. He raised his hand and signaled. "Next?"

A young woman rose, holding a child. The child's face and arms were covered with red spots. She smiled, tentatively, at the doctor.

He beckoned her in.

On his way back to Des Récollets, Yves bought the afternoon papers. Familiar faces stared from the front page. Francis Simard, Jacques Rose, Bernard Lortie. *"Quebec police issued all-Canada arrest warrants last night for three more* FLQ *suspects in the recent kidnappings."*

His heart thumped in his chest. Jacques Lanctôt, Marc Carbonneau, Paul Rose, Jacques Rose, Francis Simard, Bernard Lortie. Warrants for all of the Chenier Cell and two of us in Liberation Cell. How long will it be until my name and C.T.'s and Louise's are in the papers to complete the list? Maybe the police are already looking for me with my photograph in their hands.

He had two hundred dollars now. He took a taxi back to Des Récollets. He held the newspaper open, so that the taxi driver would not see his face.

※ ※ ※ ※ ※

"Listen to this," Jacques Lanctôt said, staring at the front page of the newspaper Louise had just brought in. "A communiqué three pages long, typed on pink paper, the information phoned to CKAC by a girl. The communiqué found in a trashcan near McTavish Street. And – get this – with the communiqué was Paul Rose's passport and his thumbprint."

"*Calice!*" Marc said.

"And it's a joint communiqué," Jacques read. "That means *we're* supposed to be co-authors."

"What's in it?"

"They don't say."

"Delivered by a girl," Louise said. "I bet that's Francine or Colette."

"He has all those kids working for him up on Queen Mary Road, the goddamn fool!" Jacques said.

"Pink paper." Louise remembered. "Colette wrote me on pink paper last summer. A couple of letters."

Later that evening, one of the French radio stations said the new communiqué was three pages long and dealt with the politics of the recent municipal elections.

"What does he think he's doing?" Jacques said. "The elections are over, Drapeau's won, what the hell does it matter? People want to know about Cross!"

"It's been ten days since we sent out word on Cross," Louise said. "Maybe it's time to –"

"No," Jacques Lanctôt said. He looked at her. "By the way, shouldn't you be in there with C.T.?"

188

She looked at him, her brother, with the resentful glare she once gave the nuns when they ordered her to do homework. He was her brother, yet he was, in a way, her boss now. How long was this going to go on?

But, obedient, she went to her duty in the dark back room.

19

A week later she was again in the back room but this time on the morning shift. Yves was with her. The prisoner, as always, was in the right-hand corner of the room, facing the television set. He seemed to be dozing over the newspaper, but when Yves got up and went to the kitchen for a cup of coffee, suddenly Cross sat up straight.

"Monsieur?" he said, not turning his head. "May I shave, please?"

"No!" she said, and felt a quick surge of delight as she saw his back stiffen. He must have thought it was me who went out. He's been waiting all morning to get Yves alone and ask him. He's afraid I'd say no. His day's ruined! Big booby! Any normal man wouldn't sit sulking all day because he isn't allowed to shave. Any workingman would be glad not to have to shave every day. The boys are far too easy on this damn diplomat! I know him, he's foxy, always trying to get a look at us, turning if you offer him a newspaper or speak to him. You can just see him sitting some day with the *flics,* going over thousands of photographs trying to find Jacques or C.T. I saw him trying to sneak a look at Suzanne that time. Jacques said he wasn't, but he was!

Why am I so mean? Oh, who wouldn't be? It's like being a babysitter, making his meals, taking him to the bathroom, watching to see he doesn't get into mischief. No, not a baby, a baby is someone you want to protect. More like an animal, a stupid animal which might run amok. She had said that once to C.T., about Cross being like a stupid animal.

"If you think that, it's because you've f-forced yourself to think it," C.T. said. "You can't afford to think of him as a man.. If you did, you wouldn't be able to b-bear what we're doing to him."

Of course that was the sort of thing he would say: unlike her brother, her husband had to make everything theoretical. Everything was analyzed to death. He's the only one who still follows the Trudeau doings and all that stuff, the debates in Parliament, all that garbage! Me, if I pick up the paper or switch on the television and it says nothing about the police finding us, I'm not interested. I'd rather do jigsaw puzzles.

And I'm right. Who cares about all this stuff they have in the newspapers saying that the editor of *Le Devoir* and a group of "influential Quebeckers" were plotting to take over the government of the province last week? What sort of takeover would that be, one set of capitalist sell-outs trying to overthrow the other? It's all a game they play, Trudeau and the guys he went to school with, years ago in Quebec, fighting old school fights, just like the rich spoiled kids they are!

And now *we're* fighting with – the Roses. That's the real bad news.

Last night, Wednesday, November 4, Jacques, C.T., and Marc had gone out at eleven p.m. It was the first time Jacques and Marc had been out of the apartment since police warrants had been issued for their arrest. But this was the big thing: a meeting betwen the cells. She and Yves had stayed behind to guard Cross.

She did not even know where the meeting had taken place; all she knew was that when they came back this morning it was nearly dawn and she was ready to weep with relief when they walked in the door. But they were in a terrible rage, all of them, raging because Paul Rose had been writing communiqués in their name, writing for both cells without ever consulting them. It didn't matter so much about the latest communiqués, they said, for the authorities had simply ignored them. What the real fight was, was the way the Roses kept holding out for *all* the ransom demands. They told Jacques they wanted Cross killed unless the authorities gave in. Jacques had told them to go screw. We're not going to kill Cross, Jacques told them. We're against the death penalty for anyone! Anyone!

Jacques and C.T. and Marc had gone to bed after breakfast, while she and Yves volunteered to do this extra duty. She had been guarding Cross for – how long? Nearly twelve hours straight.

Two days ago Marc and Jacques had begun to worry that Cross was being forgotten. So they got a Polaroid flash camera and made Cross sit on a barrel and photographed him playing a game of solitaire right here in this room. That was on Monday. Before they went to the meeting last night, they sent the picures out to *Québec-Presse,* which was the most left-wing paper they knew. They wanted to show Cross was alive just in case those damn Roses started death threats in some crazy communiqué.

But *Québec-Presse* hadn't printed the photo yet. "They aren't allowed to," C.T. said.

She looked at the prisoner. Sitting there, a danger to them. Like a live bomb. No wonder she was having migraine headaches now, day after day. If it were not for this damn diplomat, they could walk out and forget the whole thing. We are all *his* prisoners, she decided. The best we can hope for now is exile to Cuba, if we hand him over. The worst is prison for life, if we are caught.

Yves came in with two cups of coffee. She saw Cross's head jerk up, as he heard Yves enter. "Monsieur, may I shave, please?" the prisoner said, quickly.

"No, you cannot shave!" she cried out.

"Easy," Yves said. "No need to scream."

"It's my nerves."

Saturday afternoon she went out, her first time out of the apartment in four days. November; her breath was like cigarette smoke in the cold air. She took a bus and went downtown, planning to buy some groceries. Suzanne was coming back tonight and Jacques wanted her to buy a chocolate cake for their celebratory supper. Pregnancy made Suzanne want sweet food.

Keep calm, Jacques told Louise, keep calm. We just go on as if nothing happened. Get yourself some pills if your nerves are bad. And don't, please don't, make Suzanne nervous. We'll all be cheerful and have a nice supper when she comes, okay?

Cheerful. Only yesterday she had been complaining that

nobody paid attention any more, that they were all buried alive with Cross. Today she was afraid to look at another newspaper or listen to another newscast. Bern Lortie's childish features stared out at her from every front page. And this morning at the coroner's inquest, what had they done to him to make him talk so much?

The night before, Friday, November 6, plainclothes police drove up to the old-fashioned apartment building at 3720 Queen Mary Road, opposite the Canadian Wax Museum. The time was six o'clock. The phone number of this apartment had been penciled on the cover of a telephone book found in the Armstrong Street hideout. The police obtained the address from the phone company and went directly to Queen Mary Road. They went upstairs without ringing the hall doorbell. They rang the bell of Apartment 12. A girl called out to them that she was getting dressed. After a short delay, the girl opened the door. She was frail and nervous, nineteen years old and a student teacher. Her name was Colette Therrien. When she admitted the police, she seemed to be alone in the apartment. After a few minutes' search, the police found a pale, childish-looking youth hiding behind a coat in the hall closet. He was nineteen years old. He was Bernard Lortie, a student, one of the four men wanted for the kidnapping and murder of Pierre Laporte. In another room, asleep, they found Lortie's girl friend, Francine Belisle, a pretty, blonde student nurse, who was twenty-two years of age. She had been asleep, she told the police, because she worked nights at St. Justine Hospital.

The police found evidence that more than three people were living in the apartment. They arrested others that same night. They were Colette Therrien's brother, Richard, nineteen years years old and a student at the University of Montreal. And an eighteen-year-old, François Belisle, the student nurse's brother, who used the apartment weekdays and went home to his parents' house in Victoriaville, outside Montreal, on weekends. The police did not find the three other men wanted for the kidnap and murder of Pierre Laporte: Francis Simard, Paul Rose, and Jacques Rose. Later, Colette Therrien said she was in love with Jacques Rose. She said she would do anything for him.

This morning all those kids are in jail, Louise thought. We are free and the Roses are free, but those kids who helped the Roses are in jail.

And Bern Lortie this morning, saying he wanted to tell all in court, talking and talking at the coroner's inquest, telling how he and the Roses decided to kidnap Laporte and how they did it and how they brought him to the bungalow at Armstrong Street. He said he left before Laporte was killed. And told how, the day before Laporte was killed, Laporte tried to throw himself out of the window. And got cut. Which makes those newspapers liars. They said the cuts were because the men who killed him were sadists.

When she got off the bus at a big Steinberg's supermarket, she noticed a Montreal *Gazette* vending machine on the street corner. Staring at her was a front-page picture of James Richard Cross. He wore a dark sweater and open-neck shirt and sat, with playing cards in his hand, in front of a table on which were laid out more playing cards and a book. She knew what the book was, although she could not see the title in the photograph. She had placed it on the table herself when they took the flash picture of Cross. It was Pierre Vallières' *Nègres blancs d'Amérique*.

Relief that the picture had been published at last mingled with an almost primitive fear at the sight of Cross's image, released, as it were, from his dark prison, staring at her, ready to tell the police who they were and what had happened to him.

It was the Americans who had first broken the censorship. When *Québec-Press* didn't publish the picture they sent, Marc Carbonneau had the idea of sending other copies to the Associated Press in New York. Americans weren't bound by Trudeau's censorship. When the A.P. sent the photograph out on the wire, the *Gazette* took a chance and ran it. Anyway, there he was, their prisoner. Diplomat Cross.

A kidnapper with a shopping list, she went past her victim's picture, went into the supermarket, and took a shopping cart. Milk, coffee, Italian sweet sausage, bread, tomatoes, carrots, spring onions, lime drink for Jacques, and chocolate cake for Suzanne. To drift, mindless in the aisles, picking out tomatoes and putting them in a brown paper bag.

"Louise, how are you?"

If Madame Lesage had fired off a pistol behind Louise's head she could not have produced a greater reaction.

"I'm sorry. Did I make you jump?"

196

The old woman's eyes, hyperthyroid, bulging like birds' eggs. Her dyed red hair. An old gossip, whose daughter, Marie-Ange, had been at school with Louise.

"And how is your husband? Always studying?"

"Yes. How are you, Madame Lesage?"

"How is anybody these days? Soldiers everywhere with guns, people afraid to go out, the jails full. I tell you that *maudit* FLQ, I'd put them up to a wall and rat-tat-tat-tat! Oh! Excuse me! I'm sorry, I forgot. I saw in the newspaper the police are looking for your brother! Oh, he's not FLQ, is he? Poor you!"

"No," Louise said. She started at her hands which gripped the shopping cart. The awful pain, the void in her eyes, the migraine was starting. "I don't know where Jacques is or what he's doing. I've been sick."

"Ah, poor thing." Madame Lesage looked around the supermarket as though hoping for someone she could tell this to. "Imagine, when I saw his picture in the paper – it's a disgrace, saying things like that about people with no proof – you don't think he had anything to do with the death of Mr. Laporte, do you?"

"Of course not. Well, it was nice to see you, madame. Give my best to Marie-Ange."

"Yes, wait'll I tell her I met you. Where are you living, by the way?"

"In Saint Sauveur."

"And you come all the way to Montreal to shop?"

"Sometimes. Goodbye, madame."

"So, why don't we finish up here and have a coffee together? It's so long since I saw you, my dear."

"I'm sorry, but I'm in a hurry, I have to meet someone. Goodbye again."

"In a hurry?" Madame Lesage stared, like a gambler who sees the chips swept away.

"Yes." Louise fled.

Three police forces were hunting for the kidnappers of James Cross and the murderers of Pierre Laporte. The Royal Canadian Mounted Police considered itself superior to the Provincial *Sûreté du Québec*. The *Sûreté du Québec* considered itself superior to the local Montreal Police Department. All three police forces were under attack. They had unlimited powers of arrest and detention, thanks to the War Measures Act. They had, between them, arrested more than 500 suspects. They had, under their control, one of the largest manhunt forces ever assembled anywhere. Until they arrested Bernard Lortie, they had, separately and jointly, been spectacularly unsuccessful.

The Montreal Police Department found Lortie. On the evening of Friday, November 6, a month and a day after James Cross was kidnapped, a group of plainclothesmen approached the Gaston Apartments on Queen Mary Road to check on the address linked to a telephone number found in the Armstrong Street hideout. They were backed by uniformed officers, who kept out of sight in nearby streets and on the roofs of adjoining buildings. When the plainclothesmen found Lortie and the two girls in Apartment 12 and took them downtown to Montreal Police headquarters, uniformed officers made a search of other apartments in the building and a police squad ransacked and fingerprinted the suspect's premises.

Jubilation was the mood at Montreal Police headquarters that night. Lortie had confessed. Officers were ordered to say nothing to the press, as Lortie's identity would be revealed only on the following day when he would appear as a star and surprise witness at the coroner inquest. A police detail spent the night in the raided apartment, as was routine in such cases.

On the following day, Saturday, when Lortie began to tell his dramatic tale of the kidnapping of Laporte, phones started ringing on the desks of police reporters around town. The Montreal Police Department wanted it made clear that they, and not the famous Mounties or the provincial Sûreté, had finally broken this case.

On Saturday night the two uniformed officers on guard in Apartment 12 on Queen Mary Road went out at 6:30 p.m. for a celebratory supper at a nearby restaurant. By now, the apartment had been thoroughly searched and fingerprinted and photographed.

A few minutes after the officers left, a small panel slid open in the wall of the hall closet. Three men emerged from a secret hiding place. They were Paul Rose, Francis Simard, and Jacques Rose. They had all been inside the apartment at the time of the original raid and had slipped into this hiding place which they had built for such an emergency. Lortie did not have time to follow them in, which is why he was discovered in the hall closet, hiding behind an overcoat. There was a false wall in this hall closet. The Roses and Simard, aided by

Richard Therrien and François Belisle, the two young boys who normally lived in the apartment, had spent three days constructing this hiding place. Belisle went out with Colette Therrien, Jacques Rose's girl, to buy lumber. Jacques Rose, a skilled carpenter, had made the false wall, behind which they placed benches and bunks. They wallpapered the wall so that it looked like the other walls of the closet. As the entire wall was false, when the police rapped on it it gave off a uniform sound. The three kidnappers of Laporte had gone to ground here. They had hidden supplies of food, water, and blankets and so remained behind the wall for twenty-four hours while police searched and occupied and slept in the apartment. The hiding place had been constructed in imitation of the FLN hiding place of Ali la Pointe, the protagonist of the film *The Battle of Algiers*, and now, like the Arab heroes of that film, the three fugitives slipped out, exultant, and roamed about the empty apartment. Deliberately, they smeared their fingerprints over furniture and walls. Deliberately, they left the concealed panel open so that the police would know they had been there.

Then they left.

When the police returned from their celebratory supper, the opened panel faced them like a wound.

The Montreal Police Department had been unwilling to share credit for this capture with the other police forces. It was particularly hostile to the Mounties, whose headquarters is in Ottawa and which is, predominantly, an English Canadian force. So, astonishingly, the Montreal Police did *not* tell the Mounties anything about the secret hiding place and the escape of the three men wanted for the murder of Pierre Laporte. The Mounties, meantime, were searching for the Rose brothers and Simard as far away as British Columbia. And it was not until the following weekend that the Montreal Police Department was forced by an FLQ communiqué to admit to the public and to Parliament that it had, indeed, let the kidnappers of Pierre Laporte slip through its net.

Perhaps it was this police mistake which, at last, rescued the FLQ from the publicity limbo to which Prime Minister Trudeau had condemned them. Until then, press and television networks had reluctantly heeded the Quebec Justice Minister's warning that any publicizing of FLQ communiqués could contravene the War Measures Act. The radio stations, which had for a brief period been the front runners of the news, were particularly restive under the edict. This was Canada, a country which, like the United States, had never known peacetime censorship. No gentlemen's agreement of self-policing and consultation between press and government exists in the manner in which it has been employed in crises in Great Britain. And so, on Sunday, November 14, when a communiqué, handlettered in the style employed by Paul Rose, was sent to the Sunday tabloids *Journal de Montreal* and *Québec-Presse*, it was seen to contain hard news which would embarrass the police. *Québec-Presse* printed it, and, on the following day, other newspapers and radio stations also made it public. Gloatingly, the communiqué described how the Rose brothers and Francis Simard hid in the secret closet for twenty-four hours and escaped while the police went off to supper. It further said that Bernard Lortie had not acted as a traitor by giving evidence at the coroner's inquest. He had not betrayed the presence of his fellow kidnappers. The communiqué asked, therefore, that his name be added to the list of twenty-three "political prisoners" whom the FLQ wished to have flown to Cuba.

In the next few days, the huge police manhunts stalled and floundered. Most of the people who had been arrested and held in jail in Montreal and in Quebec City under the provisions of the War Measures Act were released for lack of charges against them. Fewer than sixty persons were said to be detained in jail at this time. Squabbles broke out between Government and Opposition parties as to whether there ever had been any real "apprehended insurrection" in Quebec. But in Ottawa, Montreal, and Quebec City, combat troops continued to guard homes, consulates, and public buildings. The War Measures Act was slightly amended to provide for a shorter period of detention during which a suspect could be held without charges being preferred. The state of emergency continued. For several days helicopters and Armed Forces units were used in a large search of a region in the Laurentian Mountains where the murderers of Laporte were said to be hiding.

The coroner's inquest continued. Pierre Vallières, the author of *Nègres blancs d'Amérique*; Michel Chartrand, the labor leader; and Robert Lemieux, the FLQ's lawyer, were among twenty-six persons charged with being members of the FLQ or professing to be members. They were ordered to stand trial. Bail was refused. Days passed. There was no news of James Cross.

21

James Richard (Jasper) Cross.

One week he lost a whole day. He thought it was Thursday when, in fact, they had already arrived at Friday.

He kept track of days by the newspapers. They had taken him on October 5. This was Thursday November 26. Fifty-two days, he reckoned.

One day, of course, was very much like another. And difficult to remember. They lived in what he called two solitudes. He in his little chair and they in the rest of the house. Occasionally, they would talk about something. They would, of course, discuss the communiqué, if they wanted to send a communiqué. There was not much of that, lately. In all this time – weeks it was – they had sent out just one communiqué. With some photographs.

Sometimes they would discuss with him something that happened on television, or something on the news. But these were not long conversations. There had not been many long conversations since the death of Pierre Laporte.

His wife and daughter were in Switzerland. They had left on Friday, November 6; twenty days ago, by his reckoning. They were staying with the Midgeleys, old friends who were helping his wife get through this dreadful time. Eric Midgeley was British Ambassador at Berne.

Escape? Of course one thought about it. When one was in this situation there was not much else to do. But the odds were against him, he knew. The consequences of escape were either that he would be shot dead in escaping, or that he would be confined in such conditions as to make life impossible.

They had all the means here to make life impossible. They had bolts screwed to the floor to which they could chain him. They had ropes. They had tape for his mouth. He could not go on living like that.

Besides, he knew only this room and the bedroom. He had no idea of how many people were in the rest of the house. He had no idea whether to turn right or left when he went outside of this room.

And so, every day he thought of escape. And every day he decided to hang on for another twenty-four hours. Better to stay alive.

Thoughts of death? Yes, he had them but one has to live with whatever situation one finds oneself in. One settles down to a daily routine. But almost every day one has a few moments in which one thinks, you know: Well, what's going to happen to me? Am I going to be here this week, next week? You've watched a television program and they say next week we'll be showing something or other and you wonder whether you are going to be there to see it.

Before she went to Switzerland, his wife broadcast on the local radio, hoping he would be able to hear her. He did hear her. She said she hoped the FLQ would allow him to write to her again.

He had written to her since then. Three letters in all. But

he did not know if they had posted them. Perhaps they just let him write them to keep him quiet.

Even when he wrote a personal letter to his wife, these people frequently changed the wording. They were afraid of codes. All the other letters he wrote, the official ones, were of course dictated to him by these people. He should have thought that was obvious to anyone who read them. But, unfortunately, it was not. He really got mad when he read in the newspapers that people thought those were his own thoughts in those dictated letters. He had trusted that people had *some* intelligence, outside there, in the world. But, my God, he was even less in communication than he thought!

There were two misspellings in the official letter he wrote the other week at the FLQ's dictation. He missed "questioned" – he put two *n*'s in it. The use of the double *n* is a bit difficult. Work it out some time, particularly when you've been forty days a prisoner. Another mistake was "prisonners" for "prisoners." He noticed it when he wrote it. "Prisonners" was obviously copied from the French. He left it wrong, merely to convince people reading it that he wasn't – you know – writing this of his own accord.

What he did not bargain for was the whole press proceeding in print to tell his captors what he was trying to do!

He'd had three or four very rough days after that. Not physically rough – they were never brutal with him –but rough in that, now, for the first time he felt his kidnappers had a sense of personal hostility towards him. They thought he'd been trying to trick them.

There were other bad moments, of course. Moments when one would suddenly begin to think about the whole situation and particularly about one's wife. Because, at least, he knew what was happening to him. She didn't. At times like that, one would sink into a period of complete despair.

Despair. Yet, curiously, it had nothing to do with what was

happening, or not happening, day to day, outside. The things that, funnily enough, increased one's despair were the little incidents. When they didn't allow you to shave one morning and you sat all day with rather a beard on. This, in some ways, made one feel much more miserable – it was much more real – than any news and negotiations and anything like that on the outside.

One day, of course, was very like another. He watched television. He had seen more than a hundred French films on television. He supposed it would improve his French.

Forty-eight days after his abduction, a letter, handwritten by James Richard Cross, appeared in the newspapers. It was published in the Sunday tabloids. That was the one they dictated to him, the one with the misspellings that got him in trouble. The letter said:

15 November

To whom it may concern.

I want to assure those who are interested (if there are still some) that I am in good health and being well treated. I have heard about the treatment of the FLQ political prisoners in jail and I am quite sure that I am better treated than them. I have all the information possible. Radio – TV – newspapers. I have "hot" dinners every day. I also have my pills. I can wash and have clean clothes and I have not been "questionned." But time drags very heavily after 6 weeks of imprisonment.

They consider me as a political prisonner and they will keep me in captivity as long as the authorities do not accept their demands.

I have heard my wife on the radio a few weeks ago. I know it must be very hard and painful for her. But it must be the same for the families of the FLQ political prisonners.

What more can I say? What can I expect? When and how will this bad dream end?

To whom and on what depend my liberty and my life I don't know. But I am still hoping.

J. R. Cross

P.S. I join to this public letter a private letter to my wife.

206

It was the week after this letter was published that his captors seemed to turn against him. Yes, there were four or five bad days. They were also furious with the police because their communiqué had not been released. But at the weekend it seemed easier. Things went back to that strange quiet, he in his chair, they always behind him. Two solitudes again. It was as though the world had forgotten him.

He was a Mountie. Those big boy scouts in scarlet tunics charging around Madison Square Garden on their Musical Ride were something else. Horse to him was heroin, and in the drug world when they said "horseman coming" it was time to get a transfer to another division. It had happened to him after four years and two big cases. Now they'd moved him back to Montreal where he was born, to C Division, as a constable, first class. He was French Canadian, married, and twenty-seven years old. He was five feet nine inches tall, but looked shorter. He was proud of the fact that he could kill a man with his hands. For this job he dressed semi-hippie with his hair long, but, if you asked him, hippies stank, they were "pseudo-intellectuals," which meant some type of Communist.

Combined Anti-Terrorist Squad, they called this outfit, which was a laugh when you think those Montreal cops didn't even inform the RCMP when they raided that apartment in Queen Mary Road and let the suspects get away. If you asked him, it was suicide to mix undercover squads: the difference between the RCMP and these local cops was Cadillacs and Fords. Still, cooperation was the good word now. He was a constable. The commissioner made the rules.

He and his partner had been on this case since the week Cross disappeared. The inspector put them onto the Lanctôt connection once they found out that Lanctôt was one of the names in that attempt to kidnap the Israeli consul. They went at it like family historians – interviews, interviews, finding out who was related to who and who knew who on the chessboard. They knew from the start that Lanctôt had a young wife, Suzanne, and she was seven or eight months in the family way and that she wasn't around any more. And that she had a kid, Boris, eighteen months old, who also wasn't around.

Then they scored: a casual remark by a certain person led to a woman who was babysitting with a kid full-time and who knew the Lanctôts. He and his partner kept away but set up a stakeout. On the second day she came out with the kid and she called the kid Boris. Three days later she dressed the kid up and took it to the park, to a place she hadn't been before. A pretty and pregnant girl showed up, played with the kid, kissed it and hugged it. When the girl left she said goodbye to the babysitter and the kid. His partner went after the baby-sitter. He followed the girl.

She went to an East End apartment where some hippie chicks lived. Stayed three days, and then, on the third afternoon, went back to the park. The babysitter showed up with the kid and he and his partner had a chance to say hello again. When they left the park, they split as before. He went after the girl.

This time she took the subway up to Montreal North, then went way out, by bus. He followed her to an apartment building on Des Récollets Street. There were three apartments in the building. He didn't see which one she went into.   ·

It was a quiet street, dangerous for his kind of work, a place where the neighbors noticed strangers. He called the sergeant at twenty-two hundred hours and a relief came for the night. The girl stayed inside all night. Next morning Division assigned four extra men and told them to stay with it. Trained men, his kind of squad, guys who could watch and not be seen, who could ask questions without asking them, if you know what I mean.

He was in charge. After a couple of days he went to Division to report. Told Division there was an older couple with a couple of young children living in one of the top-floor apartments. The guy was a school crossing guard. They saw him go out every morning with a STOP sign under his arm. The other top-floor tenants seemed straight, too. The man had a federal job. The tenants in the big downstairs apartment were something else. They had moved in two months ago; a neighbor said there were three young men and a girl, semi-hippie types. No, the girl wasn't pregnant. The landlord said they paid their rent on time, were very quiet. A man and wife, he said. He thought he had seen a pregnant girl there once just after they moved in, when he went up one night to fix a basement light.

The suspects had a car. Kids who lived on a street always knew about things like that. They had an old beat-up Chrysler, some kind of grayish color, used to be parked outside all the time. The little kids hadn't seen it in the past couple of weeks. Which made sense. If they had Cross in there, the car would be kept in the garage, in case they had to get him out in a hurry.

There were other things to report. The tenants of 10945 did not work at regular jobs. They went out at odd times – late evening, early morning, usually to get food and always to buy newspapers. A big kid, straight-looking, wearing thick-lensed spectacles, went out several times to make phone calls.

210

Another couple bought food and newspapers, a young couple who looked as if they might be making it with each other.

On November 26, the sergeant sent for him. Told him that St. Pierre, the Quebec Provincial Police boss, had just had a meeting with the RCMP assistant commissioner in charge of C Division. There were so many people to tail on this lead, the RCMP had been authorized to bring in twelve more surveillance men from Ottawa. "So there you are," the sergeant said. "They feel this one is important."

The sergeant sent him up to see the inspector. The inspector said they'd need a room opposite the building. "We're in luck," the inspector said. It seemed that living right opposite was a guy who was an instructor at St. Vincent de Paul Penitentiary. He had been asked for cooperation. It was given.

That evening he and his team moved into an upstairs bedroom in the penitentiary employee's house, across the street from the suspects. They had walkie-talkies, movie and still cameras, and a perfect view of the suspect apartment. Anybody who went in or out now, all he had to do was get on the phone and a man from the new Ottawa detail would follow them. That afternoon two of them went out and only one came back. Lanctôt's wife left at 16:10 carrying a small suitcase. She went to the East End apartment building where she stayed when he first tailed her himself. She stayed all night.

The other one who went out that afternoon took off at 16:38. He was the young guy who usually went shopping with the other chick. When he went out he was tailed by a man from the Ottawa squad.

"Why can't I go with you?" she asked.

C.T. did not answer.

"Well, why can't I?"

"Because it's risky."

"So," she said, "it's more risky to go downtown with you than to sit here like a rat in a trap with Cross? I don't understand your logic."

"Goodbye," he said. "Take care of yourself. T-try to have a nap this evening."

She did not answer. He went into the kitchen. Jacques and Marc had the tape all wrapped up and ready to go. The four of them had spent this afternoon making the tape. They had sat around the tape recorder, talking, taking turns, careful not to say anything which would give away where they were, or who they were, or implicate others. They had run it back twice, listening to their own voices declaiming against the system, explaining why they kidnapped Cross, saying that Washington gave all the orders to Trudeau and had forbidden him to deal with them. Listening to it, C.T. decided it was puerile: it was what happened when you got workingmen like Lanctôt and Marc in front of a mike. It sounded like a street corner political stump speech.

But try telling that to Lanctôt and Marc. They wanted him to try to give this tape to Alain, who would run off another copy. One was to be taken tonight to *Québec-Presse*, one to the weekly magazine *Choc*. They hoped that, with a prize like this – the true voices of the Cross kidnappers – the tabloids and radio stations wouldn't be able to resist. "Unless we get our message to the public again, we could sit here with Cross forever," Marc said. But C.T. wondered if this cheap imitation of a television talk show was going to do it. He thought not.

Jacques Lanctôt handed him the package. "Remember," he said. "Tell Alain we'll phone tomorrow to see if he was able to deliver an extra tape."

"Right."

When he went into the hall, she was waiting. "Why can't you let me come with you?"

"Because I'm going to a t-tavern. No women allowed."

❀ ❀ ❀ ❀ ❀

This new tip was from the Montreal Police Department, so the RCMP sergeant was skeptical. The Montreal police were so hungry for glory, he couldn't see them giving a real lead to another force. Still, co-operation was the word. As they said, the commissioner made the rules, not him. For three days they had been following it up. It was supposed to have connections with Lanctôt's sister and her husband, a guy called Cosette-Trudel. One suspect led to another. It could go on forever. In a case like this where you weren't dealing with ordinary criminals, who knew when to quit?

But tonight, just when he was thinking about turning in a negative report, suddenly something clicked. One of his surveillance men phoned at twenty-one-thirty. "I have a problem," he said. "I'm in the Boucheron Tavern with my suspect and he's met someone. I heard them talk about getting a message to *Québec-Presse*. Do you want to put a tail on the new contact?"

"What does he look like?" the sergeant asked.

The constable gave a description.

"A black windbreaker?" the sergeant said. "And he has

suede boots? Hold on a minute."

He checked his notes. He felt like he had won a very big hand at poker. "Okay," he said, "hang loose. Call me in ten minutes."

The surveillance man from Des Récollets Street had phoned ten minutes earlier. *His* suspect was in the Boucheron Tavern. The suspect was wearing a black windbreaker and suede boots. The sergeant turned to another file, smiling, despite himself. By Jesus, he thought, now I think I know who this guy is!

The inspector was locking his briefcase when the sergeant came in. "What is it?"

"Something's come up, sir."

"My wife is waiting for me," the inspector said. "I hope this is important."

"I hope so too, sir. Do you remember the Montreal police asked us to put a tail on a connection that might lead to Lanctôt's sister? She's married to a kid called Cosette-Trudel, Maison du Pêcheur type, demonstrations, the whole bit. Very possibly FLQ."

"Louise Lanctôt," the inspector said. "I remember."

"Well, right this minute, the suspect is in the Boucheron Tavern. And this is the interesting part. The man he's meeting there is one of the people from Des Récollets Street."

The inspector put down the briefcase. "Which one?"

"The one who seems to be married. I just thought. What if *he's* Cosette-Trudel?"

"We took some photographs," the inspector said. "Let's get them in. And get that picture of Trudel and Lanctôt's sister."

A few minutes later, the photographs were spread on the desk. "I'd say that's them, all right," the inspector said. "Cosette-Trudel and Lanctôt's sister. Cosette-Trudel's name was found on a piece of paper in the Armstrong Street bungalow where Laporte was murdered. Now, if *he's* in that place on Des Récollets, and Jacques Lanctôt's sister is with him, and if Lanctôt's own wife was there until tonight, I'd say we could assume that Lanctôt himself is there."

"I'd say we've found Cross, sir."

"An assumption," the inspector said, "is not a fact. But it looks damn interesting. What are you laughing at?"

"The Montreal Police Department," the sergeant said. "*They* gave us this lead."

❊ ❊ ❊ ❊ ❊ ❊

When C.T. returned to Des Récollets that evening he reported that Alain had not only made an extra tape, but that both were to be delivered to the tabloids.

"Now, we'll have to wait till Sunday," he said. "Alain said the daily newspapers are scared to print anything."

215

"What about radio, does Alain think they might broadcast it?" Jacques Lanctôt asked.

"Not a chance."

"I don't see why not."

"They'd lose their licenses," C.T. said. "They're c-capitalistic enterprises, Jacques. Don't f-forget the only reason they give us publicity is to sell advertising."

"I know that as well as you do. I'm not stupid!"

"Take it easy, *les gars*," Marc Carbonneau said. "Let's not have any fights. Nobody ever said this was going to be easy. Did you have any trouble downtown?"

"No."

"I'm worried about Alain. He's somebody the cops might follow."

"The *flics* are looking for the Roses," C.T. said. "I think they've f-forgotten about us. Now, come on, let's g-get some sleep."

❊❊❊❊❊❊

Next morning the telephone rang in the observation post. It was the sergeant.

"Send a man down to the checkpoint," he said. "We've got something for you. We found the foreman who worked on that building you're watching. He gave us the name of the architect. Now we've got a floor plan."

"Great," he said. He told his partner the news. "Only a week

216

since we came up here," he said. "And look how it's going. Nice, huh?"

"If there's any credit, Roger," his partner said, "you and me are in line for it."

"With our tongues hanging out."

❊❊❊❊❊

Sunday, November 29. Marc had asked for bacon so she was frying him bacon. The others had already eaten and now C.T. was with the prisoner, Yves had gone downtown to buy the papers, and Jacques was in the living room, hoping to hear something on the radio. Today was the day when *Québec-Presse* and *Choc* should publish the tape interview they'd sent them. Jacques said that it might, it just might be on CKLM or CKAC. Which wasn't realistic: they all knew it. But what else was there to hope for? The silence that had surrounded them for the past ten days was more threatening than the excitement, the raids, the threats and arrests in the week Laporte was taken. Who knew where the Roses were or what they were planning? Who knew anything any more?

"Do you think *Québec-Presse* and *Choc* will publish our tape?" she asked, looking down at the back of Marc's head. He sat, slumped at the table, reading last night's *La Presse*.

"Is that a church bell?"

She listened. Yes, far away.

"Remember, when we were kids, that was all you heard on

Sunday morning?" he said. "I don't seem to hear them any more."

"Why don't you answer my question? The tape. Will they publish it, today?"

"We'll see. Is the bacon ready?"

She put the bacon strips on newspaper the way her mother taught her. It drained off the grease. She served the bacon with some toast and tea. Marc liked tea better than coffee. He had a bad stomach. He worried about his food.

"Okay," she said. "Let me ask you something else. What do we do if they don't publish our tape, what do we do if they keep this up, if we're never heard from any more, if the government doesn't give in and let the prisoners go; I mean, if they just go on like this, week after week? I mean, what do we *do*?"

He picked the strip of bacon up with his fingers. His way of eating often made her look away. He had grown a scrawny beard in these last three weeks and his hair was long, what was left of it. Once she had thought he was the strong one: he was the oldest, he was a real workingman, a Communist, who had seen a lot. Now, he seemed more nervous than anyone, except her brother. Nowadays C.T. was the strong one. "Did you hear me?" she asked.

"If we don't get some action by Tuesday, I think you and C.T. should go up to the Laurentians."

"The Laurentians? What are you talking about?"

"I'm talking about the Laurentians," he said. He slurped his tea. "Alain's up there at the cottage. Maybe he'll have some money for us."

"How do you know he's there? How do you know he hasn't been arrested? The police and soldiers were all over that area."

"It says right here in *La Presse* that they've pulled out. You and C.T. could go up Tuesday, spend the night, and come back Wednesday. You'd like that, wouldn't you?"

"No. And, anyway, that's not what I was asking."

"Yves said he heard you crying in the middle of the night. Maybe if you got away from here for a day or so, it would help. Say yes. Besides, somebody has to find Alain. We're nearly out of money."

She began to cry.

"You see," he said. "It's only normal, you're only a girl, it's harder on you. Why shouldn't you get away for a day or two?"

"Oh, shut up," she said. "Just shut up!"

❋ ❋ ❋ ❋ ❋

"Well?" Jacques Lanctôt said, as Yves came in. He was sitting waiting, in the living room, his left foot jiggling in an autonomous way, as though he had some sort of involuntary muscular tic.

"No. Nothing."

"Nothing at all?"

"Here you are. *Québec-Presse. Choc.* All the other Sundays. And *The New York Times* and *Toronto Star.* Nothing."

"Marc?" Jacques called. "Come in here, will you?"

Marc came in. "Nothing in the papers?" he said.

"Correct."

"That means there won't be anything on television or radio."

"Okay, what are we going to do?" Jacques Lanctôt said.

219

His foot jiggled. His eyes were hidden by his hexagonal sunglasses. His voice was louder than normal. "Trudeau's cut off any chance we had of reaching the people of Quebec, he's radicalized the situation by bringing in these war measures, these troops, it's fascism, it's silencing all opposition, and I tell you he's doing it because he's afraid! He's afraid because we've already had a victory. Getting our manifesto on television, *that* was our victory, reaching into the homes of the ordinary people, that's why he's arrested these intellectuals, and union leaders. Robert Lemieux, people like that!"

He stopped, out of breath. Marc looked at Yves.

"Yes, Jacques, yes," Yves said. "You're right. But as you said: the point is what are we going to *do*? Do we cut our losses, give them Cross and go to Cuba – us, Suzanne and your kid, C.T. and Louise?"

"What about the political prisoners?" Jacques Lanctôt asked.

"They're not going to give in on the prisoners."

"Yves is right," Marc said. "They won't give in now."

"Well, then, suppose we ask that they let the Roses come too? And Simard."

"Oh, for Christ sake!" Yves said. "Face facts."

"What do you mean?"

"The Roses are now a murder case. Nobody's going to negotiate with them any more." He stared at Jacques Lanctôt as he said it.

"What's your reasoning?"

"Paul Rose has told the *flics* he killed Laporte. Those stupid communiqués. And he even enclosed his passport. They left their fingerprints everywhere and they boasted, didn't they?"

"That's true," Marc said.

"No government is going to let them leave the country after that. Face it, Jacques!"

Jacques Lanctôt looked at Yves. His left foot jiggled nervously, then stopped. "Yes. Yes. You mean we're on our own?"

He stared at Yves. Yves looked at Marc. "Correct," Marc said.

❧ ❧ ❧ ❧ ❧

Monday afternoon: sixteen hundred hours: November 30. He and his partner sat in an unmarked RCMP cruiser on Fleury Street, a few blocks from the suspects' apartment. The school crossing guard came along the street in his car, and, as instructed, drove up and parked behind them. His partner reached over and opened the rear door of their cruiser. The guard, an aging man, walked up, got in and sat in the back seat. He looked as though he was afraid they would shoot him.

"You made it," he said, smiling at the guard.

"Yeah."

"Well, as I think you know, we're RCMP officers working on a case. Now, we'd very much appreciate it if you could see your way to letting us use your apartment for a couple of days. We need it for our work. I'm sorry but I can't tell you more than that."

"You mean you want us to move out?"

"Yes."

"When?"

"As soon as possible."

The man sat in silence. Then, when it looked as if he was about to say no, he said, suddenly, eagerly, "Well, let's see, I could go back now and get the family and we could maybe move in this afternoon with my married daughter. She lives right near here. In Montreal North."

"That would be a big help," he said. "We certainly appreciate your cooperation. When you're ready to move, phone this number and we'll send a cab over for you. We'll pay the cab, of course."

By eighteen hundred hours there was a Mountie in the up-stairs apartment, right over the suspects. He phoned Division, to say he was in. At nineteen hundred a cab drew up and a woman got out and went upstairs. She was the Mountie's wife. It looked more normal that way.

23

When the inspector arrived at Division, the front desk told him the assistant commissioner was already in the building. The chief inspector's car would be here any minute; it had already left Sûreté headquarters on Parthenais Street. On his way up to his office, the inspector saw four or five Sûreté inspectors hanging about, middle-aged men, overweight, in olive-green paramilitary uniforms, self-consciously pulling on and off their black-leather dress gloves. Most of them were old-timers, political appointees from the Duplessis graft days. The Provincials ran Quebec: to them this building was foreign territory and the Mounties the opposition.

When the chief inspector arrived, the inspector was waiting. They went into the chief inspector's office. The inspector mentioned last night's foul-up.

"Yes, I heard something or other," the chief inspector said. "What *is* the story?"

The inspector explained. Tuesday afternoon December 1,

his men, in the observation post across the street, saw a Montreal North Police Department cruiser drive up and stop outside the suspect building. Two constables jumped out of the car and ran upstairs to the top apartment occupied by the RCMP surveillance man. Neighbors had spotted the man and his wife and, realizing they were not the normal tenants, phoned the local police. The Montreal North Police Department, knowing nothing of the stakeout, sent the squad car to investigate. The RCMP constable had to show his identification and ask the police to leave quietly. It was a very close thing indeed.

"And what about the suspects?" the chief inspector asked.

"There was no reaction. We don't even know if they saw the squad car."

"Of course they saw it," the chief inspector said. "Do we have a phone in that upstairs apartment?"

"Yes, sir."

"Right. Have someone phone the constable now and tell him to send his wife home. We don't want a woman up there if trouble starts."

The inspector called an aide and gave the order.

"As you know," the chief inspector said, "I just came back from Sûreté headquarters. Our assistant commissioner was there with me. We've had a top-level meeting with St. Pierre of the Sûreté and St. Aubin of the Montreal Department. The assistant commissioner has proposed a strategy and, I'm glad to say, St. Pierre and St. Aubin have accepted it."

"I see, sir."

"Our strategy, as the assistant commissioner sees it, will be to pick the suspects off one by one. As soon as one of these birds leave the premises, we follow him until he's safely away, then arrest him. If the people in there are who we think they are, they'll send someone out to see what happened. That way, we'll reduce their numbers. If Cross is in there, we must minimize his risk."

"Yes, sir."

"One thing is for sure," the chief inspector said. "If they're FLQ, they have dynamite, lots of it, probably enough to blow up the whole block. That's why we'll have to go at it very, very gently."

"When do we start picking them off, sir?"

"Well, it's – ten-fifteen now. I'd say we should start right away."

"I'll phone our observation post."

"Now, hold on a minute,' the chief inspector said, smiling. "I haven't finished. The drill is that this is a combined operation, remember?"

"Yes, sir."

"So we have to make the arrests in conjunction with provincial police officers. One RCMP and one provincial officer on each arresting team. That way, you know, the credit will be shared."

Bloody politics, the inspector thought. "Yes, sir, I understand, sir," he said.

"The Provincials will, no doubt, send their men up to the area and contact us," the chief inspector said. "I've told them to move on it at once."

"Right, sir."

"So, tell our men. No arrests without a Provincial police officer on hand. Okay?"

"Will do," the inspector said.

"Hey, Roger," his partner said. "Two coming out now."

He grabbed the glasses. Louise Cosette-Trudel and the husband, both wearing overcoats, she carrying a shopping bag. Christ! He went for the phone. The sergeant answered.

"Two suspects leaving now."

"Did those provincial officers show up yet?"

"No. There's nobody here but us chickens."

"I'll tell the inspector. Hold on."

He waited. He could see them going down Des Récollets. They were going downtown. He knew their form by now.

The inspector came on the line. "All right, we can't wait for the Provincials. I'm sending three cars right away."

"*Three* cars, sir?"

But the inspector had hung up.

"Hey, Maurice,' he told his partner. "You'd better get going. They're sending three cars to help you take them in."

But his partner had already moved out.

❁❁❁❁❁

At thirteen hundred hours, an hour after his partner left, he thought he saw some guys who looked like CAT Provincials going by in a VW which parked at the foot of Rue Martial. By fourteen hundred hours, his partner had not returned. One thing he knew: you could count on the sergeant: if the sergeant could pass along the drill, he'd do it. At fourteen-fifteen the phone rang.

226

"A nice little waltz-about," the sergeant said. "They took the subway and we followed them. There was a lot of shuffling, but we finally picked them up at the Berri de Montigny subway interchange. They're at headquarters now and, from what I hear, we're onto Liberation Cell, all right. So let me be the first to congratulate you, my son."

"What about the Provincials?"

"Oh, yeah, we found them at last. They're 'helping' with the investigation. I mean the interrogation."

"Well, sonofabitch! That's real nice of them."

"Be good," the sergeant said.

At sixteen hundred hours, the phone rang again. "Inspector wants to talk to you."

"Sir?"

"How are things going?" the inspector asked.

"Real quiet, sir. Our man on the top floor says they're not even playing the radio."

"Hmm," the inspector said. "Well, by tonight they'll be whistling Dixie. I just came from Westmount. We're interrogating the suspects there. The girl won't say a thing, won't even answer questions. The husband admits his part in the kidnapping, but won't say if Cross is in the apartment. Still, I'm taking bets."

"I would too, sir."

"Good," the inspector said. "Now, this is the form. We're making it a combined operation with the three police forces and the military. In the first phase we'll start moving in extra surveillance. You'll be seeing the start of that about ninety minutes from now. And by the way. We're calling it Operation Cordon."

24

Wednesday, December 2. After lunch Cross had asked permission to take a shower. Now, guarded by Jacques Lanctôt, he was toweling and dressing himself in the bathroom. As this was the only time the prisoner was not hooded and facing a corner, the guard on the bathroom detail must always wear a mask. However, when the prisoner finished dressing, he donned his own hood, pulling it down completely over his face as he had been told to do when in the bathroom or in transit. Blinded thus, he stood, with almost animal patience, waiting for Jacques. Jacques went to him, took him by the arm, and led him out of the bathroom and back into the room, lit as always by artificial light, where Cross had now spent forty-eight days. Jacques eased up the prisoner's hood and seated him in his chair before the television set.

"Do you want me to turn it on?"

"No, thanks. I think I'll read a while," the prisoner said.

Jacques rapped with his gun butt on the floor, a signal that he wanted to be relieved. Marc Carbonneau came limping in from the kitchen.

"I just want to get a coffee," Jacques said. Marc nodded and sat down on the air mattress. The prisoner, cowled, picked up that morning's newspaper and began to read it.

Sound, in an uncarpeted, unfurnished apartment, is always magnified in volume. Silence is equally distorted. This afternoon, windy, cold, with a gray sunless sky, the rooms in which Jacques moved seemed hollow and silent as an empty tomb. It was after five. Yves had been away since nine this morning: he had been trying for days to get some information on where the Roses might be hiding out. The Trudels had gone downtown, when? At noon. They were taking a long time, weren't they? No wonder, it was quiet. He looked in at the room where Marc, desultorily, had been monitoring the media. The radio was turned on, but so low he could barely hear that banal music from a Broadway show. The television had no sound; images floated across the screen like marine animals in an aquarium tank. Jacques went into the blessed brightness of the kitchen, the one room where there was clear daylight. He got a KIK cola from the fridge and went to the window with it. It was then that he looked at the man out there. And saw the man looking at him.

The man was in a backyard across the way, one of a row of backyards of houses which fronted on the adjoining street. The man wore a blue raincoat, rubbers, and a ski cap with earflaps down. He had a shovel in his hands and when he saw Jacques look at him, he began to dig up the yard. A neighbor digging in a yard: it was not a sight to frighten anyone. But when Jacques looked at the ground the man was digging, there seemed no reason to dig there. Instinctively, he drew back from the window, out of sight. At once, the man stopped digging and looked at the balcony behind him. On this balcony, ostensibly reading a newspaper, sat another man, also in a dark overcoat. There was something wrong with that. It was too cold to sit out and it was growing dark. The newspaper reader looked down at the digger and nodded. The digger turned and signaled towards the house. Two uniformed Montreal Police constables came down the lane and stood in the lee of the house. The digger pointed to Jacques' window. The constables nodded, then turned and went back up the lane.

He ran to the front of the house. In the front room the flowered curtains were drawn shut. He eased back the edge of the curtain with the barrel of his M-1. There was no one in the street. He looked at the lot up the street where the kids played ball every afternoon. There were no kids.

He went back to the prisoner's room and signaled. Marc came into the corridor. In a hoarse whisper Jacques told what he had seen. "Go and look for yourself."

Marc went into the kitchen, stayed a few minutes and came back. He nodded. He noticed that Jacques' hands tightened around the gun butt of the M-1.

Marc looked back at the front door. At any moment, the police might break down that door. The door was booby-trapped with powerfrac dynamite, set to blow.

"The booby trap?" Marc said.

"I disconnected it when the Trudels went out."

"Hook it up again."

Jacques went up the corridor, fiddled with the electric connection, and came back again. "If it's a fight they want, we'll give them a fight. We'll blow the whole damn street up."

"With four sticks of dynamite?"

"Shit."

"I wonder, have they arrested the Trudels? Or Yves?"

"Wait," Jacques said. "I just thought of something. Maybe they're searching the district, maybe they don't know we're here at all? You know as well as I do, there are thousands of places being searched."

For a few moments, this brought hope.

"So what do we do, if they do come in?" Marc asked.

"Take Cross down to the garage. Put him in the car. You drive, I'll open up the garage door. And we blast out!"

❊ ❊ ❊ ❊ ❊

At seven that evening Yves Langlois walked up Des Récollets Street and entered the apartment. When he had admitted him, Jacques Lanctôt locked the door again, then put down his M-1 and gripped Yves in a bear hug. "Christ, you're back! Christ, I thought for sure they were going to arrest you there in the street."

"Who?"

"The *flics*. They're all around us."

"I didn't see any," Yves said. "You're imagining it."

Jacques stared at him. "They're out back. But you can't see, it's too dark now."

"Where are the Trudels?"

"That's what I mean. They never came back. They left at noon."

"Take it easy," Yves said; but felt himself infected with this fear. He went in to see Marc, who was with the prisoner. Marc's eyes looked grateful when Yves came in; like a dog who's been locked up.

"Anything on the Roses? Where were you all day?" Jacques said, coming after him.

"Just stooging around town. Everybody under the sun is in

232

jail or just out of jail. All kinds of people and, the joke is, ninety per cent of them never heard of the FLQ. It's ridiculous."

"Anyone seen the Roses?"

"No, Alain thinks they're still up north someplace. Did you eat yet?"

"I forgot," Jacques said. "Christ, man, we're worried. I tell you we saw *flics* out back."

"I'm going to eat," Yves said. He went into the kitchen and found some bread and peanut butter. As he was spreading the peanut butter, Jacques called:

"Hey!"

He went into the front room. Jacques was crouched by the window, his gun barrel poking the curtain aside. "Look out there."

Yves knelt and peered out. There were six men standing across the street. Six big men in overcoats and hats staring at their building. Cops. They couldn't be anything else.

"They *know*," Jacques Lanctôt said.

Yves drew back, squatting on the floor, staring at Jacques. Jacques' large hexagonal sunglasses hid his eyes, so Yves could not see if he was afraid. Yves felt sick: it was like a Western, the posse across the street, the law; now for the shoot-out. "Oh Christ!" Yves said.

"They must have arrested the Trudels."

"Yes."

"Why didn't they pick *you* up then?" Jacques said.

"Maybe, when I went out this morning they hadn't found us yet. When I came back tonight they didn't know where I was headed. When I turned in here, it was too late for them to grab me."

"But why?"

"If they know," Yves said, "then they know Cross is here. They don't want a shoot-out in case he gets killed."

Jacques sat in the darkened room in silence. Then knelt again and peered out from under the curtain.

"Still there?" Yves asked.

"Yes. We'll have to tell Marc. Will you take his place?"

A moment later Marc came in, knelt, looked out, let the curtain drop. "Come in the kitchen," Marc said to Jacques.

In the kitchen it was dark. Jacques peered out, then pulled down the blind and switched the overhead light on. Marc lit a cigarette. His lips were dry; he kept moistening them with his tongue. "One thing that's good," he said. "The girls aren't here."

"Yes. We're in for a fight."

Marc smoked in silence. Then: "You know. There's still the Cuban consul down there at the Expo grounds. And that plane at the airport. Supposing we ask them to send us Suzanne and the kid? And release the Trudels and let them come too?"

"It's too late for that," Jacques said. "All those *flics* want now is to put us in a position where they can take a good shot. They want to send us to hell – not to Cuba."

"But they won't want to send Cross back to Britain air freight."

"They don't give a fuck about Cross! If they'd cared about Cross we wouldn't be here two months!"

"Okay, okay, take it easy," Marc said. "I'll go check with Yves. See you in a minute."

"Wait. What are we doing, sitting here like dopes? You watch the back, I'll watch the front. If they rush the building we'll put Cross in the car. We'll show them the dynamite and pretend we've got enough to blow the block up. Remember, these *maudits flics* are fond of their skins."

Marc shrugged. He took the Beretta pistol from his belt and went to the window. "All right, you take the front room."

234

❄❄❄❄❄

Shortly before ten that night they heard a sudden tramp of feet on the sidewalk; it sounded like men coming on the run up from Rue Martial. Jacques Lanctôt backed into the corridor, holding his M-1 at the ready. "Get the handcuffs on Cross!"

In the prisoner's room, Yves rose and swiftly handcuffed Cross. "What's wrong?" the prisoner asked. Yves did not answer. Minutes passed. There was no further sound. After fifteen minutes Marc came in, took the key from Yves, and uncuffed Cross.

"What's the matter?" Cross asked again.

Marc looked at Cross, who sat, as usual, his back to them, facing the wall. There was a silence.

"The police know where you are," Marc said, softly.

The prisoner's head jerked up.

Marc beckoned Yves and whispered, "They're moving people out of the buildings around us."

"Are they?" Yves said. Suddenly, inexplicably, he had lost his awful fear. "It's going to be a shoot-out after all. Rat-a-tat-tat! Bonnie and Clyde."

"Bonnie who?" Marc asked. He did not go to English-language movies.

"Never mind."

"What are you laughing at?"

"I don't know," Yves said. "I guess I'm hysterical."

Marc looked at him, then went back into the kitchen. Yves saw him settle by the window, his Beretta cocked.

Suddenly, at two a.m., all the lights went out. Marc lit matches and checked the downstairs fusebox. "They've cut the power," he reported as he came up from the garage and was joined by Jacques in the dark corridor. "Get Cross up," Jacques called to Yves. "Bring him here."

The prisoner, lying on his mattress, was not asleep. He heard them say the power was cut. The one guarding him got him up and led him into the corridor. They told him to sit on the mattress which they dragged into the corridor. Then handcuffed one of his wrists to a doorknob. It was a painful posture. When they had tied him up like that, all three ran into the front room.

They had heard a noise. Marc edged towards the front window and poked the curtain aside. A man in plainclothes was creeping on his hands and knees, coming from the sidewalk towards them. He was trying to reach the valve which connected the building's water supply just below the front window. Marc opened the window and stuck his M-1 barrel out. "Get away from there, you sonofabitch!" he said.

The man looked up, then, rising to his feet, turned and walked quickly back across the road.

"All right," Jacques said. "That's it! If they want a fight, they'll have to kill me. I'm not going into those cells!"

He put his gun down and ran back into the kitchen. On the top shelf of the cupboard was a small can of pale-blue paint. He took it and ran back into the front room. With a rag he daubed huge letters on the windowpane: F L Q.

He ran into the other front room and repeated the maneuver: F L Q. He was excited, sweating, trembling in rage. "Okay," he said. "Let's mark off the shooting territory."

"There's still Cuba!" Marc said.

Jacques stared at him.

"That's right," Yves said.

Marc was holding the flashlight; it made a big moon circle

on the bare floorboards. They stood, three shadows in the dark room, staring at each other in the cone of light.

"We still have Cross," Marc said. "We still have a chance."

"What if they pretend to make a deal and, when we leave some guy dressed as a civilian comes up in the crowd and shoots us in the back?"

"Sure, there'll be risks," Marc said.

"Yves?"

"Cuba or a shoot-out," Yves said. "It's all the same to me."

The seconds dragged into a minute. Jacques Lanctôt's left foot began its autonomous jiggle. Then stopped. "All right," Jacques said. "*Cuba.*"

"Let's throw out a message," Marc said. "There's a piece of hollow pipe in the garage."

"Get it."

❈ ❈ ❈ ❈ ❈

The FLQ stationery he had once designed with such pride, the logo of the *habitant* farmer, the words OPÉRATION LIBÉRATION Jacques stared at the familiar sheet of paper as, the flashlight balanced on the table beside him, he began this, his last communiqué. He wrote it in his own hand.

"Hey, what's the name of that other lawyer, the one who helped Vallières and Gagnon?"

"Lemieux?"

"No, not Lemieux. The Jew."

"Bernard Mergler. He's the civil liberties lawyer."

237

"Yeah, that's him. Robert's still locked up, they'd never let him out to help us, would they?"

"I don't know."

"Get Mergler," Yves said. "When I worked in the courts our guys said he was honest and a great lawyer."

"Will he come?"

"Yes. He's a good guy, I tell you."

"Okay. How does this sound, then?"

```
Communiqué:

    If you try anything (guns, gas, etc.), Mr. J.
Cross will be the first to die. We have several
sticks of powerfrac dynamite. If you want to
negotiate send us a newspaperman from Québec-Presse
or Le Devoir. Plus Lawyer B. Mergler.
                We shall conquer.
                      FLQ
```

"That sounds good."

Jacques rolled it in a cylinder and slipped it into the foot-long length of lead pipe.

"Open the window."

"Right."

The pipe was hurled out onto Des Récollets Street. They heard it clang on the pavement. Feet pounded suddenly.

"*Calice!*" Marc said, laughing. "They thought it was a stick of dynamite."

"Did they get it yet?"

"Here they come. Oh! Oh! They're scared shitless. It's not dynamite, don't worry, *les flics!* Pick it up, yes, that's the brave *flic.* Look inside. Right. Now, go back to Führer St. Pierre and tell him what we say."

❊❊❊❊❊

238

At dawn they uncuffed Cross from the doorknob in the corridor and allowed him to lie down on the mattress. Then handcuffed his wrists and put a blanket over him. He was weary, but could not sleep. When they had settled him, they went to the windows to watch. For the first time in the long weeks of this kidnapping they no longer relied on radio and television for situation reports. The media were still silent, but the world, at last, was happening right outside their windows. From dawn onwards there were signs of movement and, at eight a.m., suddenly, it all began to come together. Army transport helicopters chattered like giant crows, passing and repassing over their roof, landing troops in the grounds of the nearby École Benjamin de Montigny. Files of gray ambulances passed at the foot of Rue Martial. In the distance, on the adjoining Avenue Gariepy, they could see uniformed police moving men, women, and children from nearby houses. Plainclothesmen with high-powered rifles patrolled the roofs of surrounding buildings. A fire engine arrived and was stationed at the foot of the street beside a blue truck from the Montreal Police Bomb Disposal Squad. At 8:30 a.m., one hundred and fifty armed policemen were deployed at the four connecting intersections surrounding the block, while combat troops armed with FN automatic rifles and Stirling submachine guns stood in long lines along the spines of each adjoining street.

All of these elaborate and excessive preparations were made in the manner of a primitive tribe marching on a distant hilltop to terrify its enemy. The final move, directly aimed at terrorizing the terrorists, was the appearance of small groups of plainclothes policemen wearing red armbands and carrying automatic rifles, walking up and down Des Récollets Street, directly opposite the kidnappers' hideout.

Shortly after nine, the local radio stations came alive, reporting that Montreal Transportation Commission buses had been placed at the intersections of a four-street area, around Des Récollets Street, making it impassable to traffic. Spectators were being kept back at barricades. Even the press was being held several streets away from the suspect building. Nearby residents had been evacuated. Schoolchildren from both adjoining schools had been sent home for the day. Armed Forces medical teams and field kitchens were being set up in case this operation turned into a siege.

Slowly, as though wakening from a two-week sleep, the news media regained their air of excitement. At 9:30 that morning, Thursday, December 3, the radio announced that Quebec Justice Minister Choquette would be flown by helicopter from Quebec to Montreal Police headquarters and from there would go directly to the scene of the operation. Robert Demers, the lawyer who had earlier acted as government negotiator, was on his way to Montreal North, together with a negotiator who would act for the kidnappers.

"A negotiator," Marc said. "And they say the Cuban consul is on his way to the *Man and His World* Pavilion."

"Maybe we won't have a shoot-out after all?" Yves said.

"Don't count on it," Jacques told him. "If those *flics* can get their hands on us for five minutes we won't be worth sending to Cuba."

"It's some right-wing lunatic that worries me," Yves said. "Some right-wing Oswald out there with a gun, waiting to avenge Christ-knows-what."

"You're not kidding," Jacques said. "What chance have we got?" His left foot began to jiggle nervously. Marc noticed it. "Look, we still have a *good* chance," Marc said. "And do you realize that if we get out of here and they shoot us down, the television will be on us? One thing we're going to get is coverage."

"That's right." At mention of coverage, Jacques' nervousness seemed to disappear. "I've often thought about that," he said. "If we escape today we'll be escaping on television. The whole world will see what we've done! The whole damn world will see this happening! It will be fantastic!"

"Yes," Yves said. "It's like we wrote the script. The Cuban consul waiting and the cops, and the plane – Jesus!"

For a moment they stared at each other. Marc realized that he was trembling. Jacques' eyes were hidden by his shades but his face lit in a smile. Yves kept punching his thigh, a trick of his when excited.

"So let's get out there where we can show them, right?" Marc said. "If those fascist pigs shoot us down, they'll make us martyrs, do you realize that?"

"*Saint Marc!*" Yves said and made the sign of the cross.

Marc turned, aimed a mock punch at Yves, then went into the front room. He knelt and peered out under the flowered curtain. Soldiers and plainclothesmen armed with rifles were on the roofs opposite, facing in his direction. But the only figures now on the street were two small clumps of the mysterious plainclothesmen, wearing red armbands and carrying automatic rifles.

Then, slowly, cleared through the police barrier at the far end of the street, a car approached. It came on cautiously, stopping some yards away from their building. Three men got out. One of them pointed to the building where Marc knelt behind the curtain. Then pointed to a house across the street. One of the other men nodded and began to walk towards Marc's building. The other two men turned, crossed the street, and went in at the side door of the house across the way.

The man coming towards Marc's building wore a dark overcoat and hat, a white shirt, dark tie, and darkish suit: he did not look like a cop. Dark hornrims, mustache, about forty-five or fifty, Marc estimated. Yes, he could be the lawyer, all right. He did not seem to be armed.

A few moments later, there was a knock on their door. Marc positioned the others, then went cautiously towards the front door.

"Who is it?"

"It's Mergler and I am all alone."

Marc signaled and Jacques undid the bolt, unhooked the chain, and opened the door. Both he and Marc raised their guns.

The lawyer, seen close, was pale but composed, with a wary manner and too-perfect teeth. He asked Marc if he was Jacques Lanctôt.

Marc said he was Carbonneau. He pointed to Jacques. "This is Lanctôt."

The lawyer then asked them if Mr. Cross was there and if he was all right. They led him down the hallway to the corridor where Cross lay on a mattress, a blanket over him, guarded by Yves, who was holding an M-1. In English, the lawyer asked Cross if he was all right. Cross smiled and said he was fine. The lawyer then said he recognized Cross from his photographs but had been asked to make a positive identification.

"I am to make a positive identification of you by asking you the name of the bull terrier you had when you were posted to Delhi."

"Garm," said Cross. "The name was Garm. G-a-r-m."

That seemed to satisfy the lawyer. He told Cross, in English, that he hoped to have him out in an hour or an hour and a half. Then he turned to Jacques Lanctôt.

Jacques and Marc led the lawyer into the empty front room where he gave them paper which he said was the government's plan for their safe conduct to St. Helen's Island where a temporary Cuban consulate had been set up. Jacques began to read the document. Cross was to ride with his captors to St. Helen's Island and remain there in the consul's custody until the plane carrying the kidnappers touched down in Cuba. But Jacques was searching for something else in the document. "What about the wives and children, does it mean they can go along?"

The lawyer said it did.

"What about the Trudels? Are they included?" Jacques said, asking the question he most feared to ask. For if Louise and C.T. could not go, how could he live, later, with their abandonment?

The lawyer said the authorities had promised that the safe conduct would include the Trudels. Then Jacques asked about persons now held under the War Measures Act, and, of course, the lawyer said no. Marc could have told Jacques that and thought it childish to have brought it up at this point.

"What about press coverage?" Jacques asked. "I want this to be fully covered by television and radio. I mean our ride to the Cuban consulate, our handing over Cross, and our departure. That way it's safer for us and it gives publicity for our cause."

The lawyer did not agree. He said in his view they shouldn't quibble but should try to get to the Cuban consul at St. Helen's Island as quickly as possible. The bigger the crowds became, the greater danger of some trouble, some incident which might provoke shooting.

"But that's just what I'm talking about," Jacques said. "How do we know we won't be shot down before we get there?"

Yves had brought Cross into the room and now Cross, relaxed, no longer with the air of a prisoner, smiled and said to the lawyer, "These chaps seem to be afraid of right-wing terrorists."

"No," Marc said. "We're afraid of a police ambush."

The lawyer then offered to go downtown in the car with them, if that would help.

"Look," Cross said, smiling. "What's the matter here? Am

I not important enough? Or do you think the authorities don't care about me? Surely you realize the entire world is watching and the authorities here will certainly not want anything to go wrong."

"Okay," Jacques said. "We'll leave in our own car with our own weapons, clothes, and so on. We'll get into the car downstairs, drive out, drive nonstop to St. Helen's Island, and hand Mr. Cross over there."

The lawyer turned to go. "Remember, we expect you back in ten minutes," Jacques said. "We don't like the way things are shaping up out there. Who are all those people with the red armbands?"

"Well, they're certainly not Red Guards," Yves said.

Marc was at the window. "Why *are* they wearing the armbands, then?"

The lawyer said he thought that if shooting started, the authorities wanted to be able to distinguish between plainclothesmen and the FLQ.

They let the lawyer out. Watched him as he crossed the street and went in at the side entrance of the house opposite. There were special phones in there, connecting with Choquette, the police, even with Trudeau himself.

Yves kept staring at Cross. This man, now, uncowled, standing up straight, talking to them as an equal, was so different from the man they had kept handcuffed, the man they had guarded day after day, the man they led about this little apartment. Cross had lost about twenty pounds and was pale from lack of sunlight, but now he seemed a younger brother to that heavy, aging man they had taken from the mansion on Redpath Crescent. Smiling, suddenly confident, for the first time he saw them unarmed, unmasked, saw them as they really were. Now, it was they who were trapped, surrounded by enemies. Cross seemed free.

"He's coming back," Jacques reported, from the front room.

The lawyer knocked and was admitted. He said the authorities warned that if they had booby traps or timing devices in their baggage they would have to be de-fused and removed. He said the police would enter the house as soon as they went out. If anything happened – any explosion – the getaway car would be stopped en route.

They bargained. Jacques insisted on their taking the twenty pounds of dynamite with them in the car. He would surrender it only to the Cuban consul.

The lawyer went back across the street, returning some minutes later. They went over the documents one last time. Because the Chrysler was in such poor condition it was arranged that an empty police car would follow behind them in case they broke down or had a flat. Marc would then take over and drive the police car. It was their last condition. The lawyer went across the street to check, then came back and told them to get their baggage ready. Yves and Marc started throwing clothes into three suitcases and there was a discussion about the big portable television set, the one valuable thing they had in the place. "Isn't it going to seem real bourgeois to arrive in Cuba with a television set?" Yves said. But they took it with them, all the same.

"Ready," Jacques said, at last.

Yves brought the prisoner out, handcuffed.

"Why the handcuffs?" the lawyer asked.

"Well, it's only until we get to St. Helen's Island."

"I don't like handcuffs at all," the lawyer said. "And even less under these circumstances."

"Okay," Jacques said. "We'll take them off as soon as we get to the car."

"I'll drive this wreck," Marc said. "Yves and Mr. Mergler should sit up front with me and Jacques, you sit with Mr. Cross in the back seat."

But as they began to go down into the garage, Jacques grew

245

nervous again. "Supposing the *flics* have some sharpshooters hidden in there, waiting to pick us off?"

The lawyer, who was in a hurry to get going, bravely suggested that if they were worried about sudden ambush, they let him go first into the garage. "All right," Jacques said.

The lawyer entered the garage, dark, quiet as a grave. Their old Chrysler stood silent, in the fine dust of two months' inaction. Jacques followed the lawyer in, cautiously, his M-1 at the ready. The garage was empty.

Then they brought Cross in and Jacques unlocked the handcuffs, taking them off, throwing them on the concrete floor, with a loud clatter which grated in the tense gloom of the darkened garage. He and Yves began to load up their luggage in the trunk. That big Jesus television set, how would they get it in? "*Calice!*" Marc swore. "We should have left it behind." But the lawyer suggested they put it in the back seat where it would act as a shield for Cross. They put Cross in beside it and then Jacques and Yves began to stick pieces of newspaper up to screen the other windows from view. But the lawyer, impatient, said they must hurry. They *must* go now.

Marc sat behind the wheel, worried about whether the old car would start after all these weeks. Yves got in with him, and Jacques got in back with Cross, holding onto the right rear door which would not close properly. "Let's go, then," Jacques said. Marc engaged the ignition. The old engine turned over, died, coughed, coughed, coughed and then, with a rusty noise like oil drums dragging across a brick floor, it caught and roared into splendid life. The lawyer, who had been waiting beside the car, went over to the garage door, pulled it up and walked up the driveway onto the street alerting the police that the kidnappers were coming out. Marc gunned the old car; nervous, so nervous that he scraped the side of the car against the garage wall and got stuck. A sliver of chrome tore off the rear fender as he backed up, went in again, and then came out.

246

With a bump of its undercarriage, the old Chrysler came up over the hump of the ramp and stopped on the street. It was 12:55 a.m. The lawyer, waiting on the sidewalk, opened the front door of the car and got into the front seat beside Yves. The old Chrysler, jerking forward, then turned down Des Récollets Street, as motorcycle police, straddling their machines like mechanical cowboys, slammed down six riding boots, six engines catching at once in a roar of disciplined thunder, and the police bull team moved into position, three to ride shotgun around this Very Important Automobile, three to leapfrog ahead, holding traffic at intersections, sidelining all other cars, bulling the motorcade through. Overhead, with a loon's lurch, an Armed Forces helicopter moved out to chart the traffic pattern while behind the bull team, eight other automobiles moved into gear. Cross, seeing his first real sunlight in sixty days, blinked painful red-rimmed eyes at the sky as Marc hit the floorboards with the accelerator and they were off, past the first whirring, blinding bank of cameras and flashbulbs, past the shoulder-to-shoulder lines of combat troops, past the police barricades at the bottom of the street, slipping and sliding in the turns as they pushed out through the tangle of side streets, more police motorcycles joining them as they came out now, sixty-miles-an-hour fast, onto the big north-south lanes of Pie IX Boulevard. Rows of police lines and massed crowds, hundreds of faces lifted to watch their passage like daisies opening to the sun, a crowd so great that Marc shouted – "It looks just like the Santa Claus Parade! – and it did, for they *were* a parade now, twenty-two motorcycle police surrounding a motorcade of eight automobiles, all with their headlights on, first an unmarked Montreal Police car, then the Chrysler, then four more Montreal Police cars, red flashers turning (one, empty but for its driver, in case the Chrysler broke down), then the provincial police in their car, and, lastly the car of the Royal Canadian Mounted Police.

And, all around, bright sunlight, crash helmets, uniforms,

cleared streets, crowds, traffic lights stopped in midsignal, cops waving them through. Racing nonstop across the city at sixty miles an hour, their route laid down by the police, acting out this script they had helped to write, escaping as no fugitives in history have ever escaped before: *live, on television.*

Yes, live. Even their enemies were, at that moment, giving prime time to the televising of the motorcade. In Parliament, Prime Minister and Cabinet, Opposition and rank-and-file members, all eschewed lunch to sit by television sets, munching sandwiches and watching this drama. In Montreal, Quebec Justice Minister Choquette, the man directing this police operation, sat at a set, watching, accompanied by Lord Dunrossil, the ranking British diplomat involved. For, at last, the bad guys had surfaced, the terrorists were out in the open and running, and the word came that Carbonneau was jockeying the old Chrysler like a crazy stock-car racer, that they were armed and had dynamite, that they were coming off the big boulevard into the harbor area, that an order had gone out to shut all harbor entrances, to block all other traffic, to slip a new lead dog into the car pack, this time a National Harbors Board police cruiser, driven by a dock veteran, which raced in ahead of the former police lead car, leading it and the entire motorcade at expert breakneck speed through the narrow maze of old waterfront streets towards Concordia Bridge, which leads to St. Helen's Island and those shut-down exhibition buildings erected for Expo 67, in summer a permanent fairground exhibit called *Man and His World*; in winter an abandoned, snowdrifted silence, a manmade island, remote from normal pursuits, impregnable to casual violence. At the very tip of this island is the building which was the Canadian Pavilion at Expo, an improbable huddle of white roofs clustered together like fallen paper airplanes. Now, by diplomatic fief, this building was a forgotten land, a temporary consulate of the Republic of Cuba where the acting consul waited to play his intermediary role.

248

Cuba: Fidel, machetes, sugar cane, cigars. Yves' mind mused on these images as the Chrysler raced in and out among the old streets of the waterfront. Suddenly, he thought of the passports which the government had promised would be issued to them today, thought of the Cuban consular visa, the necessary red tape. He, of all of them, was the only one known by a name which was not his. He was Pierre Seguin and the others had carefully continued to call him Pierre before the lawyer and the prisoner. But who *was* Pierre Seguin, this man he had invented? What if they asked him where Seguin was born and where he had lived? He had once used the name for false papers and now, remembering, he opened the glove compartment. But the registration and license were not there.

"Where's the car registration?" he asked Jacques. "Where's the license, do you have the owner's license? The owner's license is not here."

The lawyer, not understanding, laughed. "Don't worry. There's one thing you can be certain of. You're not going to be arrested for driving without a license."

But Yves was looking at Jacques, who shook his head. God knows where the license was.

Now, once again, there were huge crowds. Only twenty minutes after their wild ride began they were racing along the docks, passing the backdrop of a huge oil tanker offloading right by the road, and in that moment, with the big ship behind them, they leapt again onscreen.

For, in this place, television had grouped forces for a last great encounter. This was where, earlier, cameras had recorded the passage of a car driven by a young man wearing dark glasses, a man identified as Ricardo Escartin, a Cuban Embassy first secretary who had driven across the no man's land of Concordia Bridge to that pavilion which, when he entered it, became Cuba. And now, as zoom lenses picked up the old battered wreck of a Chrysler, surrounded by its police outriders, going hell-for-freedom towards the bridge, a classic

249

piece of television film was created, a moment like that sinister frame as Jack Ruby moved out of the crowd to shoot Lee Harvey Oswald, or the long view of that other motorcade as it came up towards the book depository in Dallas.

But this moment was not tragic, it was a classic movie finish, the old car racing up to the opened barrier, not slowing down as it fled past onto the bridge, suddenly alone, the outriding motorcycles and police cruisers stopping, turning back. On it went, up that lonely road towards the abandoned fairground. On St. Helen's Island, at the end of the bridge, two cars waited to meet it. In the lead car sat the last representative of the Canadian law, a Montreal Police captain called Marquis. Standing beside the other car were the Cuban, Escartin, and an English Press Officer, William Ashford, representing the British government. Ashford looked into the back seat of the Chrysler and recognized Cross. Then Ashford and Escartin got into their car and, led by Marquis in the police cruiser, the small procession of three vehicles drove along the narrow strip of island to the far end where the white roof cones of the former Canadian Pavilion gleamed in the December sun. At a predetermined point, the police cruiser made a very deliberate U-turn and Captain Marquis drove away, going back across the bridge, back to Canada.

Now, they were in Cuba.

Escartin stopped his car. Ashford got out and walked back towards the Chrysler, which had also stopped. Jacques Lanctôt got out first, followed by James Richard Cross. Ashford, an old friend, threw his arms around Cross, embracing him in a most un-British manner. Then they shook hands.

"Hello, Jasper, how are you?"

"Fine, Bill."

The consul was waiting. Cross shook the Cuban's hand and said: "Thank you."

The idea was for Cross to get into the Cuban's car, and

Ashford, worried about his condition after fifty-nine days in captivity, took hold of his arm to guide him. Amused, Cross pulled his arm free. "What's the matter with you, Bill?" he said, jokingly. Ashford smiled, embarrassed. Cross walked briskly to the car.

The procession moved again; only two cars now. At the former Canadian Pavilion, everyone got out. Bernard Mergler, the kidnappers' intermediary, walked across from the Chrysler to confer with the Cuban consul. The Cuban pointed out a door to Ashford and Cross, who walked away and went into the pavilion. For a moment the three kidnappers stood in the open, in the cold, near-winter sunlight, alone. Three young men, poorly dressed in T-shirts and slacks, untidy, in need of haircuts, carrying automatic rifles, a pistol, and four sticks of dynamite. Three faces now staring about them, confused, nervous: Jacques Lanctôt, handsome, clean-shaven, his eyes hidden by hexagonal rimless sunglasses; Marc, older, disheveled, with scrawny beard and long hair curling over his bald patch. Yves, peering through thick-lensed spectacles, a big, boyish monk, his hair cut in a heavy bob.

Escartin left Mergler and went towards the kidnappers, holding a large leather bag in which, later, he would collect their weapons. He told them to come into the pavilion. They were led to a room at the opposite end of the building from the room used by Cross and Ashford, and there Escartin faced them, holding out the bag. "Give me your weapons," he said. With the easy skill of a former guerrilla, he unloaded the M-1's and the pistol and put them, with the dynamite, into the leather bag.

"You can telephone your relatives from here," he said.

"We want to call *Québec-Presse* and *Le Devoir*," Jacques said. "We want to – "

"You may *not* call the press. That is official."

Escartin turned to Bernard Mergler, the lawyer, and asked

251

him to help make the arrangements. Telephone communication was established with Robert Demers, the government negotiator. Mergler and Demers, both reasonable men, anxious to end this without bloodshed, set up a method of bringing the other Cuba-bound passengers to St. Helen's Island: Suzanne Lanctôt and her child from the South Shore and the Cosette-Trudels from their cells at RCMP headquarters in Westmount.

It all took time. The afternoon dragged on.

At the far end of Concordia Bridge, restless, unsatisfied, television zoom lenses went in on the white inverted cones of the pavilion, far away, too far for them to pick up any human figures. The world seemed to wait, at intermission, while kidnappers, victim, and intermediaries prepared backstage for the final act. Other cameras, like spies, poked into the front seats of cars, scrutinizing all comings and goings across the bridge. Again and again, on film, the networks reran their shots of the wild ride downtown, as voices reassured listeners to stand by, for "this is live CBC coverage in Montreal of the final chapter." Again, the zoom lens went in, enlarging the faraway roofcones, again it pulled back to the fixed long shot.

Canadian passport officials went across to the island in their car, equipped with the paraphernalia to make out passports for the kidnappers. The cameras, restless at the wait, went up to the federal capital, Ottawa, for interviews with politicians who, like everyone else, were watching their television sets. "We are all waiting breathlessly for you and others in the media to inform us that Mr. Cross is being released."

Radio was more enterprising. Shortly after three, radio reporters announced that a well-dressed man was at police barriers trying to get through. Earlier he had appeared at police barriers in Montreal North on a similar mission. He was Gérard Lanctôt, father of Jacques and Louise. Years ago he he had been a liegeman of that Adrien Arcand who saw Canada's troubles as inspired by the Jews. No, his son had not asked to see him. He had not seen Jacques since the boy was seventeen. Eight years ago. He was there, he explained, in case he could do something to help if his boy did something rash, He waited; he did not get to see his son.

At four p.m., negotiations were still going on. The television cameras went, in relief, to a familiar face. In Ottawa the Prime Minister faced television with a Cheshire cat smile. He had just talked to Cross on the phone, he said, and added: "I couldn't help saying 'God bless the Irish.'" For Trudeau this distasteful affair was over. He had won. Although he was to keep the War Measures Act in force for six months, on that day, in victory, he simply told the nation that Cross was free and that "the rest is now, I think, a nightmare which has passed into history."

At five-ten, in the beginning darkness, television cameras picked up the outline of a car, cleared through police barriers speeding across the bridge towards the island. Inside were three Mounties in plainclothes, together with a girl and a young man. The girl was Louise Cosette-Trudel. The young man was C.T. When they got out of the car at the pavilion and hurried in side, Jacques Lanctôt caught Louise and kissed her, while C.T. and Yves Langlois performed an impromptu war dance.

253

"Hey, where's Marc? Is he okay?"

"He's over there," Yves said pointing. "But don't disturb him now. He's on the phone."

Slouched by the receiver, running his hand through his straggling hair, Marc Carbonneau sat, talking quietly to the wife he had left three years ago when he decided this revolution was more important to him than a family. She still lived here in Montreal with his four children. Yes, she said, she had been watching the television. He tried to explain: "If I took part in this kidnapping it's because I love you and the kids." Did she understand? He tried to say that this was not forever. "One day I'll come back and you'll understand," he said. And the kids, how were they? He sent them his love. "I'll come back," he said again. "I love you." He heard her weep. "*Nous vaincrons,*" he said.

A second car was coming onto the island. They knew, because its approach had already been reported on television, and now, moments later, it drew up outside the door. Two young girls got out. One was a girl who had agreed to go and fetch Suzanne Lanctôt from the South Shore apartment where she was staying. The other girl, Suzanne Lanctôt, now very, very pregnant, walked into the pavilion, holding her little boy by the hand. When Jacques Lanctôt saw his wife, he hugged her, and caught his little son, holding him aloft in joy: his son whom he had not seen since that day, weeks ago, in the park; the child who, in his bad moments, he had thought he might never see again.

In a nearby room Consul Escartin stood with Canadian passport officials affixing sealing wax and important red ribbons to new Canadian passports specially issued for the kidnappers. Passport photographs had been taken with a Polaroid camera. The special Cuban visas, unlike the facsimile documents of our age, were florid and handsome, fit for ambassadors or queens.

254

And now, at last, with Suzanne's passport completed, they were ready to leave for the airport. It was dark outside. In a room at the far end of the pavilion Cross had finished a meal of chicken brought over by the police cruiser, and was drinking wine with his friend Bill Ashford. His afternoon had largely been spent making phone calls, first to his wife Barbara in Switzerland, then to his daughter Susan, in Montreal. Afterwards he telephoned his superior, the British High Commissioner in Ottawa. Then, and only then, did he consent to take the calls which waited, one from Premier Bourassa and one from Prime Minister Trudeau. Now tired but happy, wearing an open-necked shirt, an old sweater and slacks, he sat on a sleazy couch in front of a television set in this strange lounge – again, as he had been so often in this curious affair, a spectator at his own drama, waiting for the next act.

Outside the pavilion two Cuban official cars were waiting. The small procession – Escartin and the kidnappers, Suzanne and the child – drifted out into the darkness. Marc tried to open the rear of the old Chrysler to remove their bags, but the lid was jammed shut. So they left their clothes and belongings behind and, carrying only three small suitcases and a rucksack, containing clothing belonging to Suzanne and the child, they got into the cars and were driven to a helicopter landing pad near Concordia Bridge. At six-fifty, an Armed Forces Sikorsky helicopter lifted them into the darkness and whirled them for the last time across their native city. Seven minutes later the helicopter landed at Montreal International Airport on a heavily guarded runway, well away from press and public, where Military Flight 602, a Canadian Armed Forces Yukon transport plane, waited ready for takeoff to José Marti Airport, Havana, Cuba. The Cuban ambassador was there: he had flown in from Ottawa to supervise this strange event.

At bay, too far away, the banks of cameras focused hopelessly in long shot, recording the appearance down there of two police cruisers which picked up a small knot of people and moved them from the helicopter, up under the bronto-saurean rump of the Yukon. They stood there, a forlorn little group, lit by the flare lights, waiting as a few pieces of baggage were lifted aboard by the plane's loadmaster. The pilot was already at the controls: a major, he normally flew people like the Prime Minister or the Queen. There were similarities on this flight: very few passengers, large official aircraft, high priority of takeoff and landing.

They were all assembled now, the men from the Depart-ment of External Affairs who would go as Canada's repre-sentatives on the flight; Escartin and an assistant, for Cuba; a military surgeon in case Suzanne gave unexpected birth en route; the plane crew. There was some joking among the kid-nappers as they stood waiting to board, and then, as they went in at the tail of the aircraft, a silence. Their group sat together, down front – Jacques and Suzanne and little Boris, Louise and C.T., Yves and Marc. The time was seven-thirty. They did not know it but already, because of their delay in pro-viding the television audience with that last dramatic liftoff, their prime time had been pre-empted. The networks had moved on to a grandstand press conference at which Justice Minister Choquette introduced the three police chiefs – RCMP, provincial, and city – who had become the official heroes of this tale. There were many questions, many congratulations: there were the usual complaints about non-cooperation with the press.

The kidnappers waited on the runway. While the world no longer stood by for takeoff, banks of cameras remained focused to film the departure for later telecasts. Engines warmed up, the plane's flashers began blinking and it moved along the runway into position. Inside the cabin all was very quiet.

The Roses and Francis and Bern are probably watching us

right now, Marc told himself. He imagined them sitting at some television set, wishing that they too were on this freedom plane. He wondered if they, too, would one day see Cuba.

They would not see Cuba. The snows were coming, the brutal Quebec winter, long as a death. Laporte's gravestone would be buried in that drifting snow on the slope of Mount Royal Cemetery. The men who killed him were to be hidden under that same snow in a lonely farmhouse at St. Luc, thirty miles from Montreal, buried, literally, underground in a tunnel beneath the farmhouse basement from which, three weeks from now, in the quiet days just after Christmas, police would flush them out, manacle them, and bring them down to Parthenais Street and into court. Paul Rose, Jacques Rose, Francis Simard. They might insult the judge, shake their fists and cry *"Nous vaincrons"* and *"Vive le* FLQ," crying it out in that special disfiguring French accent which is their heritage from those disgraceful French Canadian slums which made them who they are. They might rise and yell "injustice" and call the judge a whore and refuse the court's lawyers, seeing themselves as politicals and martyrs. But when the heavy-set, uniformed provincial police beadle calls out *"Tout le monde debout!"* and all stand obediently and the judge walks in and the beadle cries *"Assoyez vous!"* and all in court are seated and the charge is read: the charge is murder, foul, sordid murder, three against one. Was it their self-hatred which made them able to kill so pitilessly a French Canadian, one of their own; to strangle him with the chain of his holy medal? No, they are not martyrs. They are slum boys, caught. The cops will now prosecute. And the judge will sentence.

❊❊❊❊❊

The noise of the Yukon's engines changed. The captain gave it throttle, wings trembling, brakes on, waiting the go signal from tower. Yves opened the passport they had handed him and looked at the name typed there: *Pierre Seguin*. At last he had become that other he set out to be. The Yves Langlois of that middle-class respectable family, numbering High Court judges in its family tree, was now Pierre Seguin, revolutionary; Cuban resident. I am no longer that student, the boy who was a court stenographer, a hotel clerk, a drifter. I am become another. And that former me is dead.

"We're going to take off," Jacques Lanctôt told Suzanne, taking her hand in his, his other hand holding the pudgy fist of his child. He was elated: he had done it. They were here, safe at last, and they were now in history. We will be remembered, he told himself. He thought of today. As the old Chrysler had swept towards Concordia Bridge he had seen a knot of young people standing behind the police barrier, giving the clenched fist signal of the FLQ. Now, he told Suzanne

258

about it. "I shouted out the window – *Nous reviendrons* [we will come back]," he told Suzanne. "And we will, you know. We will!"

Suzanne did not speak. The plane had bunched itself like a bull ready to charge out once the gate goes up. Now it charged, and suddenly, light as a leaf, lifted into the air. She looked across the aisle at Louise. Louise was crying.

Louise wept: it was over. They were off the ground. In six hours they would land in Cuba. She would never again see Montreal, never go to the cabin at Prevost in those hot summer days when the mosquitoes drove you into the warm water at the side of the lake, never throw snowballs with the kids at Easter, never stand by the ski tow, waiting for one last run, never sit on Maman's double swing in the backyard or drive to Quebec City for Christmas. It was over, they were safe, they had done something, yes, and C.T. was speaking to her now, saying it's all over, don't cry, we're safe now, everything will be great, yes, yes, and he was right, she mustn't cry, they had done something for history, Cross was alive, they were alive and all Canada, all America now knew that there was injustice in Quebec, we had our manifesto read on television, after all. It was a revolutionary act, wasn't it? It was, it was!

But she wept, she wept.

Two days later, James Richard Cross went home to London. His captors were in Cuba in that special limbo which awaits revolutionaries before their time when, at last, they are hauled aboard the mother ships of rebellion. Cross, released by the Cuban consul as soon as the Yukon landed in Havana, had remained in seclusion in a Montreal hospital for more than twenty-four hours. Now, on the morning of Saturday, December 5, exactly two months after the day of his abduction, he was leaving Canada for a new post.

At eight-thirty a.m. a roomful of reporters and cameramen assembled at Montreal International Airport. A Canadian Armed Forces 707 Boeing jet, the plane used by Prime Minister Trudeau on official journeys, waited to fly Cross home. He entered, flanked by the British High Commissioner and other British and Canadian officials. They were seated, facing the cameras. The High Commissioner, an impressive tub of a man with eyebrows thick as whole cigar ash, rose to introduce Cross. "Ladies and gentlemen, Mistah Jasper – Mistah Cross!"

But it was Cross everyone had been staring at all along; these features familiar from hundreds of newspaper photographs, now a real face they were seeing for the first time, a face they would be unable to place a year from now; an ordinary man become, briefly, a celebrity. He spoke, first in English, then in French. All was diplomatic banality until he mentioned the death of Laporte: then his voice faltered. Perhaps only he and the dead Minister had finally understood this thing: to them it could not be a theatrical event, staged and performed by would-be actors. For whose life was ever ended by a play?

Outside, in a fine dust of snow, the 707 waited on the tarmac. When the press questioning threatened to drag on, the High Commissioner rose and handed Cross his hat and coat. Swiftly, he was removed from the room like a man who has created a disturbance. The official party hurried out, under a new grouping of television and newsreel cameras, past Mounties in beaver hats and brown-and-yellow tunics. Cross said his goodbyes, ran up the ramp and, at the top, turned and waved to the assembled cameras in the amateur manner of a man who has never done it before. The plane door shut. The ramp was wheeled away. The plane moved out and, far away, lifted into the morning sky.

It was, perhaps, the final irony in this Canadian drama. Two men had been kidnapped. The French Canadian lay dead. The Englishman went free.